Praise for *In ...*

"Combines effortles... ...s-pense and plenty of stimulating romance."

—*Publishers Weekly*

"Readers will savor the growing romance between two disparate people and the dash of mystery."

—*RT Book Reviews*

"Fast, clever, and romantic, with lovable and rewarding characters. A very entertaining read."

—*Booklist*

"Full of powerful emotions, great characters, and a sexy romance."

—*Fresh Fiction* Fresh Pick!

Praise for *One Rogue Too Many*

"A merry romp... Grace captures the essence and atmosphere of the era."

—*RT Book Reviews*

"Filled with humor and witty repartee... Grace woos readers in true Regency style."

—*Publishers Weekly*

"Grace's flair for crafting engaging characters and light touch...result in another sexy, Regency-set historical."

—*Booklist*

Praise for *Lady Vivian Defies a Duke*

"Another winning marriage of romance and wit. This classic love story is absorbing and endearing."

—*Publishers Weekly* Starred Review

"Sprightly, amusing, fun, and quite charming...everything a love-and-laughter romance reader could desire. The characters shine and Grace's talents sparkle."

—*RT Book Reviews*

"Captivating, thrilling... A must-read for anyone who is seeking a wild, romantic adventure!"

—*Night Owl Romance* Top Pick!

Praise for
Miss Lavigne's Little White Lie

"The suspense and intrigue are well tuned and the humor is subtle and charming, much like the novel as a whole."

—*Publishers Weekly* Starred Review

"The characters are colorful, the research on target."

—*RT Book Reviews*

"It's official. Author Samantha Grace has proven it's impossible for her to disappoint. A dazzling historical romance!"

—*Romance Reviews* Top Pick

Praise for
Lady Amelia's Mess and a Half

"Full of love and betrayal, passion and scandal...well researched and entertaining."

—*RT Book Reviews*

"Anything written by Samantha Grace deserves a coveted spot on my 'keeper shelf.'"

—*Romance Reviews* Top Pick

"Clever, spicy, and fresh from beginning to end."

—Amelia Grey, *New York Times* bestselling author of *The Duke in My Bed*

Praise for
Miss Hillary Schools a Scoundrel

A *Publishers Weekly* Top 10 Romance

"With heart and humor, Grace delivers a rich and winning Regency debut. Clever and charming, this tale brings in everything Regency fans love."

—*Publishers Weekly* Starred Review

"Grace's fabulously fun debut will dazzle and delight readers."

—*Booklist*

"An absolute must-read. I loved it, I adored it, and I can't wait to read more from this author."

—*Romance Reviews*

Also by Samantha Grace

THE *Best* OF BOTH ROGUES

SAMANTHA GRACE

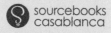
sourcebooks
casablanca

Copyright © 2015 by Samantha Grace
Cover and internal design © 2015 by Sourcebooks, Inc.
Cover art by Judy York

Sourcebooks and the colophon are registered trademarks of
Sourcebooks, Inc.

All rights reserved. No part of this book may be reproduced in any
form or by any electronic or mechanical means including information storage and retrieval systems—except in the case of brief
quotations embodied in critical articles or reviews—without permission in writing from its publisher, Sourcebooks, Inc.

The characters and events portrayed in this book are fictitious or
are used fictitiously. Any similarity to real persons, living or dead,
is purely coincidental and not intended by the author.

Published by Sourcebooks Casablanca, an imprint of Sourcebooks,
Inc.
P.O. Box 4410, Naperville, Illinois 60567-4410
(630) 961-3900
Fax: (630) 961-2168
www.sourcebooks.com

Printed and bound in Canada
MBP 10 9 8 7 6 5 4 3 2 1

In memory of Eddie, a true gentleman at heart

Prologue

EVE THORNE HAD NO MORE TEARS TO SHED. HER BODY had become heavy, sinking into her bed as if it might swallow her. The coverlet beneath her cheek was damp and cool. Subdued afternoon light cast her normally cheerful bedchamber in shadow.

Her maid's sympathetic frown and the porcelain plate she held out to Eve made her eyes burn, dispelling the notion she had cried herself dry. The plate was filled with dishes meant for Eve's wedding breakfast, food that would spoil in a day with no guests to enjoy the feast.

"Lord Thorne will be cross if I cannot coax you to eat something, miss," Alice said.

"Has he returned?" Speaking required more effort than Eve thought possible; her voice was raspy and her throat tight.

Alice shook her graying head. "May I speak freely, miss?"

"Please," Eve said on a sigh.

"You don't want your brother to find you this way. The baron is on a tear as it is."

Sebastian was scouring London for Eve's runaway groom now, determined to defend her honor. Finding her in tears would only make matters worse, but how did one hide the shattered pieces of one's heart?

She blinked up at Alice. "I will try."

Her lady's maid answered with an encouraging smile and placed the plate back on its tray. "Very good, miss. Allow me to help you sit up."

Eve leaned forward while Alice fluffed the pillows and watched in a numbing fog as her maid placed the tray across her lap.

The sight of red grapes made Eve's vision blur again. "Oh, bother," she mumbled. Why did everything have to make her think of Ben?

It was hard to believe it had only been last night when they had teased each other.

Ben's smoky blue eyes—the perfect blending of dark blue and gray—had twinkled with mischief as he'd wrapped her in his arms when Mama had allowed them a rare moment alone for Eve to bid him good night. It was to be their last good-bye, for tonight he should have taken her to his home. *Her* home.

Once we have spoken our vows, I will expect many things from you, Miss Thorne.

Is that so, Mr. Hillary? Let me hear these expectations, so I might decide if I wish to meet them.

She had been teasing. In that moment of blind devotion, she would have done anything he asked. His amused chuckle had washed her in warm tingles.

Do you want the entire list?

She had nodded, expecting him to recite the usual duties involved with managing a household. Instead, he'd made her laugh and planted the most delicious vision in her mind to take with her to bed: Ben lounging on a fainting couch like some hedonistic god, wearing nothing but a loincloth and laurel wreath in his golden brown hair, while Eve fed him grapes.

Eve had felt so cherished and happy when he'd stolen a kiss and whispered in her ear. *I love you, Kitten.*

She swiped at the wetness leaking from the corners of her eyes. What could have happened between nightfall and this morning at the church to change his mind about her? Or had she been too smitten to recognize reservation in his actions?

He had come to St. George's Church, and by all accounts, seemed prepared to marry her. Surely the love she had felt in his touch last night was no lie. Yet her limited imagination didn't allow for any other excuse for what he had done. Ben left her at the church, humiliated her in front of her family and friends.

A soft knock sounded at her door and Alice swept across the room to answer. Eve's mother paused in the threshold. Her dark gaze flickered over Eve as a small frown formed on her lips. "Eve, there is a gentleman here to see you. Mr. Cooper says Mr. Hillary sent him."

Eve's heart leaped. She knew Ben hadn't truly abandoned her. Something of the utmost importance must have occurred to make him leave so suddenly.

More important than your wedding?

She ignored the logic in favor of having Ben back.

"Should I have Milo tell him you are not receiving?" Mama asked.

"No!" Eve nearly knocked over the tray in her haste, but Alice grabbed it before it tipped. Eve mumbled an apology and scrambled from the bed. She stopped at the washstand to clear the evidence of her tears from her cheeks, although she wouldn't be able to hide the redness of her eyes and nose. "Did Mr. Cooper indicate how he knows Ben?"

Mama came up behind her to place her hands on Eve's shoulders. "He only said he made his acquaintance at the docks this afternoon. Mr. Cooper was seeing his cousin off to India on one of Benjamin's ships."

Why would Ben be at the docks on their wedding day? Eve swallowed against the panic welling up at the back of her throat. There must be a reasonable explanation, and it appeared Mr. Cooper was here to deliver it. She couldn't get ahead of herself.

Draping the cloth over the side of the basin, she took a deep breath. "I suppose I should see what the gentleman has to say before drawing conclusions."

Mama's smile reflected in the looking glass appeared more like a grimace. "That seems wise, dearest."

With her mother at her side, Eve made her way to the drawing room where Mr. Cooper was waiting. He stood as they entered, a friendly grin on his round face. A quick glance at his sturdy brown trousers, plain jacket, and simply tied cravat revealed he was a gentleman of little means, but a gentleman all the same.

Mama came forward to perform an introduction. "Mr. Cooper, this is my daughter, Eve. Mr. Cooper is a parish chaplain at St. Saviour's Church."

A chaplain? Eve refrained from rubbing away the tightness at her temples. A man of the cloth was often employed to deliver distressing news, but that certainly wasn't the case today. Still, she couldn't stop from asking, "Has something happened to Mr. Hillary? Has he been hurt or become ill?"

His kind smile didn't fade. "No, miss. He was all in one piece when last I spoke with him, although he was a bit pale and shaky, now that I consider it. I am certain there is no cause for alarm, however." He reached into his jacket and pulled a long box from an inside pocket. "Mr. Hillary charged me with a task, and I promised to deliver this to you straightaway. He said this belongs to you."

Eve accepted the gaily wrapped box and allowed her mother to guide her to the settee. Her fingers shook as she tore open the gift. The rip of paper seemed to echo in the silence.

Mama sat down beside her. "Will Mr. Hillary be calling at Thorne Place soon?"

A slight shifting of the man's jaw made Eve's heart race. "I do not believe that to be the case, my lady." When Mama raised her eyebrows in a gesture of irritation, Mr. Cooper cleared his throat. "What I mean to say is Mr. Hillary departed on his ship, ma'am. He is traveling to Delhi, as is my cousin."

Eve fumbled the box and it fell to the Turkish carpet. A gold necklace with yellow gems spilled out, winking up at her in the fading sunlight. Her breathing had ceased the moment Mr. Cooper said Ben was gone, but it returned on a ragged inhale.

"Allow me, Miss Thorne." The gentleman bent

to retrieve the necklace before holding it out to her. She stared at the unusual piece lying in the worn palm of his glove. A small circular gem—perhaps a yellow diamond—sat atop two larger, identical ones, creating a pyramid. The necklace itself was composed of two strands of tiny black pearls, perfect and elegant.

Her hand shook as she accepted the offering. "D-did Mr. Hillary say anything? Was there a message for me?"

"I am sorry, miss. I was charged with delivering the package, but Mr. Hillary sent no word other than this belongs to you."

"But I've never seen it before, or anything like it." How could it belong to her?

Mr. Cooper shifted his weight to get a closer look at the jewelry. "It is an exotic piece. I saw similar ones when I toured India. I believe it holds special meaning."

Eve's fingers closed around the necklace, and she gazed up at the man in interest.

He seemed to recognize her curiosity, because he went on to explain. "I attended a wedding during my stay in Calcutta, and the groom presented a similar necklace to his bride before securing it around her neck. A fellow wedding guest explained that the necklace is believed to protect the marriage and serves as a symbol of love, trust, and marital happiness."

A low growl came from her mother, the unladylike sound shocking. "Mr. Cooper," she snapped. "Do you realize the cruelty of your words? My daughter was abandoned at the altar today."

The poor man's jaw dropped, his complexion suddenly bloodless.

"How dare you speak to her of marital happiness at a time like this?" Eve's mother was on her feet and moving toward the bellpull. "Have you no sensitivity?"

"Mama, Mr. Cooper meant no harm. He could not have known."

Her mother would accept no defense of the man, however. "What type of gentleman agrees to perform the devil's errand without question?"

"The devil?" Mr. Cooper's pale skin began to glisten in the afternoon sunlight.

"Mama." Eve's soft reprimand went unnoticed.

Her mother scowled in Mr. Cooper's direction as she yanked the bellpull cord. She had never seen her mother in such a state. Eve had always assumed her brother had inherited his temper from their father, but Mama seemed as unstoppable as Sebastian had been earlier that day.

When Milo entered the drawing room, Eve's mother instructed him to see Mr. Cooper to the door.

"Forgive me, Miss Thorne." The clergyman ducked his head and made a hasty retreat from the drawing room before Milo needed to lay a hand on him.

"Thank you, sir," Eve called after Mr. Cooper.

Once the door closed, Mama swung toward her. "Why should you offer your thanks? Of all the nerve, marching in here without an invitation and…"

Eve blocked out the rest of her mother's rant as she contemplated the necklace. Why would Ben tell Mr. Cooper the jewelry belonged to her when she'd never before laid eyes on the piece? A necklace that symbolized love, trust, and happiness?

Unless…

Hope flared in her heart. He was coming back for her. She couldn't fathom any explanation for his desertion today, but he must have a good reason, one she would understand as soon as he returned from dealing with whatever had called him away to India. She hugged the necklace to her chest, close to her heart, and prayed for his swift and safe return.

One

BENJAMIN HILLARY—BEN TO HIS FAMILY AND FRIENDS; "that damned heartless rogue" to most of Society— tried the back gate leading to the Eldridges' garden.

"Locked," he muttered. Of course it was. He'd had nothing but bad luck since his return from Delhi almost a month earlier.

"Balderdash." Crispin Locke, Viscount Margrave, shouldered him aside and grabbed the weathered iron handle. Gas lamps flanking the gate bathed the stone wall in a golden glow. "You have to put some brawn into it. These old gates stick." Ben's old schoolmate shot him a superior look before yanking with a loud grunt.

The eight-foot-high gate didn't budge.

"Peculiar." Margrave's strong brows dropped low as he smacked his hands together to clear the orange residue from his riding glove and proceeded to soil both gloves. "Why do you suppose Lord Eldridge had the gate secured?"

"To keep out unwanted guests?"

Perhaps the Earl of Wellham had warned Lord Eldridge that Ben might show up tonight. That would explain the small army of footmen at the front door. If Wellham would stop turning Ben away when he called on him at home or hiding in his club where Ben was not a member, he wouldn't be reduced to sneaking into the assemblies.

An invitation might be nice too, but he understood the reason his name was omitted from most guest lists. He had unintentionally destroyed the reputation of an innocent young lady—a lady he still pined for two years after walking away from her. Fortunately, he'd been able to set things back to rights for Miss Eve Thorne upon his return to Town. She was back in Society now, and Ben was determined to win her back into his arms.

Eventually.

She claimed she wanted nothing to do with him, but Ben possessed the letter Mr. Cooper had sent to him in India stating otherwise. Eve and the clergyman had developed a friendship when she began calling on him at St. Saviour's Church soon after he had delivered Ben's wedding gift. Mr. Cooper's letter implored Ben to return to England immediately, as it seemed only Ben's presence could end her misery. Until that time, Ben had believed he was the only one still suffering.

"You won't be getting in through the gate." Margrave swiped a lock of blond hair from his forehead and left a smudge.

Ben really should tell his friend, but the idea of Margrave bowing over Lady Eldridge's hand, all pristine and proper except for an orange smear on his face, made Ben grin.

"Why do you look so pleased?" Margrave grumbled. "I thought you wanted to get inside."

"I do, and I *will*."

Ben's sister had warned him away from the Eldridge Ball, because Eve would be here. And even though Ben had come for Wellham, she was the reason he wouldn't allow a locked gate to defeat him. He walked alongside the wall, searching for a way over.

A tree branch hung over the stone wall just low enough that he could reach it with Margrave's help.

"Give me a leg up?" Ben said.

His friend made a stirrup with his hands for Ben's foot and hoisted him into the air. Ben grabbed the branch, and when Margrave stepped out of harm's way, he swung his legs to build momentum, hooked one over the branch, and hauled himself up to straddle it.

"Well done. Wellham is in for a surprise, I think." Margrave saluted him, as if assisting a friend to scale a wall was nothing out of the ordinary.

"This seems like old hat to you, Margrave. What were you up to while I was away?"

He flashed a jaunty smile up at Ben. "Oh, you know. Things and such."

That barely qualified as an answer, but Margrave had never been the chatty type. As his friend moved on silent feet and faded into the darkness, Ben worked his way toward the tree trunk. Once he'd cleared the wall, he dropped to the ground with a teeth-rattling thump. He rolled his neck and shoulders, then brushed off his breeches and coat.

"I am too old for this nonsense."

At three-and-thirty, he was hardly in his dotage, but he wasn't a young buck to be kicking up a lark anymore either. He located and followed a path that wound through the garden and ended at the terrace stairs.

Several guests had retreated outdoors, taking advantage of the light breeze off the Thames. A lively melody floated through the opened French doors and flashes of color appeared through the bank of windows. Ladies dressed in crimson, plum, and emerald skipped around the ballroom floor on the arms of their gentlemen partners. Ben hadn't danced a quadrille since he'd left London, but the steps came back to him in an instant.

A footman stood just inside the doors and, noting Ben's approach, held out a silver tray. "Champagne, sir?"

Ben grabbed a glass and adopted a swagger as he entered the Eldridge ballroom. If he behaved as if he belonged there, no one would question him. They never did.

∽

"You mustn't fret," Eve Thorne's sister-in-law murmured in her ear. "He will be here."

"I'm not fretting."

Helena's blue-green gaze dropped to the handkerchief Eve hadn't realized she'd been twisting into a tight coil. It was an accurate reflection of what Sir Jonathan Hackberry's tardiness was doing to her insides. Her fiancé had promised to arrive early to Lord and Lady Eldridge's ball, where their betrothal would be announced within the hour, and he had yet to make an appearance.

A thread of apprehension wound its way around Eve's heart and held it captive. What if Jonathan didn't come?

Giving up on following the conversation between Lady Eldridge and two ladies from the Mayfair Ladies' Charitable Society, Eve stole another glance over her shoulder.

"Sir Jonathan will be here," Helena repeated.

Eve repaid Helena's kindness with a halfhearted smile. Her brother's new bride was more than a sister-in-law to Eve; she was a dear friend. Eve didn't want Helena to know her reassurance did nothing to calm the tempest brewing inside her.

Everything will be well. There is no cause for worry. Eve had learned long ago these were empty platitudes people tossed around when they didn't know what else to say. But Helena meant well, and Eve loved her for trying to ease her worries.

Sebastian wore a scowl as he reentered the ballroom. He pulled Eve and Helena aside when he reached them. "Hackberry wasn't playing cards."

Eve had known it would be a pointless trip. Jonathan was not a gambling man. He was an intellectual, more interested in archaeology and anthropology than loo, but Sebastian seemed to need something to do, so she had suggested he check the card room.

Helena looked back and forth between Eve and Sebastian, then forced a bright smile, her dimples showing. "We haven't searched the refreshment room yet."

"An excellent idea. Shall we?" Sebastian held his arm out to his wife, but Eve shook her head.

"I will wait with Lady Eldridge in case Sir Jonathan arrives and cannot find me."

"Are you certain?" Her brother drew Helena closer as if their short separation while he visited the card room had been days instead of a half hour. Helena tipped her head and gazed at him from beneath her lashes.

Eve couldn't help smiling at the newlyweds. She appreciated their attempts to include her, but it was obvious they would rather be alone. "I am certain." She shooed them away. "Go. Sir Jonathan will be here any moment."

She said a silent prayer that he wouldn't make her out to be a liar. Being abandoned by a second husband-to-be would be too mortifying to bear.

This time when she scanned the crowd, her heartbeat skipped when she thought she saw Ben. She almost wilted on the floor when she realized it wasn't him. Lady Eldridge swore Eve's former betrothed wouldn't step one foot into Eldridge House, even though he had been turning up like a bad penny at the assemblies ever since his return to London. The earl had taken extra precautions tonight and hired additional men to guard the doors at his wife's request. Nevertheless, Eve had learned never to underestimate Ben's ability to get in wherever he wasn't wanted.

And she didn't want him here tonight.

She had waited far too long for Ben to come back to her. In two years, he hadn't sent a single word of explanation, and now that he had returned, she no longer cared what he had to say.

Liar. Eve huffed in response to the whisper at the back of her mind. Well, she didn't *want* to care. That must count for something.

Lady Eldridge and her guests moved on from discussing their latest charity efforts and began gossiping together. Having been the topic of wagging tongues too often, Eve had no desire to join them. She wandered a few steps away before checking to see if the countess had noticed. She hadn't.

The sea of familiar faces around Eve began to blur as she resumed the lookout for Jonathan. Perhaps he was lost again. He may be perfectly capable of traveling to Egypt without incident, but he couldn't navigate a town house to save his life. He often took wrong turns on his way to the men's retiring room and wound up in the host's library. Sebastian had even retrieved him from the corridor outside Lord and Lady Sethwick's family rooms once.

Eve couldn't search their hosts' town house for him, but a quick circle of the ballroom might be wise. With Lady Eldridge occupied, Eve slipped into the crowd. She wouldn't go far, and she would be back before Sebastian and Helena returned, hopefully with Jonathan at her side. She weaved her way toward the perimeter of the room where there was no traffic and stopped to get her bearings. If she headed toward the bank of French doors at the back of the ballroom and looped around, she could make quick work of her search.

She squinted at the guests crowded into the ballroom dancing a quadrille, even though she knew

Jonathan wouldn't be on the dance floor either. He preferred to observe from the sidelines. Oh, how she missed dancing with a skilled partner. A sigh slipped past her lips.

Heavens. She hadn't meant to sound so wistful. Jonathan was a good man, a fine gentleman who accepted her just as she was, scandalous past and all. And she cared a great deal for him. A life without dancing was a small price to pay for his amiable company.

With a decisive nod, she swung in the direction of the French doors and squeaked in surprise. Benjamin Hillary, the blasted rat, was headed her way. She froze, not knowing which way to go but certain she didn't want to talk to him. He hadn't tried to speak with her since that night at Lady Chattington's ball three weeks earlier, and she liked it that way.

Or she *should*. She hated that she was a tad bit disappointed he'd been keeping his distance.

Ben hadn't spotted her yet, since his gaze was fixed on the dance floor. Whipping her head around, she searched for a place to go.

The alcove. No, the plant!

She didn't have time for debate. Without another thought, she dashed for a deserted corner of the ballroom and squeezed behind the potted palms and ferns.

Saints above, what if she missed her betrothal announcement because she was hiding in a corner? Or worse, what if the evening ended with her brother challenging Ben to another duel? She couldn't hope to intervene a second time to save Ben's life.

Damn the rogue. He was going to ruin her wedding again.

Two

BEN MADE A SLOW CIRCLE OF THE BRIGHTLY LIT BALL-room, stopping occasionally to study the couples as they sashayed past, their cheeks pink from exertion. After several moments, he was satisfied Lord Wellham wasn't among the dancers, not that Ben was surprised. If his memory served, the earl favored gambling over gamboling.

Reaching a secluded corner near a dark alcove, he paused to check once more for his quarry before he sought out the card room.

"What are you doing here?" a voice hissed. "You are not on the guest list."

"Pardon?" Ben spun toward the speaker and came up short. His eyebrows veered toward each other. "How do you know?" he whispered back to the mass of green palm fronds.

"Because I helped make the list." The plant's fronds parted, and Eve Thorne's stern glare greeted him.

What the devil was she doing?

Her frown deepened when he simply stared, at a loss for words. "Do you wish to die, Mr. Hillary?"

The corners of his mouth twitched. "Let me guess, you've been attacked by a man-eating plant. Are you in need of rescue, Kitten?"

She growled softly and the fronds snapped back into place. Ben checked the surrounding area to be certain they hadn't earned any unwanted attention, then peered around the massive greenery. Eve was wedged against the wall, her yellow chiffon skirts crushed against the large pot. Her chest rose and fell in rapid movements, drawing his attention to the modest swell of her breasts peeking above her lacy neckline. A rosy glow infused her ivory skin, making the sprinkling of freckles across her cheeks almost unnoticeable.

God, he had missed her—her freckles, her pouty lips, her soulful brown eyes. He had been smitten from the moment he had spied her at the theater during the little Season, and two years on a faraway continent had done nothing to cool his ardor.

"What are you doing back there, Miss Thorne, and shouldn't you have a chaperone?"

She crossed her arms as if erecting a wall between them. "God only knows why, but I am trying to save your skin, Benjamin James Arran Hillary."

Damnation. He had almost forgotten he'd been burdened with so many names, and that she had a habit of invoking every one when she was perturbed. His smile expanded. Despite her pretense of indifference, she was worried for him. "Am I to conclude your skulking about means you still care?"

"I *care* about Lady Eldridge, and I do not want to see her ball ruined by you and Sebastian coming to fisticuffs. You really must leave before he sees you and demands another meeting on the field."

Crossing paths with Sebastian Thorne didn't concern Ben. Her brother's need to defend her reputation after Ben jilted her had been satisfied three weeks earlier in a duel, and Thorne would not issue a second challenge for fear of losing. Ben suspected neither of them wanted to risk looking like fools again either. Instead of dueling with pistols or swords as any other normal men would do, they had allowed Eve to choose the weapons. She had chosen gloves.

He scowled. "Do you have any idea how ridiculous it looked for two men to engage in a slapping match?" The gents at Brooks's hadn't stopped talking about the duel for days, and Ben had endured the brunt of the teasing since he'd followed his youngest brother's advice and allowed Thorne to win.

Eve's smile radiated with self-satisfaction. "Since no one died, I would say I made an excellent choice."

He grudgingly admitted her cleverness had managed to resolve the conflict without bloodshed—or much, anyway. Ben had walked away with a cut on his cheek and a nasty bruise, thanks to her brother filling his glove with pebbles. But bruised pride and a bruised mug were small prices to pay to see Eve's position in Society restored.

Eve pursed her lips before her scolding continued. "Just because I saved you last time doesn't mean I can stop Sebastian from killing you if he finds you here tonight. You really must leave before he realizes you have sneaked in. How did you make it past the footmen?"

Ben casually scanned the crowd, uninterested in discussing his undignified entrance into Eldridge House or her brother. "I don't see Thorne, which means he is unlikely to see me."

"Sebastian escorted his wife to the refreshment room," Eve said, "but they will return any moment."

Ah, yes. Her brother had taken a wife recently, a young widow from Scotland. "I expected matrimony to tame the beast."

She wrinkled her adorable turned-up nose at him. "Do not speak of matrimony and beasts in the same sentence. It reminds me to keep my distance lest I strangle you. *Accidentally*, of course."

"Completely by accident, I'm sure." He chuckled under his breath. "Although I imagine you would employ a hefty dose of cheerfulness in the process, wouldn't you, Miss Thorne?"

"Yes, well." A touch of mirth slipped past her stony facade, making her eyes shine. "Mama always said happy is she who performs a good deed."

"Why, Miss Thorne!" he said with mock surprise.

A laugh slipped from her—no dainty fairy's titter, but a hearty sound that made him fall in love with her all over again.

"You never could stay cross for long, Eve. I always admired that about you."

"I am *still* cross with you, Mr. Hillary." And yet she was still smiling too. This was the Eve he remembered: joyful, witty, and capable of chasing away any darkness lurking about.

"I see I've managed to improve my standing already," he said. "I believe when we last spoke you were furious and declared me a loathsome, fork-tongued serpent of Hades."

The pronounced arch of her brow said she stood by her opinion, even if her fury had died down to a mere irritation.

He'd missed this, bantering with her. No one had ever challenged him like Eve. He extended his hand, needing to touch her. "Will you please come from behind the plants before someone notices me talking to them and thinks I have formed an attachment?"

Her smile faded. "Ben, you cannot stay. I'm sorry."

She had no cause to feel sorry, but he did. Ben had been living with regret every day since he'd left. He owed her an apology even though words could never make up for what he'd done.

"Stand up with me, Eve. Grant me one dance and I won't ask you again."

At least not until the next set. He had no plans of walking away from her again, but a gentleman never tipped his hand when setting his sights on a young lady.

She licked her lips, hesitated, then shook her head. "It wouldn't be right."

It wouldn't be right? Because it would displease her brother? Thorne could go to hell. Ben had things to say to Eve, and he would say them one way or another. He dropped his hand to his side. "Very well. If you will not come out, I will join you."

She gasped as he made a move to wedge himself into the crowded space. "Wait!"

He halted and smiled indulgently. "Yes, Miss Thorne?" The beginning of a waltz drifted across the ballroom, a merry composition he didn't recognize after his time away.

Eve loved the waltz. When he had courted her, he'd waited close to the entrance in order to sign her dance card first. He hated the thought of another man holding her close, her beautiful eyes sparkling as some eager buck led her around the floor. Ben wanted to be the only man to ever hold her.

He offered his most charming smile. "It is a waltz." He drew out the last word, trying to tempt her.

Interest flashed across her pretty face, but she didn't budge from her hiding spot.

"Come on, Kitten. We were always perfectly matched for this dance."

Her dark lashes fluttered like the wings of a moth drawn to a flame. She looked toward the ceiling as if searching for an escape, but eventually her gaze settled on him. "If I dance with you, then will you leave?"

He fought back a victorious smile. "I will." After he found Wellham and had a word with the earl.

Eve's eyes narrowed on him. "*One* dance, Mr. Hillary, then you must leave. I will not be charmed into allowing another, and you cannot work your way back into my good graces. I would advise against even trying. Please, give me your word."

He wouldn't make a promise he couldn't keep, not again. "The dance will be over before you negotiate the terms. I suppose I must join you after all." Shrugging his shoulders, he moved to squeeze into the corner with her.

"No!" She held up a hand. "I am coming, but first make certain no one is watching."

Ben glanced around the room. No one seemed to be paying him any notice, but it was a dark corner. And rather dull. Or it would be if Eve hadn't chosen to surprise him. "No one is looking."

"One more thing." Her cheeks turned scarlet as she slipped from her hiding place. "Please don't call me Kitten. I am not that girl anymore."

He nodded in understanding, sobering. Two years had changed him, and the scandal he'd created seemed to have changed her as well. Eve seemed stronger. More capable of making him toe the line, if she wished it.

He held out his arm. She hesitated to touch him. Once she had made her decision, however, she gripped his arm and attempted to drag him toward the dance floor.

"You are an eager one, Miss Thorne. Missed my company on the dance floor?"

He caught a glimpse of her dismayed frown before she ducked her head and urged him toward the middle of the floor. He followed, dodging couples as they went. Once they reached the thick of the crowd, he took her in his arms to lead her around the floor. A shocking scarlet blush had invaded her cheeks. Her gaze shot around as if looking for someone. The meaning of her odd behavior dawned on him, and a bitter taste coated his tongue.

"You don't want to be seen with me, do you, Miss Thorne?"

He expected a clever retort, a denial, or a frank affirmation, not the quivering of her bottom lip as her shimmering brown gaze lifted toward him.

"Oh, Ben. Why didn't you just stay away?"

❧

Eve silently cursed the break of her voice. She no longer wanted to have butterflies in her stomach when Ben was near, or for her heart to drum a rapid staccato. She didn't want to sigh with pleasure as they glided around the ballroom floor, moving together as if they were one, or to cling to him as the gentle pressure of his hand on her back made her bones feel as if they were dissolving. And she certainly shouldn't *revel* in the sensations she didn't want to feel.

Ben's eyes darkened to a stormy blue as she held his gaze through the turn. She forced herself to look away, her gaze landing on his chest as a reminder that no heart resided beneath his charcoal gray waistcoat— the one that molded to his lean muscles and fit him like a second skin.

Lud! Why must he look like heaven dished up with a silver spoon tonight? She swallowed another sigh. Desire was a voracious creature that couldn't be trusted. The true measure of a man was the kindness of his soul, and she was certain Ben's soul was as dark as night.

His fingers tightened on her back as if he sensed she was teetering on the edge of running away. "Eve," he said on a breath, "I owe you an apology. Not a day has passed that I haven't regretted walking away from you."

She snapped from her trance; the fire that had been smoldering inside her sparked to life. "*Walked*, Mr. Hillary? I heard you dashed. Your brother sported a black eye for coming between you and the door."

"I know, and I hate myself for it." His Adam's apple

bobbed and a flush invaded his face, disappearing into his hairline.

Her eyes widened. Ben hadn't blushed a day in his life. She was certain of it. Forever the flirtatious rogue, he turned ladies into blithering idiots. He'd never been vulnerable with her, but now... Her heart lurched at the thought he, too, might be capable of being hurt.

His thumb skimmed her shoulder blade, causing tingles to travel through her body. "I understand if I botched my chances at earning your forgiveness," he said softly, "but you still deserve an apology. It is too long overdue."

No one in her right mind would allow a few spoken words to soften her heart, and yet her resentment began to melt like a Gunter's ice on a warm day. She had always been too forgiving, ever since she was a little girl. When Father had yelled at her for being too noisy, a simple pat on her head later soothed her injured feelings. Or when Sebastian was a boy and charmed Cook into giving him a treat meant for Eve, forgiveness came as soon as her brother offered to play a game with her.

She had always considered her compassionate nature to be a virtue. Now it felt like a liability. She didn't want to forgive Ben. Holding a grudge was the only protection she had to keep from falling under his spell. The rogue would never turn *her* into a blushing, blithering idiot again.

A rush of heat flooded her body as she recalled diving behind the palms when she'd spotted him circling the ballroom. That might have been a touch idiotic, but she had panicked, which she supposed made her blithering as well. *Very well.* Beginning *now*, she would no longer allow him to affect her.

She cleared her throat, striving for a dignified mien. "I will take your apology into consideration, Mr. Hillary."

"I suppose your consideration is all I can ask, Miss Thorne. Perhaps in the near future, you might even consider starting over as—"

The music ended and Eve dropped her hands to her sides, steeling herself against him. "The dance is over. You promised you would leave now."

His mouth hung halfway open, the rest of his sentence lost. Recovering from her lapse in manners, he offered a strained smile and held out his arm. "Of course, Miss Thorne."

"Thank you, but I do not require your escort." She surged into the crowd before she changed her mind.

Ben was her past. Jonathan was her future. There was no such thing as starting over.

Hurrying with her head down, she made her way back toward Lady Eldridge. She didn't know how she would explain her absence, or even if any explanation would be required. If someone had spotted her waltzing with Ben and told her brother already, she was in for a row. She understood Sebastian only wanted to protect her, but her brother would never understand her position. No matter how hard she tried, she just couldn't hate Ben.

A lady backed into her path and Eve bumped into her. "Pardon me," she mumbled, tried to sidestep the woman, and accidentally stomped a gentleman's toes. A surprised grunt reached her ears.

"Sorry." She tried to forge on, ducking her head even more to hide her embarrassment, but two firm hands grabbed her shoulders. She gasped.

"Here you are, darling."

The voice filled her with relief, and she nearly collapsed in Jonathan's arms. Looking up into her fiancé's warm turquoise gaze, she smiled. "You've arrived."

His cockeyed grin was aimed back at her. "Of course I have. Where else would I be except by your side this evening? Forgive me for being late. I—uh—I ran into an unexpected delay."

Eve's assessing gaze took in his untamed brown curls and rumpled cravat. Her heart lost some of its lightness. Jonathan had a tendency to become absorbed in his studies at times, but surely he wouldn't forget about their betrothal ball. "Did you lose track of time at the museum?"

His smile faded. "No, darling. I swear to you. There was an incident along the way this evening, but all is well and I am here."

"What kind of incident?"

"I'd rather not worry you," he said, two lines appearing between his brows. When she didn't shift her curious gaze or offer to let the matter drop, he sighed. "A pickpocket tried to take my watch in Covent Garden."

"A pickpocket?" The shock of his answer made her light-headed. When she swayed slightly, he took her by the arm to steady her.

"He was just a boy. I gave chase, but he was too quick. There really is no cause to worry."

She frowned. "Why were you on foot after dark?

It may have been only a boy *this* time, but you cannot expect to be so fortunate next time."

"I know; it was foolish. I promise never to repeat my mistake. Forgive me for being late?" His sheepish expression lent him a boyish air, and she didn't have the heart to scold him further.

"You are forgiven. And thank God you were not hurt." She linked arms with him. "Now let's find my family. Lord Eldridge will make our announcement soon."

Throwing one more anxious look over her shoulder, she prayed Ben was already leaving Eldridge House. Her stomach ached at the thought of him finding out about her betrothal as if he were a casual acquaintance rather than the man she had loved and mourned for so long.

She should have told him about Jonathan when they danced. Even though she had every right to make a happy life for herself, she couldn't shake the sense she was betraying Ben by keeping her impending marriage a secret.

Three

A PUNGENT FOG HUNG ON THE AIR, CASTING A GRAYISH tint over everything in the card room. Ben cursed under his breath. He would stink of cheroot when he returned to the ball. If the Earl of Wellham were not among the loo players, Ben would make another sweep of the ballroom. And if he happened to cross paths with Eve again, he didn't want to give her one more excuse to run from him.

He frowned, unhappy with their parting this evening. At the end of the dance, she had bolted like a racehorse when the starter waves his flag. She hadn't even bothered to say good-bye.

Just like you, jackass. Ben scratched his neck where prickles crept along his skin. The day he left for India, he'd had so many thoughts swirling in his mind, but when Mr. Cooper asked if Ben had a message for Eve to accompany the gift, he'd become too choked up to speak. He had never said good-bye to her either.

Ben was likely a fool to believe it was possible to win her back after what he'd done, but her pull was undeniable. He still loved her. He didn't deserve her—never had—but he would do everything he could to earn her favor again. Now, however, he had a task to complete. If he wanted to help Charlotte's family, he needed to propose a deal with Wellham, which required an actual conversation with the man.

Charlotte Tanney. Ben's first infatuation. He still pictured her from the day they tried to elope. *Golden hair tucked beneath the fashionable new bonnet he'd bought with his allowance, her wide smile plumping her rosy cheeks.*

"In only a few days, I'll be Mrs. Benjamin Hillary," she whispered in his ear as they crammed into a mail coach with a mother and her brood of five children. *"I have never been happier."*

He grinned and discreetly brushed his hand against hers to convey his agreement. He'd never been happier either. At fifteen, no one would ever convince him love couldn't transcend social class. Charlotte, the sweet and innocent baker's daughter, was his perfect match.

As the carriage pulled away from the coaching inn, the boy beside Ben dug his bony elbow into his ribs. Ben grunted under his breath and shifted closer to Charlotte. The boy's mother stared blankly from across the coach as she cradled her fussy baby against her chest. The town of Eton hadn't disappeared on the horizon before the baby began screeching loud enough to explode his brain. The stench of a dirty nappy crept up on him and soon overpowered the spices clinging to Charlotte's silky hair.

He never traveled in such a manner, accustomed as he was to the luxuries his father's wealth afforded. How anyone survived such conditions was beyond him.

Charlotte lifted her face toward him and smiled in commiseration. "Thank you. I realize this is beneath you."

"No, it isn't." He refused to acknowledge any differences between them. They belonged together, no matter what his father believed, and once Charlotte was his wife, his father would see he was wrong.

He'd never had a chance to change his father's mind, since Father and his older brother Nicholas caught up to them before the end of their second day. Ben hadn't been allowed a moment to say good-bye to Charlotte before she was bustled into another mail coach headed back to Eton and Ben was forced into a hired coach that carried him back to his family home.

The faint sounds of Charlotte's anguished cries encroached on his memory, and he slammed the door in his mind.

Ben returned his attention to searching for the Earl of Wellham at the overcrowded gaming tables. Margrave caught his eye and waved him over to a table wedged in a corner of the drawing room. As usual, his friend had chosen a position that allowed him the best view of his surroundings. Ben's brother Jake was seated next to Margrave.

Ben ignored the glower his brother directed toward him. No doubt Jake had heard about his back-door entrance and came to the card room to deliver another lecture on etiquette. Jake thought attending parties without an invitation was beneath Ben. Ben thought his youngest brother should remove the stick from his arse.

Signaling a footman to bring him a drink, Ben scanned the various groups of men gathered around the tables. Wellham wasn't there. Ben's source—one of Wellham's servants—assured him the earl would be here this evening, so he couldn't have gotten far. When the footman approached with a crystal tumbler on a small tray, Ben offered his thanks and headed toward Margrave and Jake's table to wait for the earl to make an appearance.

As Ben approached, Margrave's dark gaze remained locked on his cards. He was likely calculating the odds of holding a winning hand. The viscount was a genius with numbers and never forgot what cards had been played, which was the reason Ben hadn't sat at his table since their days at Oxford. He was pleased to see his brother hadn't fallen prey to Margrave's trap either, choosing to observe rather than join the game. Three of their fellow gents were not as bright.

Jake lifted an eyebrow in reproach. "I tried to speak to the earl on your behalf, but the second he saw me, he dashed out the door. Someone saw him leaving the ball on foot. I would have told you when you entered the room if you hadn't given me the cut direct. I'm guessing Wellham will not be back."

A low growl rumbled in Ben's throat. "What the devil is wrong with the man? I barely know him, so what is his objection to me?"

Jake shrugged. "He wasn't exactly enthused to speak with me either. Whatever his objection, it seems to extend to our family, although I cannot guess at what that might be."

Ben took an angry swig of his brandy and remained standing. He didn't see a point in staying in the card room if his quarry was gone. He nodded toward Jake. "Thank you for making the attempt anyway. I know you prefer remaining by your wife's side at these sorts of events. Should we go find her?"

Ben didn't know his sister-in-law well since he'd been in India during his brother's courtship of her, but in less than a day, he had noted Jake's devotion to Amelia and the son she had given him. He tried not to envy his brother.

At Jake's grim expression, a ripple of unease passed through Ben. "Perhaps we should stay where we are," his brother said, "or better yet, why don't we leave the ball and find a tavern?"

Something was amiss. To leave early would risk offending Lord and Lady Eldridge. Jake would no sooner abandon his wife than he would his priggish manners.

"What has happened? Why have you really sought me out?"

Jake tugged at his cravat. His nervous silence did nothing to stop the sense of dread building in the pit of Ben's stomach.

"Is it Mother? Father?" Ben misjudged the distance of the table and accidentally slammed his glass against the surface.

Jake's eyes widened, clearly surprised by his alarm. Margrave and his opponents halted their game to stare. Heat engulfed Ben.

"Nothing has happened," Jake said. "What would make you think—?"

Ben waved off his brother's question, irritated that he'd drawn attention to himself. He needed to keep his wits about him, especially around others. It was too undignified to have one of his attacks here. "If you've not come bearing bad news, then you were sent to keep me occupied. By whom?"

His brother smiled sheepishly. "I am to keep you out of the ballroom. And do you truly need to ask who sent me?"

"Lana," Ben grumbled. Their younger sister. The only person capable of bending Ben and his three brothers to her will. Being a soft touch when it came to Lana, however, didn't mean he would allow her to run roughshod over him. Even if Wellham had evaded him again, as Jake reported, Ben wasn't ready to leave. "Unless you intend to tie me up, you've no way of keeping me in the card room."

Jake chuckled. "Do not give our sister any ideas, or she may start carrying rope in her reticule." His brother's grin faded, and he stood to draw Ben away from the table, affording them more privacy. "Perhaps it would be best if you heeded Lana's wishes tonight. She wants to spare your feelings. Eve Thorne's betrothal is to be announced in a moment."

Ben's breath left him in a whoosh.

"You must have heard Sir Jonathan Hackberry has been courting her. The contract was signed last week." Jake's voice sounded far away and his lips were still moving, but Ben was no longer listening.

He had learned of Hackberry's interest in Eve the night her brother challenged Ben to a duel. When he hadn't heard Eve's and the baronet's names linked again, he'd assumed Eve had discouraged the odd man.

"Amelia said Miss Thorne genuinely likes him, which must be some comfort."

Ben was ripped from his dazed state by his

brother's ridiculous words. "She *likes* him? How is that comforting?"

Several pairs of eyes swung in their direction. Anger seared his veins, and he wanted to shout for everyone to mind their own damned affairs, but he didn't care to be the topic of tomorrow's gossip. Ignoring their curious stares, he motioned Jake to follow him into the corridor. The door closed behind them with a soft snick, shutting out the rumble of voices from the card room.

Ben crossed his arms to keep from hitting something. "Did you say she likes the man?" One *liked* one's Aunt Mabel or mincemeat pie or the rare sunny day. Eve couldn't bloody well marry Hackberry just because she found him amiable. Furthermore, Hackberry's likability was a point for debate. Ben didn't care for him one bit.

"Eve will only marry if love is involved," Ben said. "She was steadfast on this."

"Circumstances change. People change." The dim lighting couldn't hide Jake's pitying look. Ben gripped his biceps to keep from wiping the look off his brother's face with his knuckles.

"You know nothing about her. Why am I listening to you?" He turned to stalk toward the ballroom, but Jake's hand on his shoulder stopped him.

"Can you truly say you know her anymore?"

Ben jerked free of Jake's hold. He hated having the truth tossed back in his face. "This is her brother's doing. She would never compromise her values. I need to speak with her."

"Ben, please do not make a scene. Hasn't Miss Thorne suffered enough embarrassment at your hands?"

His brother's words cooled the flames that were consuming his insides, and his shoulders slumped as his anger slowly died away. Damn Jake for being right. He was too big for his breeches as it was.

Sebastian Thorne wasn't to blame for Eve's circumstances. This was Ben's doing. Just as he had destroyed Charlotte, he had crushed Eve's dreams of a love match. She was settling for less than she deserved because of him.

He exhaled and dragged his fingers through his hair. "Must you always act as my conscience?"

"I hope not. I have better ways to spend my time."

Jake had advised him well when he'd convinced him to lose the duel with Eve's brother to restore her reputation, but to surrender her to another man? Even though he knew his brother was right—Ben *should* let her go—the decision hung heavily over his head.

Eventually, he nodded. "I won't make a scene."

Jake smiled and slapped a hand to Ben's shoulder. "Splendid. Shall we rejoin Margrave?"

Ben spun out of Jake's grasp and stalked down the long corridor en route to the ballroom.

"Devil take it." Jake's long strides soon matched his. "I thought you weren't going to cause any trouble."

Jake cursed under his breath as Ben reached the ballroom door.

"I gave my word," Ben said, "and I will not break it. Thank our sister for trying to spare me, but I can't stay away."

When Ben entered the brightly lit room, Jake sighed. "Blasted martyr," he grumbled and followed him inside.

The musicians were playing a raucous tune, sawing at their instruments as the dancers spun around the floor at dizzying speeds. Lord Eldridge moved to the edge of the dais, his posture stiff as he awaited the end of the set. The earl's slicked-down silver hair, as well as his height, made him stand out in the crowd. A determined set to his jaw hinted he had a task to perform.

Ben's fingers began to tingle. He shook his hands to drive away the irritating sensation, but it didn't help. His chest was growing heavy, as if trying to squeeze the life from him. Inhaling deeply, he fought against the feeling of suffocation creeping up on him. *Hell, not now. Not here.* He couldn't allow the panic to get the best of him this time.

Jake's forehead creased, and he grabbed Ben above his elbow. "Come with me."

He didn't argue as his brother drew him toward a darkened alcove. They dissolved into the shadows, the wall catching Ben's weight as his legs almost buckled. He clawed at his cravat, managing to rip the knot free, and gasped for air.

"Slow down," Jake urged in a quiet voice. "Take your time breathing."

Ben focused on his brother's soothing tone, closing his eyes and silently repeating "all is well," as he'd learned to do in Delhi when he woke from a nightmare, struggling to breathe.

Jake's hand on his shoulder supported his weight. "Gather your wits, Ben." Although Jake's tone wasn't chiding, his meaning struck Ben, and he glared at his brother as indignation flooded his body, restoring his strength.

"I'm not a bloody Bedlamite," he said through gritted teeth. "Gather *your* wits before I beat your arse."

Jake held his palms up in surrender and chuckled. "I only meant to help. No need to resort to violence."

"I beg to differ," a familiar voice snipped. Their little sister stood at the alcove entrance with her hands planted on her slim hips, the light behind her setting her auburn curls ablaze. Her fiery gaze locked on Jake. "I told you to keep him in the card room."

Lana had been a willful chit since birth. As soon as she was old enough to speak, she'd begun ordering around her four elder brothers, and she had never outgrown the tendency. Jake was almost as difficult to tolerate with his overzealous sense of honor and justice.

Jake squared his shoulders, ready to go toe to toe with their sister. "I would like to see you try to corral him for once. He's as stubborn as Daniel."

"That is a lie," Ben said, his humor returning bit by bit. "I surpass our brother at most everything."

Lana's brow lifted, mirroring Jake. "I would not boast, Benjamin. Vulgarity and stubbornness are not virtues."

Ben grinned. He never thought he would miss his younger siblings trying to manage him, but he had. They had no chance at succeeding. Nevertheless, it was heartwarming to know they cared enough to try.

The music faded from beyond the alcove, only to be replaced by the din of laughter and chatter. Lana's husband appeared at her side, his hand sliding possessively to the small of her back. "Lord Eldridge is signaling for everyone's attention."

She dropped her arms to her sides with a weary sigh. Her eyes glittered in the dim light. "Ben…"

Her voice was filled with such sorrow that he forgot about his own distress. She'd always had a tender heart, and her sisterly love left him speechless.

Lord Andrew smiled down at her. "Your brother can muddle through well enough without your aid, Peach."

"How reassuring." Lana rolled her eyes and leaned into her husband as he placed a kiss at her temple.

Ben nodded his thanks to his sister's husband for trying to cheer her. "And if I make a grand mess of my life, I will come to you straightaway. Then you can put things back to rights for me."

"Marvelous," she grumbled, but the beginnings of a smile turned up her lips.

A hush descended over the ballroom, and Ben eased forward, bracing to hear the words he dreaded. Eve was marrying another man. She would be lost to him in a matter of moments.

He cursed under his breath. He'd lost her two years ago when he'd lost control of himself the first time. His heart beat heavily, a small reminder of their wedding day when his heart had taken off on a wild gallop. Dizziness had threatened to overtake him, blackness encroaching on his vision. He'd thought he was dying, and so he had run, heedless of his brother standing in his way.

Ben stood up straight, his spine like iron as Lord Eldridge's voice rang out in the large room as he called for attention. "We are gathered together on this joyous occasion to announce the betrothal of Miss

Eve Thorne and Sir Jonathan Hackberry." The words
sounded as if they traveled through a long tunnel to
reach Ben. A dull ache pulsed beneath his breastbone
as the earl encouraged everyone to congratulate the
couple. When the festivities resumed, the words
hadn't fully sunk into Ben's awareness yet.

While he was in India, Ben believed Eve would
receive another offer of marriage. He never imagined
she would remain unmarried, not a lovely young lady
who'd turned heads any time she walked into a room.
Acceptance of her marriage to another man had come
easier from a distance, but reality hadn't been standing
within his sights. And it hadn't had tousled hair and a
wrinkled coat. A man couldn't be judged by appearance alone, but Sir Jonathan Hackberry could not be
any more unsuitable for Eve. Ben couldn't be the only
one to notice.

"What does she see in him?" he asked of no one
in particular.

His brother shrugged. "I cannot say. He and
Amelia's friend grew up together, so we have dined
with him twice. He is a hard man to know, although
my knowledge of ancient ritual drumming has
greatly increased."

"Pardon?"

Lana turned away from the scene in the ballroom.
"Sir Jonathan spent several years in Syria, Egypt, and the
surrounding area studying the use of drums in religious
ceremonies. He can speak on the subject at length."

"Yes," Lord Andrew drawled. "He makes one want
to stuff a handkerchief in his mouth and ship him
back there."

Ben chuckled. He liked his sister's husband. "I own a fleet of ships. Something could be arranged."

"*We* own a fleet," Jake said with a touch of drollness. Their maternal grandfather had willed his shipping company to Daniel, Jake, and Ben, allowing them to become independent from their father.

"And do you also have a handkerchief?" Ben asked.

Lana tugged off her glove and waved it like a flag. "Will this do?" She and Jake shared a laugh. *In for a penny, in for a pound.* Those two had always been quick to scheme together, and Ben was happy to see their marriages hadn't weakened their bond.

The quartet returned from a brief intermission and began tuning their instruments. Jake held his arm out to her. "We should find Amelia and offer our best to Miss Thorne."

"But not to her betrothed." Lana winked at Ben before they walked away.

Lord Andrew stayed behind. The mischievous glint was gone from his eyes. "Obviously, you can't send Hackberry back to Syria, but you shouldn't step aside if you want the lady." The younger man rarely took anything seriously, but affairs of the heart appeared to be the exception.

"Your opinion is at odds with my brother's. Jake believes I have caused enough trouble for Miss Thorne."

Lord Andrew's grin returned. "It must be difficult for your brother, so often being wrong." He clapped Ben on the shoulder and lowered his voice. "Earlier, Thorne was in a temper because the groom-to-be hadn't arrived yet. He doesn't fully trust Hackberry."

The baron had always been suspicious of others' motives. Ben leaving Thorne's sister at the altar would have only reinforced his paranoia. "He trusts me even less."

"Perhaps, but if you prove him wrong, he isn't too proud to change his mind. He cares about his sister and only wants her happiness. Can you make her happy?"

Ben didn't know. If a strong desire to please her guaranteed success, then he was miles ahead. "How do you propose I proceed? Miss Thorne is promised to another man. Doesn't honor dictate I should leave her be?"

A wicked smile swept across his brother-in-law's face. "Honor makes for a poor bed partner, doesn't it?"

What was he implying? That he'd been unfaithful to Lana? Ben's fingers curled into a fist. "If you have dishonored my sister, I will knock that smirk from your face."

Lord Andrew shook his head, chuckling to himself. "You Hillary men are a hotheaded lot, always prepared to defend Lana with your fists, but there is no need. I adore your sister. Besides, she is scarier than any of you."

Ben relaxed his stance, laughing at himself.

"Honor receives a lot of lip service," Lord Andrew continued, becoming serious once more, "but when it keeps you from the woman you love, honor brings nothing but misery."

The gent had a peculiar way of looking at things, but he made a good argument. What was the sense in honor when it left one feeling hollow inside? And since when had Ben become concerned about behaving honorably? He had just climbed the garden fence and walked into the Eldridge Ball uninvited.

Until Eve spoke her vows, she was available, and Ben had only a short time to convince her that she belonged with him instead. He just needed to find a way to get close to her without her betrothed or her brother getting in his way.

He smiled at Lord Andrew as an idea began to form. "I'll be by to speak with my sister tomorrow, and I may need to borrow her soon."

"As long as you promise to bring her back."

Four

WHEN EVE WOKE THE NEXT MORNING, SHE WAS surprised her jaw wasn't sore. She must have smiled for hours while she and Jonathan accepted congratulations at their betrothal ball. She had laughed and smiled even wider to hide her distress whenever Lady Eldridge had glanced her way. The earl and countess were very kind to host a ball in her and Jonathan's honor, and she hadn't wanted to appear ungrateful.

She had been anticipating the evening with great excitement. Betrothal balls were usually joyful occasions with dancing, pleasant conversation, and perhaps a stolen kiss between the happy couple. Instead, she had gotten Ben. Former beaus did not attend a lady's betrothal ball. Granted, most ladies didn't have a former beau to trouble them, because engagements led to actual weddings, not jiltings.

Ben deserved a solid facer for ruining her evening, and she was certain Sebastian would oblige her if she asked it of him. She wouldn't, though. It was best to forget the evening, and she would do just that when she joined her friends for a trip to the foundling hospital within the hour.

Too restless to wait for her maid, she gathered the basket of children's clothes from her desk and sailed out her chamber door. She and a small group of ladies were delivering clothes and blankets to the orphans that afternoon.

Eve was proud of her needlework. She had taken extra care to make her stitches perfect, believing no effort should be spared when it came to the children. When Amelia Hillary spoke of her time with the foundling hospital's wards, her blue eyes always lit up and a soft smile graced her face.

Amelia was one of the most generous ladies Eve had ever met, and her efforts to improve upon the foundling hospital's living conditions were inspiring. Eve's only objection to the lady was her husband, but she couldn't blame Amelia for falling in love with one of the Hillary brothers. Eve had been unable to avoid falling under Ben's spell, so who was she to cast stones? Besides, Jake Hillary seemed a decent sort of gentleman, and he treated her friend well.

As Eve descended the stairs, her sister-in-law's voice floated up from the foyer. "Where is your bonnet, young lady?" Helena was speaking to her younger sister, Gracie. The girl had come to live at Thorne Place after Sebastian and Helena's wedding, and she quite livened up the house.

"Why do I need a bonnet? There is no sun out today," Gracie said, using her ten-year-old reasoning.

Eve reached the landing where the staircase curved, bringing the pair into view. Helena was tying the satin ribbons of her bonnet under her own chin, but paused to glance away from the round looking glass hanging on the wall. "Ladies always wear bonnets and gloves when they leave home."

Gracie's head tipped to the side, as she seemed to ponder her sister's statement. "Is that an order from the Prince Regent?"

Helena laughed and turned fully toward her sister. She caught Eve's eye, and her smile broadened. "It isn't a royal declaration as far as I know, but you still must wear your bonnet."

As Eve reached the foyer, Gracie called out her name and greeted her with an enthusiastic hug. With the bulky basket in the way, Eve couldn't return the hug as she would have liked, but she placed a kiss on top of the girl's honey-colored head. The two had become fast friends the moment they had met. "Someday you will love wearing new bonnets and then you will be told to stop spending all your pin money on them."

Gracie shook her head, jostling her sweet curls. "I will buy a fishing pole with my money."

Helena held out the bonnet to her sister. "I believe Fergus and I must have a little talk."

The good-natured Scot entered the front door in time to overhear Helena. "Has the lassie landed me in hot water again? You must always do as your sister says, Miss Gracie." He winked at the girl behind Helena's back, and Gracie covered her giggle with her gloved hand.

Fergus was Helena's land steward in Scotland, but he had come to London as her protector when Helena wanted to reunite with her sisters. He was as close to Helena as family.

He doffed his hat toward Eve. "Afternoon, Miss Thorne. The carriage is waiting."

With Gracie's bonnet in place at last, they walked out of the town house and climbed into the carriage. Fergus closed the door, scrambled to take his place on the box next to the driver, and then they were on their way.

The sky was a dingy gray and a trace of dampness hung on the warm air. "We may see a storm before the day is over," Eve mused.

Gracie screwed up her nose, apparently unhappy with her prediction.

"But not until after your picnic."

The girl's smile returned, as if Eve could dictate the weather.

Helena and Gracie had plans to visit a park on the outskirts of the city, where another of Helena's sisters was meeting them for a picnic, but first they were carrying Eve to Amelia Hillary's town house. With Sebastian at the House of Lords until the evening and Mama having taken to her bed with an arthritis flare-up, Eve would be without a chaperone.

When the carriage turned onto Park Street, Helena picked at her glove as she was prone to do when uncertain. "I wish I could have canceled the picnic, but there wasn't enough time. I feel as if I am disappointing you and Sebastian."

"Don't be silly." Eve flicked her wrist, mentally directing her sister-in-law's guilt out the window. "You have not seen Lavinia since before your wedding. Certainly she misses you both. I will be fine without you."

"I could leave Fergus—"

"Helena, please stop fretting. I will be on a charity mission. What possible trouble could I get into at the foundling hospital?" Eve was certain Amelia Hillary knew about Ben's appearance at the ball last night and might question Eve about him. The last thing Eve wanted was a hovering Scot listening to every word spoken. "Besides, Sebastian would be in a temper if you went without protection."

Helena stopped nibbling her bottom lip and sighed. "I suppose you are right."

"Of course I am." Eve smiled in reassurance as the carriage slowed to a halt at Verona House. After kissing her companions' cheeks and wishing them a pleasant afternoon, Eve accepted Fergus's hand down from the carriage and thanked him for his escort to the door. He handed her the basket of children's clothes as the Hillarys' butler invited her to follow him to the drawing room.

Eve was early, but she wasn't the first to arrive. Lady Bianca Norwick—Amelia's dearest friend—and Lady Fiona Banner were already having tea. Their faces lit with smiles when the butler announced her.

"Eve, how lovely that you could come." Amelia crossed the room to embrace her. "Please join us."

Eve's heart expanded at the warm reception. It was hard to believe at the beginning of the Season she'd had no friends, and now these three ladies had become her closest confidantes. Bianca—better known as Bibi among friends—had been the first to take Eve under her wing, securing an appointment for her with the most sought after modiste in London. Then the countess had gone the extra step and secured a husband for her as well. Eve smiled in memory of their recurring jest. Bibi might have arranged an introduction between her and Jonathan, but Eve had brought him up to scratch.

Fiona, Bibi's sister-in-law, perked up as Eve approached the sitting area with her basket in hand. "You've brought your sewing. May I see?"

She was pleased with Fiona's request, for the baroness's skill with a needle was unparalleled. Setting the basket on a side table, Eve lowered into a refined damask chair and retrieved a snowy white gown from her basket. She had painstakingly embroidered yellow daisies around the hem. As Fiona tipped her ash-blond head to the side and inspected her stitches, Eve held her breath.

Her friend murmured with approval as she flipped over the fabric to check the opposite side. "Impeccable work, my dear." Placing the gown on her lap, Fiona aimed a teasing look at her sister-in-law. "It is good to know *someone's* little darlings will be well dressed."

It was common knowledge in their small circle that Bibi abhorred needlework, and having seen some of her creations, Eve agreed it was probably wise to leave the embroidery to others.

"Lud!" Bibi shot back, her brown eyes twinkling. "Little Fi is the best-dressed girl in England, thanks to her auntie."

Spots of color appeared on Fiona's thin cheeks, and she tittered with pleasure.

Eve watched the ladies' exchange with a touch of envy. Jonathan had no family, having lost both parents while he was away at Cambridge and two brothers to the war. Her betrothed had no extended family either, which left him quite alone in the world. It was no wonder he had turned to books and study.

Feeling sorry for herself was too selfish by half—she had a small and loving family of her own—but she had always longed to be part of something bigger. It wasn't to be, though. Swallowing a wistful sigh, she pulled a blanket from the basket.

A commotion in the foyer captured the ladies' attention. "Stop complaining. I told you a footman would carry it, but you insisted."

Eve couldn't make out the reply or place the masculine rumble. Curious, she shifted on the chair for a better view of the door.

"It sounds like Lana and Lady Phoebe have arrived," Amelia said as she rose from her seat. "We should depart soon. Otherwise, we will interfere with the children's dinner hour."

The new arrivals appeared in the drawing room doorway side by side, blocking the foyer behind them. The ladies came forward to exchange greetings around the circle, everyone seeming to talk at once as they asked after each other. Amelia was presenting Eve to Lady Phoebe when a man cleared his throat behind her.

Lana swung toward the doorway. "My apologies, dear brother. You may set the trunk over there."

Eve turned with a smile for Jake Hillary and gasped. Ben flashed a grin, his eyes locked on her. A small trunk was perched on his shoulder as if it weighed nothing; one arm curled up to help balance it, stretching the fabric of his jacket tightly over his bicep. Eve's mouth was suddenly dry, and she couldn't look away.

He sauntered into the room to place the trunk out of the way, his buckskins hugging his backside as he lowered it to the floor.

"Thank you, Benjamin." Amelia's voice broke his spell on Eve, and her gaze dropped to the carpet as heat consumed her. "I am afraid Jake is not here. He is taking exercise at Gentleman Jackson's Saloon."

"I'm not here to see Jake."

Eve stole a peek at him from beneath her lashes and discovered him watching her. His smile widened, one side of his mouth hitching higher.

"I heard about the renovations at the foundling hospital. Since I didn't have the opportunity to contribute to the worthy cause, I thought I would accompany you today to see how I may be of service now."

Amelia's elegant blond brows veered toward each other, but before she could respond, Lana linked arms with him. "And what an excellent idea. I'm certain the board appreciates your interest in the children's welfare."

Amelia's sea-blue gaze flickered back and forth between Eve and Ben. Unable to bear her friend's discomfort, Eve gave a slight nod of agreement. Amelia exhaled loudly, as if she'd been holding her breath. "Yes, the board will be very pleased by your interest, I am sure."

Splendid. The board could have his interest all they liked, but the way his blue eyes darkened when he looked at Eve, she suspected they would have a difficult time capturing his notice. She made a point of ignoring him as she resumed her seat, but her skipping heart wouldn't allow her to fool herself. Every nerve ending in her body tingled with awareness of him. Too aware.

If she managed to survive the afternoon, she might just hide until her wedding day.

Five

BEN ATTEMPTED TO MANEUVER HIS WAY INTO THE SAME carriage with Eve for the ride to the foundling hospital, but Lady Bianca Norwick and her sister-in-law cut him off. Linking arms with Eve, they directed her toward the Norwick carriage. Eve didn't spare him a backward glance while she chatted with the ladies and climbed inside. Other than the one time he'd caught her ogling him in the drawing room, she had done a convincing job of pretending she was oblivious to him.

He ground his teeth in frustration. He hadn't expected a *tête-à-tête* with Eve would come easily, but he hadn't anticipated interference either. Although Ben's brother *had* mentioned Lady Norwick enjoyed a friendship with Sir Jonathan Hackberry, so it should come as no surprise the lady was guarding Hackberry's interests.

Ben needed a moment alone with Eve. The charge when they'd locked gazes earlier had all but knocked him on his arse. Attraction did not equal love—Ben was wise enough to know the difference—but Eve had desired and loved him at one time. His drive to

learn if that love still existed was as powerful as anything he had ever experienced.

After assisting the three remaining ladies into his
carriage, he settled on the seat beside his sister. Lana
could always be counted on to be an accomplice, but
he was uncertain where his sister-in-law's loyalties
lay. Amelia's assistance might be needed today, but he
didn't wish to make her uncomfortable by asking her
to go against her best friend, Lady Norwick, who had
clearly declared herself on Hackberry's side.

He studied Amelia across the carriage seated next
to Lady Phoebe. His sister-in-law regarded him with a
pleasant smile in return. She was a strikingly beautiful
woman with high cheekbones and dainty features.
He understood his brother's fascination with her. She
was also a master at hiding her thoughts. If she was
flustered by his unexpected arrival this afternoon, she
gave no indication.

Lana remained silent. It figured the moment he
desired his sister's interference she would choose to
hold her tongue.

"I hope my presence today hasn't shocked you,
Mrs. Hillary," he said, mindful to address her formally
with Lady Phoebe present.

Amelia shrugged slightly. "There is nothing shocking about the Hillarys' generosity, sir. Your family has
been a foundling hospital benefactor for some time.
I must admit I am pleased with your interest in the
children themselves. They are dear to my heart."

The carriage wheel dropped into a hole, knocking
Lana against him. His sister's eyebrows lifted as if to
remind him of her warnings earlier that morning.

Amelia was not to be trifled with when it came to the orphans, and it felt as if he was treading on unstable ground. Even though his actions were a ploy to secure time alone with Eve, he had to admit he admired Amelia's devotion to her charity work. Another lady might have lost interest after having her own issue, but not Amelia. His desire to support her efforts was sincere, even if his true aim in accompanying the ladies was less lofty.

"Please do not hesitate to request anything of me on the children's behalf. I am at your service," he said.

She sat up straighter, her blue eyes twinkling happily. "How marvelous. The nursery will be pleased to learn they have a volunteer today."

Ben's blood froze in his veins. "The nursery?"

Amelia nodded, her smile as enigmatic as always. "The babies are very sweet, and they respond well to being cuddled. I will have a nurse show you the way."

He looked wildly at his sister for help, but her face was turned toward the window, her shoulders shaking. If he didn't know better, he might think she was laughing at him.

The carriage arrived at the brick gates of the Woodmore Home for Foundlings before he could formulate an excuse to bow out of nursery duty. He had nothing against infants, but he didn't know the first thing about entertaining one. As far as he could ascertain, babies held no interests beyond eating, sleeping, and making messes. And they *cried*. What if he made a baby cry and couldn't convince it to stop? Eve might think him a horrible person if he frightened a baby.

His stomach churned the closer they drew to the massive four-story building, and he broke into a sweat before the carriage rolled to a stop in front of the arched entry. He wiped his brow with his handkerchief, then haltingly climbed from the carriage to gawk at the forbidding structure. "Amelia…"

"It is impressive, isn't it?" His sister-in-law linked arms with him and whisked him inside while the carriage carrying Eve and her companions was still rolling up the drive. The determined set to Amelia's jaw convinced him no help would come from her.

Inside the lobby doors, she released his arm. The place was deserted and so quiet, Amelia's voice startled him. "Everyone must be occupied."

Which meant no one was available to provide him with an escort. Ben's shoulders slumped with relief.

"Fortunately, I know the way to the nursery." She headed for the curved staircase, the heels of her shoes clicking against the bare stone floor. Reaching the stairs, she paused with her hand on the iron balustrade and glanced over her shoulder. "You will want to follow me, Ben."

There was nothing commanding in her tone. Otherwise he might have protested. Instead, he closed the gap between them as she started up the stairs. The foundling hospital was nothing like he had expected. It was clean and cheerful with buttery yellow walls and amateurish paintings displayed in gilded frames along the upper gallery. A fresh bouquet of colorful flowers sitting on a half-round table greeted them as they reached the top floor.

"It is even better than Jake led me to believe, and

he sang your praises. Are you responsible for all of this?" He gestured to the paintings, which he now suspected were the children's artwork, the large windows allowing sunlight to spill on the warm wood floors, the flowers.

She was blushing but held her head a bit higher. "The Mayfair Ladies' Charitable Society has taken on Woodmore as our special project. I cannot take all the credit."

Her modesty was refreshing. Jake had told him Amelia was the driving force behind the renovations long before she garnered the other ladies' support. He wanted to ask what role Eve played in the project—if she came to the hospital often and how she spent her time there—but they'd arrived at the nursery.

He blinked in surprise at the number of cribs in the room. He counted ten, and most appeared to be occupied. Only two nurses tended the nursery, each working with expert efficiency before moving on to the next fussy baby. The babies' crying echoed off the walls.

"Babies need to be held too," Amelia said loud enough to be heard over the commotion.

He nodded, understanding the reason she thought he could do some good here.

She met his eyes and smiled before moving to a crib to lift a baby who was on the verge of screaming. Her tiny arms and legs flailed as her cries rose on a crescendo. Once Amelia had soothed the little one, the racket in the room died down considerably.

"Is Daisy hungry?" she asked someone behind him.

He spun on his heel and discovered a wet nurse sitting in the corner feeding two babies.

"No, ma'am. Mrs. Hudson fed her ten minutes ago."

He looked around, expecting to find another wet nurse, but she seemed to be the only one there at the moment.

"Perhaps Daisy would like to go for a walk," Amelia said. "I will take her around with me. This is my brother-in-law, Benjamin Hillary. He is here to offer his assistance."

"Yes, Mrs. Hillary."

One of the bedside nurses barely glanced at him before returning her attention to changing the babe in her care into a clean nappy.

Amelia nuzzled Daisy's damp hair and whispered sweet words to her.

He nodded toward the baby girl. "Looks like crying requires much effort. Daisy has broken a sweat."

"Yes, I believe that's the way of it. It is her only way of asking for attention." She nudged him. "Go on, then. Find a baby to hold and talk to him or her."

Ben balked. "Talk to one? What do we have in common?"

"You will think of something." Amelia chuckled as she left him standing in the nursery, frightened out of his wits.

He did nothing at first. Just stood rooted to the floor. But as the women slanted curious glances in his direction, he began to feel silly. He was a man. He had traveled the world—faced dangers on sea and land with equal bravery. A tiny person was no cause for alarm, even if a baby could shatter eardrums and produce enough drool to drown a man.

He ventured farther into the nursery, wandering down the aisle of cribs toward the quieter section of the room. He passed sleeping infants with their bottoms in the air or sucking on their fingers. Sometimes both. All of them boasted rosy, plump cheeks that made them undeniably adorable.

Tension melted off him with each step. The little ones appeared so peaceful when they slept. Ben couldn't remember what it was like to sleep soundly without bad dreams or waking in the wee hours for no reason and being unable to fall asleep again. Perhaps the babies' innocence made them sleep without a care. Whatever it was, he wished he could recapture those moments in his life when he hadn't a care either.

Reaching the last crib in the row, he encountered two serious brown eyes staring up at him. A hand-lettered sign hung on the wall above the crib. *Boy: Tobias.*

"What a large name for a tiny boy."

Tobias didn't fuss or smile or give any other indication he expected anything from Ben. In truth, the tot's expression said he didn't expect anything from anyone, as if he had resigned himself to being forgotten.

A frisson of anger passed through Ben. The babe was too young to have learned such a lesson, and Ben meant to correct it. He leaned slightly over the crib railing, smiled, and wiggled his fingers at him. Tobias simply blinked.

Another failed tactic. Perhaps Ben should follow Amelia's advice and talk to him. He cleared his throat, trying to think of something relevant. He meant to say something along the lines of "what a strapping lad you are." Instead squeaky gibberish poured out of him. "Where is the good boy? Where is Tobias? There he is. *There* he is." The gents at Brooks's would be mocking him for days if they overheard him.

Tobias, however, was more forgiving of Ben's silliness. A toothless grin broke across his round face.

Ben's smile grew. "You like that, do you?" He gibbered more nonsense and made funny faces at him. Tobias's first giggle startled Ben, and he gasped softly.

"Do that again?"

The baby obliged him. The sound filled him with happiness. Repeating the act elicited more tiny giggles that soon transformed into belly laughs. The more Ben made a fool of himself, the harder Tobias laughed. Ben was laughing too. He forgot his shyness and lifted the baby from the crib to hold him close to his chest.

When he turned, he caught the women smiling at him, their expressions soft. Under normal circumstances, their bearing witness to his childish antics might have embarrassed him, but he found he didn't care. The only one who mattered was little Tobias, and his heartwarming coos between giggle fits said he was happy.

And at that moment, so was Ben.

He bounced Tobias gently in his arms, singing an old sailors' song, much to the boy's pleasure. His eyes twinkled up at him, and it struck Ben that he could be holding his own son like this, looking into rich brown eyes just like Eve's, if only Ben hadn't given up. It didn't matter if he thought he was doing the right thing at the time. He'd made a mistake letting her go, and he wouldn't make the same mistake again.

Ben sang a little louder, hopping a bit from foot to foot in an old dance he'd learned from the seamen aboard the ship. When he added a small stomp and twirl, he stopped, the words dying on his lips. Eve stood in the doorway, her brown eyes shimmering with tears. The little girl Daisy was asleep in her arms.

Six

EVE BRUSHED AWAY A TEAR THAT FELL ON HER CHEEK and strode into the nursery without looking at Ben. The heavy warmth of the sleeping babe in her arms, and then seeing Ben playing with a little one, ripped off the scab from an old wound. All the pain from two years ago, when she realized her dreams of being his wife and bearing him children were dead, flooded her. She held tightly to Daisy to keep from drowning in emotions she wanted to forget and fought to control the trembling of her body.

With the nurses occupied, Eve searched for the baby's crib herself, reading each sign posted on the wall above the cribs. She would return the baby as Amelia had requested and hurry back to the parlor where the other ladies were sorting through clothes with the head nurse.

She had been looking forward to helping in the nursery ever since Amelia mentioned it last week. Eve loved babies: their silky tufts of hair, soft cheeks and plump thighs, and the sweet little mewing sounds they made in their sleep. As long as she could remember, she'd wanted to become a mama. She craved mother-hood as some ladies craved a cup of chocolate in the morning. In three weeks, she would marry Jonathan, and her baby dreams could finally come true.

She ignored the niggling voice whispering in her ear that she wanted more. More was no longer pos-sible. At one time, she'd thought love was as necessary as food, the air she breathed, or a safe place to lay her head. Love had done nothing but break her heart. She preferred kindness and comfort to sorrow any day.

Finding Daisy's crib, she gently laid her on the stark white bedding. The baby rolled over with an audible huff and puckered her mouth several times as if she were still nursing, but she didn't wake. Once Eve was satisfied Daisy was settled, she turned on her heel to make her escape, but a burst of frustration surged through her. Why should *she* be the one to leave the nursery? Ben wasn't even supposed to be here today—just as he wasn't supposed to be at Lord and Lady Eldridge's ball last night.

She marched back down the aisle of cribs, each step fueling her anger. Ben was still talking to the baby, lift-ing him overhead and babbling nonsense. With hands on her hips, she opened her mouth to take Ben to task when the baby tossed up his accounts, splattering the lower half of Ben's face, cravat, and coat.

He groaned.

"Oh dear," she muttered and rushed forward to take the baby. Ben handed him over with a grimace before retrieving a handkerchief from an inside pocket of his coat and wiping the mess from his face.

The baby watched with round eyes and chewed

uncertainly on his fingers as if trying to anticipate Ben's reaction. Even Eve was holding her breath, fearful of an angry outburst. Not that Ben had ever shown a temper in her presence, but her father never would have remained calm in similar circumstances. Of course he never would have been in a similar situation, because he'd possessed the good sense not to hold a baby above him.

No. That wouldn't have been the reason. Papa had never shown interest in children, not even his own. Her heart softened toward Ben, just a tiny amount, but enough to make her want to come to his aid.

"I will take the baby back to his crib, then I will find water and a cloth."

He stopped her with a touch to the elbow. "No, let Toby Boy stay." When he reached for the baby, Toby flashed a gaping smile and giggled low in his throat. Ben took care to hold him in his left arm to avoid the wet spot on his fine coat. "I will, however, accept your kind offer, Miss Thorne."

She shook her head, smiling in spite of herself. "Why were you holding him overhead? Don't you know a jostled baby is probably going to erupt like Mount Vesuvius?"

"I do now." His crooked grin stole her breath. Why must he show good humor at a time like this? It only made him more appealing.

She turned away before he noticed the flush that must be stealing into her cheeks. "Find a place to sit and I will be back in a moment."

One of the nurses directed her to a back room where she found a small pitcher of water, a basin, and extra cloths. With the supplies in hand, she returned to tend to Ben, but he and the baby were no longer in the nursery. She wandered into the empty corridor, wondering where the two could have gotten off to in the short time she had been gone.

A baby's squeal echoed from the end of the passage and around the corner. Moving more slowly than normal so she wouldn't spill, she headed toward the sound, a smile tugging at her lips. When Ben had arrived at Amelia's town house earlier, Eve had believed his interest in the orphans was a trick to get close to her. Now she felt a little foolish for doubting his sincerity. And more than a touch arrogant for thinking she mattered enough that he would go to such trouble to see her.

When she rounded the corner, she could see Ben had located a wooden bench in front of a large window at the end of another corridor. He wasn't sitting, but rather pointing out things to Toby beyond the window and talking to him as if he were an adult and could understand him.

She cleared her throat to get his attention, not wanting to startle him. Ben had another smile for her. "You left the nursery," she said as her knees knocked together.

"You told me to find a place to sit."

"I meant in the nursery." Where there were others and she wouldn't be forced to be alone with him.

He shrugged and lowered to the bench, sitting the baby on his knee. "Thank you for coming to my rescue."

She rolled her eyes as she placed the basin and

pitcher on the bench beside him. "This is hardly a life-threatening event." Maintaining an air of efficiency, she poured water into the basin, wet the cloth and wrung out the excess water, then held it out to him. Ben's eyebrows lifted.

"My hands are not free, Miss Thorne. Will you do the honors?"

Her eyes narrowed when he offered her another charming smile. She might have fallen for his handsome looks once, but she was a lot wiser now. *I am.* Despite her claim, she moved to stand between his thighs and touched the cloth to his cheek. Surely her heart was pounding loud enough for him to hear.

Pretending he didn't send her mind and body into a spin, she dragged the cloth down to his chin and quickly scrubbed his lips, nose, and jaw.

He winced. "Not so rough."

She pursed her lips. Perhaps she was being less careful than she might be with someone else, but he needed to be convinced she felt nothing for him. Or she needed to convince herself.

The baby arched his back and craned his neck toward the window. "You want to see outside, don't you, Toby Boy?" Ben tucked him over his shoulder, eliciting more happy coos from Toby.

Eve returned her attention to wetting the cloth and wringing out the water. "I never realized you had a fondness for children."

"Is that true? I thought we had discussed having several." If his voice held even a hint of teasing, she would have marched away, but he seemed genuinely surprised by her assumption.

"*I* discussed wanting several." She still wouldn't look at him while she set to work on the stain on his cravat, scrubbing it even harder than she had his face. "I have always loved children. When I was a girl, I dreamed of having a big family. I love my brother dearly and I would never trade him for a dozen siblings, but I always wondered what it would be like to have more than one."

"Noisy and annoying."

She wrinkled her nose.

"But also reassuring," he said, his voice taking on a softer tone. "Imagine if you had four siblings just like your brother, always ready to tell you what to do or defend you."

She hazarded a glance at his face, and the sincerity she saw in his smoky blue eyes chipped at the wall between them a little more. This was a bad development. The wall was in place for a reason.

A strand of hair slipped from her coiffure as she returned to vigorously scrubbing his clothing. He reached to tuck it behind her ear. She jumped, shocked by the intimacy of his touch. His hand fell to his lap, and she took a step back for fear she wouldn't have it in her to discourage him if he touched her again.

"I wanted everything you wanted, Evie. I still do. A large family of our own. A home in the country… I want *you*."

Her heart leaped into her throat and she wasn't sure she could speak. She shook her head.

"Yes." His voice sounded hoarse. "I came back for you."

Who did he think he was to waltz back into her

life—after she had given up on him ever returning—and claim he had come back for her? She dropped the cloth in the bowl, splattering water on the bench and floor. "You are two years too late, Ben."

He captured her hand before she could leave. "I came back for you the day of our wedding. I tried to see you at your brother's town house." His eyes had darkened, and she didn't know how to read his expression. "I encountered your brother on the street before I could reach you."

Eve's breath caught. Sebastian had seen Ben? Her brother had led her to believe Ben had run without looking back. "No, Bastian would have told me if he had spoken with you. You are lying."

Ben's jaw muscles twitched, a red flush invading his face. "Ask him yourself, Eve. Your brother refused to allow me to speak with you, even though I told him I was desperate to marry you. We still could have sent for the vicar. Thorne swore I would never see you again, then he called me out. And I wanted to meet him on that field. Nothing was going to keep me from you, especially not your damned brother."

Now she was certain he lied. She jerked her hand free. "There *was* no duel."

"No, there wasn't." He met her gaze, his unwavering, pleading with her to believe him. "I realized no matter what happened, I would lose you. Either I would die or I would kill the brother you love."

The gravity of such a loss slammed into her. Nausea welled up inside her, leaving a sickening taste in her mouth.

He reached for her again, but she backed away.

"I chose the least destructive path, Evie. At least I thought the damage would be minimal compared to the loss of life. I never anticipated you would be treated as you have been, and I am wracked with guilt."

His admission rang with truth, but she didn't want to believe him. If she had misjudged him... Her hand covered her mouth as her vision blurred. *Good God.* If she had misjudged him, she had given up too soon.

And now it truly was too late, for she had given her word to marry Jonathan. She could never inflict pain on him—or anyone—like she had experienced. Even if she wanted, she couldn't go back.

"Ben." Her voice broke on a soft cry. "I am betrothed," she choked out before spinning around and running from *him* this time.

Seven

BEN'S YOUNGER BROTHER DROPPED INTO A LEATHER chair in front of Ben's desk without waiting for an invitation. Since Ben had already overlooked Daniel's unscheduled arrival at his Cavendish Square town house—not to mention his brother barging into his study unannounced and helping himself to a brandy—he held his tongue. Complaining would prove a waste of time, for Daniel rarely worried about inconveniencing anyone. And his brother's sudden appearance *now* was damned inconvenient.

Ben checked the mantel clock and sighed, replacing his quill and abandoning his ledger. His next appointment would arrive in a quarter hour, and he didn't need his brother bumping into Mr. Armstrong and Viscount Margrave on his way out. There wasn't much time to get to the heart of the matter, then send his brother home.

Daniel scowled at the contents in his glass; his ankle was propped across his knee. Only one thing could bring about a surly mood like this: a problem with Hillary Shipping. What could it be this time? A squeaky hinge on the shipping office door? A loose shingle on the roof? Ben had never met a more obsessive man, and although Daniel's fastidiousness had helped to make their joint shipping company successful, it could become tedious.

Ben drummed his fingers against his cherry wood desk. "Tell me the bad news, so we can sort through it. *Quickly*."

With only thirteen months separating them, the two had been figuring things out together since they were both old enough to walk and talk.

"I don't think we will be sorting this one. Lisette has charged me with inviting you to dine with us this week. She is planning a small dinner party tomorrow evening."

"Egads!" Ben chuckled.

His brother was correct. There would be no escaping this one, although Ben didn't greet the invitation with the same dread Daniel would have if the situation were reversed. Ben liked Lisette and her kin, and socializing had never been the same hardship to him that it was for his brother. Daniel abhorred playing the gentleman, preferring the simple life of a seaman, but he was a husband now. And his willingness to play host at his wife's behest was a testament to how much he loved Lisette.

"You may tell your wife I accept."

"Very good." Daniel seemed to have no control over his jiggling foot. "Family is to arrive an hour before dinner. She wants to see everyone before we retire to Brighton for the winter."

If his brother couldn't live on the sea, he could at

least be close enough to enjoy the salty breeze and never-ending crash of waves on the shore. Their father's Brighton house would be the only property to suit Daniel for a long stay.

"I see." Ben tried to control the twitching of his lips. "A tiny sailor is on the way, aye?"

"How did—?" Daniel's gaze snapped up, his blue eyes dancing with undisguised pleasure. He laughed. "I swear to God, if you speak a word to anyone, I will break your nose. No ruining her surprise."

Ben laughed too as he pushed away from the desk to come around to congratulate his brother. "I would not dream of stealing her thunder. Congratulations. Fatherhood suits you, I think."

Daniel had been a father figure to Lisette's younger brother for some time, so he'd already gotten a taste of what the job entailed. Daniel rose to accept his hearty handshake before they gathered each other in a rough hug. They were still pounding on each other's shoulders when Ben's man of business appeared in the doorway.

Mr. Davis adjusted his spectacles and cleared his throat. Ben bid him to come in. "Pardon the interruption, sir, but Lord Margrave has arrived with Mr. Armstrong."

Daniel's eyebrows shot up. "Harvey Armstrong, the Bow Street Runner? Why do you require the services of an investigator?"

So much for no one outside of his trusted staff knowing his business.

Ben inclined his head toward his man. "Allow me a few moments with my brother, then you may show them in."

"Yes, sir."

After the outing to the foundling hospital, Ben felt defeated. Eve was marrying another man, and he could do nothing about it. How could she possibly know enough about Sir Jonathan Hackberry to know she wanted to marry him? He'd only been courting her a few weeks. And then Ben had gotten an idea, one he didn't want his brother knowing about. Moving to pour himself a drink, he tried to deflect his brother's questions. "How is it *you* are familiar with Mr. Armstrong?"

"I hired him to locate a missing person. Lisette's cousin, Xavier Vistorie."

Ben swung back around, his interest piqued. "And did the man find him?"

"Hell no. It's as if the earth opened up and swallowed Vistorie whole. Odd business, that."

"Oh." That didn't inspire confidence. Ben wandered back to his desk and perched on the edge. "How difficult could it be to uncover a bloody American in Mayfair? He would be as conspicuous as a boar dressed in Sunday best."

Daniel smirked. "Are you referring to Vicar Dowden?"

"And everyone says you are not clever," Ben drawled. "Tell me, do you think Armstrong is a competent sort, or have I wasted my money?"

"Assuming you haven't misplaced a person, it should be money well spent. I hired Armstrong because of his reputation for getting results." Daniel sipped his drink. "Nice attempt to distract me, but I haven't forgotten my original question. Why do you need an investigator, and how did you hear of him?"

Heat crept into Ben's face. It was none of his brother's concern, but Daniel wouldn't cease his badgering until he got an answer. "Margrave recommended him. If you wish to know of my dealings with Armstrong, you are welcome to stay. It could be a long interview, however, so if you have other matters requiring your attention—"

"Very well." Daniel sank back in the chair with a sly smile.

Damn! Ben had been certain his brother would lose interest if it meant sitting through an interview. Daniel was a restless man and not one to voluntarily sit still.

"Splendid," Ben grumbled as his office door swung open and Margrave appeared with Mr. Armstrong in his wake.

While Ben's old chum ambled in without an invitation and made his way to the sideboard to pour a drink, the investigator halted at the threshold.

"Come in, Mr. Armstrong," Ben said. "Have a seat."

The man moved with efficiency and assurance, nodded an acknowledgment to Daniel, and sat in the twin chair in front of Ben's desk. There was nothing extraordinary in the investigator's appearance. He wore a functional gray coat, trousers, and beat-up black boots. Mr. Armstrong looked like any man one might pass in the street, which likely accounted for his vaunted reputation as one of the best. And yet he couldn't find the American?

Margrave returned with a drink in hand and positioned himself behind Armstrong's chair.

Ben launched into the reason for the investigator's

visit. It seemed wisest to get it behind him, like diving into a cold lake without stopping to consider how uncomfortable it would be. "What have you learned?"

Armstrong pulled a paper square from his jacket pocket and unfolded it. "As requested, an accounting of Sir Jonathan Hackberry's activities over the past twenty-four hours."

Daniel uncrossed his leg, his boot landing on the wooden floor with a thump. "You had Miss Thorne's betrothed followed?"

Ben ignored him, easing forward to catch every word, and motioned Armstrong to continue. He detected the hint of a smirk on Margrave's face.

"At one o'clock yesterday, Hackberry left his town house en route to the lending library where he spent two hours and thirty-five minutes browsing. He purchased two books: one on Ancient Egypt and *Travels to Discover the Source of the Nile, In the Years 1768, 1769, 1770, 1771, 1772, and 1773,* volume two. After his departure from the lending library, he visited the hatter to commission a top hat, but he couldn't decide between black and dark gray. When the shopkeeper suggested he choose both, Hackberry said perhaps he would make a decision after he thought on it a day. Next he made a visit to the glove maker, where he debated the merits of two pairs of riding gloves versus three. From there—"

"Argh!" Daniel groaned loudly and dropped his head back on the seat.

Ben chuckled. "Is there a less boring account of the man's comings and goings? For my brother's sake, of course." Although, in truth, Ben wasn't any more interested in Hackberry's shopping excursion than his brother was.

Armstrong's eyebrow twitched, but otherwise his stony expression wasn't altered. "No, sir."

"No?" Ben pushed from the desk to pace a few steps, then turned to point. "No, as in you are disinclined to deliver your report with more flair, or Hackberry's activities remain mundane and uninteresting?"

"Both statements are correct, sir."

That can't be. Every man had his secrets, a touch of darkness lurking inside. Ben held out his hand for the paper, then wiggled his fingers impatiently when the investigator didn't comply at once. "Let me see. Surely Hackberry cannot be that pedestrian."

Margrave shrugged one shoulder when Ben looked to him to support his assertion. "I'm not acquainted with the man."

Armstrong passed him the paper and sat stiff-backed on the chair. "I am afraid you are mistaken about the gentleman's tediousness, Mr. Hillary."

Ben read the list aloud. "The printer, reading room in Bloomsbury—" He dropped his arm to his side. "What does this mean? Hackberry went missing for an hour?"

The investigator shrugged. "Sir Jonathan took a wrong turn and accidentally locked himself in the museum storage room. When he was discovered among the cataloged exhibits, he stuttered an apology and bumped into a miniature porcelain bowl that shattered on the floor."

Daniel laughed and shook his head before downing his drink.

"I am certain the museum librarian was not amused," Ben said by way of scolding his brother.

"He was not," Armstrong confirmed. "Nevertheless, the bowl was of no value, so Sir Jonathan was only escorted from the premises by two porters instead of being taken into custody."

"Egads." Ben thrust the list back at Armstrong. There was nothing remotely debauched in his report. Hackberry had even retired early on the day in question. "You may go. Mr. Davis will see to your fee on your way out."

"Yes, sir." The man tucked the paper back into his pocket and left as somberly as he'd arrived.

"Well, that was disappointing," Margrave said and lowered his lean frame into the vacant chair next to Daniel.

Ben pinched the bridge of his nose. "Christ," he said on a breath. What had Eve been thinking when she accepted Hackberry's proposal? Surely she realized she was betrothed to a dolt. As his wife, either she would die of boredom or chronic embarrassment.

"What are you doing, Ben?" Daniel asked. "Spying on Miss Thorne's fiancé serves what purpose? She has made her choice."

Ben squared his jaw and met his brother's stare. "I intend to change her mind. You heard the investigator's report. Hackberry is all wrong for Evie."

"Is that so? And you were able to determine his suitability from a list of activities?"

"Yes. Yes, I was." Ben circled his desk, dropped into his chair, and retrieved his quill to finish his recordings in the ledger. In his mind, the matter was settled. His brother and friend could see themselves out.

Daniel cleared his throat. Ben's quill kept moving.

"Ahem!" Daniel stood and planted his hand in the middle of Ben's page.

Gritting his teeth, Ben looked up at his brother looming in front of his desk.

"How?" Daniel's eyes were wide with curiosity, no longer mocking him. "How do you know he is wrong for Miss Thorne?"

Ben dropped his quill on the desk. "For twenty-four hours there wasn't a single activity listed that showed he thought of Miss Thorne once. No lingering over the bonnets at the milliner shop. No box of her favorite sweets. He didn't even call on her, and he chose to retire early rather than escorting her to whatever event she attended."

"Ah." Daniel nodded, discarding his glass on Ben's desk. "And a day is too long for any man to go without calling on his lady if the heart is involved."

"Exactly, which is the reason Miss Thorne cannot marry Hackberry." Ben pretended not to notice Margrave rolling his eyes.

Daniel said nothing for a moment, as if mulling over the situation. He crossed his arms and his scowl returned. "How are we planning to stop her?"

"We?"

"You know putting our heads together reaps the best results."

Ben smiled. Perhaps Daniel was correct. His assistance could come in helpful. "First of all, Hackberry should be added to your wife's guest list. Just

Hackberry. What I have in mind requires privacy, and I wouldn't want Evie catching wind of our conversation."

"I wouldn't miss this for the world," Margrave said with a grin. "No need for your lady wife to issue an invitation, Daniel. You may let her know I'm available."

"She will be relieved, I am sure."

Eight

EVE WASN'T TESTING SIR JONATHAN. TRULY, IT HAD not entered her thoughts when she'd asked if Gracie could join them on their stroll through Hyde Park. Nevertheless, Eve found herself studying her fiancé's interactions with the young girl and comparing him to Ben and the baby boy at Woodmore Foundling Home.

She had never seen a man *hold* a baby, much less serenade and dance with one. It piqued her curiosity about fatherhood in general, but especially about what type of father Jonathan might become—the type of father she suspected Ben would be.

Gracie walked ahead a few paces as they headed back home, twirling her parasol. "Sir Jonathan, what is your favorite flavored ice?"

This was her fourth question in a row, and Eve imagined Jonathan was tiring of supplying answers to the girl's trivial questions. When Eve slanted a look at him, however, he sported the same affable grin he always wore.

"Another excellent question, Miss Gracie. Allow

me to think on it a moment." His smile broadened, and he winked when he caught Eve's eye.

Warm affection filled her heart. Jonathan was a good man. He would make a decent husband and father. And someday she expected she would come to love him. Perhaps not as much as she had loved Ben two years ago, but at age nineteen she had been prone to mawkishness. Now she was prepared for a more mature type of love, one of admiration and companionship. She was making the right decision in forgetting about Ben and moving forward with her life.

Her throat grew tight, and the necklace she wore seemed heavier all of a sudden. She touched Ben's parting gift, wondering what had possessed her to pull it from her jewel box and don it this morning.

"Burnt filbert," Jonathan announced at last.

"Ew!" Gracie spun around, walking backward for a couple of steps, her face screwed up in a show of disgust. "Burnt filbert smells awful. How can it be your favorite ice?"

Jonathan shrugged. "Have you ever tasted it?"

Gracie shook her head before spinning back around to see where she was going.

"Then you cannot make an informed decision. You must give something a chance before declaring it all wrong for you. Do you like burnt filbert, Miss Thorne?"

"Not especially, I'm afraid." She cleared her throat. "Sir Jonathan is correct, however. One must give something a chance in order to form an opinion."

Jonathan tossed a satisfied smile in her direction, and she tried to ignore the sinking feeling in her stomach.

She had been perfectly content with Jonathan before Ben arrived at her betrothal ball, and ever since their conversation at the foundling hospital, she had been unable to think of anything else.

Why had she listened to his claim of having come back for her on their wedding day? It was a lie. Sebastian would never keep them apart. Her brother knew how much she had loved Ben.

Ask him. Eve knew she should question her brother, but trepidation kept her from broaching the subject with Sebastian. If he confirmed Ben's account, where did that leave her? *Them?* She was promised to another man, and she couldn't break her word, especially when Jonathan had done nothing to displease her.

Then there was the question of how she would ever forgive Sebastian for his interference. She adored her older brother and abhorred the idea of anything coming between them. Perhaps it was best if she remained in the dark since his answer wouldn't change the past or her future.

Ask him, the voice whispered in her head. She pushed the thought aside. Now wasn't the time to dwell on the past. She wanted to enjoy Jonathan's company. They hadn't spent time together since their betrothal ball. He had sent his regrets yesterday, canceling their plans for a picnic in the park.

Jonathan claimed correspondence and reconciling his accounts were keeping him busy, but she suspected he was engrossed in his studies and used his business as an excuse. She should be very cross with him, but in truth, she had needed the time to sort through her feelings about Ben.

As they neared Thorne Place, Gracie raced ahead and bounded up the stairs to disappear inside.

"Would you like to take refreshment?" Eve's invitation was a habit of courtesy.

Jonathan stopped on the walkway and turned to face her. His eyebrows shot up on his forehead. "Would you like me to accept, Miss Thorne?"

She forced a smile. "Why would I ask if I did not?"

"Why indeed?" Apparently he didn't expect an answer and offered his escort inside.

In the foyer, Eve surrendered her bonnet and parasol to Milo, then requested the butler arrange for a tray of tea and sandwiches to be delivered to the drawing room.

"Yes, miss."

Jonathan followed suit, handing over his hat, and trailed behind her. As a betrothed couple, they were allowed some liberties, such as relative privacy and an innocent touch. Eve left the door open wide and chose a chair across from the settee. Jonathan paused, his gaze passing back and forth between the chair next to Eve and the settee. Eventually he sat on the settee, facing her.

Eve folded her hands in her lap and tried not to stare at the lock of hair sticking up on his head from him removing his hat. Her fingers itched to set him back to rights, but touching him in such a way would feel too intimate. When she stopped to consider the length of time they had known each other, she realized they were barely acquainted. She and Ben met four months before he proposed, which seemed like a lifetime in comparison.

Jonathan propped his elbow on the armrest and aimed a puzzled frown in her direction. "Miss Thorne, might I make an observation without overstepping my bounds?"

"How am I to answer when I have no notion of what it is you have observed?"

"Fair enough." He nodded slowly as if considering how to proceed. "Then perhaps an apology will be in order after I speak freely anyway. You seem different today, and I've wondered if I might be the cause."

She sat up straighter, her heart skipping. "Different? How so?" Her troubled thoughts couldn't show on her face.

He leaned forward to rest his forearms on his knees and scrutinized her. "You seem less lively, quite unlike yourself. Have I done something to upset you?"

"Heavens, no!" Her hand flew to her chest, her fingers grazing the warm metal of the necklace.

His gaze seemed drawn to her neck. He sat up and inclined his head. "Is that a new piece of jewelry? I haven't noticed you wearing it before."

She enclosed the pendant in her palm as if to shield it from view. "No, it's nothing special. Just a trinket from an old friend."

"May I see?" Without waiting for permission, he left his seat to crouch in front of her. She swallowed hard, debating how she would answer if he asked for her friend's name. "I am sure I've seen one like it in my travels."

Eve slowly uncurled her fingers with a shaky sigh. His interest was simply a matter of curiosity. To him, the necklace was nothing but an artifact for study.

To her, it had been a promise—one Ben had broken when he stayed in Delhi and never wrote to her. Even a short letter to tell her that he would not be returning would have sufficed, although she would have been crushed. She'd held on to the hope that he would come back much longer than she should have.

Not even the kindhearted Mr. Cooper had been able to convince her to move forward with her life in their weekly conversations. When she learned the chaplain had written to Ben imploring him to return because he was worried for her, Eve had felt betrayed and angry. One glimpse into the man's sorrowful eyes, and she knew Mr. Cooper had intervened with the best intentions. If she had expected Ben to grant Mr. Cooper's request, perhaps she wouldn't have been so quick to accept Jonathan's offer for her hand.

That's unfair. Jonathan had an endearing quality about him. He wasn't Ben, but that was to his credit. Unclasping the necklace, she placed it in her betrothed's upturned hand. He held it closer for inspection then traced the three round yellow stones with the tip of his finger before sliding the black pearls through his hand.

"Beautiful," he murmured. "Excellent artistry. This is an expensive trinket."

She lifted one shoulder in a noncommittal shrug. "It is nice, but it means nothing to me."

He held it out to her, his mouth curving into a half smile. "In some parts of India, the groom gives such a necklace to his bride to symbolize their lasting bond."

"I wasn't aware, but how fascinating." She retrieved the necklace, shoved it into the crack between the cushion and chair, then smiled brightly. "Have you studied Indian culture?"

"My early studies involved Brahmanism." That was all the invitation Jonathan needed to return to the settee and launch into tales of his time at various archaeological sites during his childhood. When his father was alive, archaeology was Sir Reginald Hackberry's passion, and he dragged his wife and son to all the dusty places of the world, passing on his love for antiquities to Jonathan.

Eve's heart beat a little faster when he talked of his life abroad. It all sounded intriguing and exciting. Perhaps she would like to see these places too. "Do you wish to follow your father's example and involve your own son in your work someday?"

"No." All traces of lightheartedness vanished. "What I do is too dangerous for a family. I would never place my wife and children at risk."

Her breath caught at his answer. That he would abandon his first love for her and their future family created a lovely tingle along her skin. "You love your work, Jonathan. Can you truly give it up?"

He screwed his mouth to the side as if contemplating her question. Eventually, he exhaled, almost deflating on the settee. "That has been my intention since returning to England and seeking a wife, but I cannot say if I will be able to remain here always."

Eve's jaw dropped. She wanted to demand he tell her why not. What call was there for him to leave their homeland, other than his silly obsession with drums and sacred dances and trancelike states? His was a boy's fascination. It wouldn't do for him to run off in order to satisfy his whims while leaving her behind. It wouldn't do at all.

He flashed a broad smile. "Now don't fret, dearest. I have no desire to leave you."

She didn't return his smile. Having no desire to leave was not the same as promising to stay.

Milo preceded a footman with a tray into the drawing room and instructed the man to place it on the low table. "Will there be anything else, miss?"

Eve didn't trust herself to speak, so she simply shook her head. Jonathan helped himself to tea and a sandwich, then nattered on about his day. When there was no more mention of leaving England, Eve began to settle, and half an hour later, she had almost forgiven him for making her worry.

Once they finished their refreshments, Eve rose from her seat to see him out. He held her hand and placed a chaste kiss on her cheek as they reached the drawing room door. "I'm sorry for what I said earlier. I truly didn't mean to upset you. Forgive me?"

Her back lost its rigidness and she smiled softly. "Of course. I realize it must be an adjustment to go from well-traveled bachelor to husband. I promise to allow you more leeway in the future."

"Thank you, Miss Thorne. For my part, I will try to do better. Is there a way I might make up for my gaffe?"

She squeezed his hand. "You may sign my dance card at Almack's tonight."

He winced. "I forgot tonight was Almack's."

"You forgot?" She dropped his hand. "It is but one night of the week."

He raked his fingers through his hair, leaving his light brown waves standing on end. "Yes, about that… I've received an invitation to speak on Mesopotamia this evening."

Eve crossed her arms, tapping the toe of her slipper against the floor as she bit her tongue.

"Miss Thorne, I… The invitation…" A scarlet flush spread up his face. "I am sorry. I did not think. I was flattered anyone would find me fascinating enough to warrant an invitation based on my own merits. Lady Norwick has been kind enough to assist me these last few weeks, but…"

She knew what it was like to be excluded, although that did not excuse his forgetfulness. She really wanted to dance, blast it all. No more standing on the sidelines wishing her fiancé would ask her to stand up with him. And she certainly couldn't go around woolgathering about waltzing with Ben all the time. It wasn't well done of her.

Eve sighed. "I hope you enjoy a pleasant evening, but make certain to get plenty of rest tonight, because tomorrow you will begin taking dance instruction."

"Dance instruction? But I don't dance."

"Which is a problem," she said, hands landing on her hips. "I need a dance partner. I don't want to be one of those wives handed over for the young bachelors to entertain."

Jonathan scowled. "Nor do I like the idea. Very well. Send around a message with the time and location, and I will be there."

That was more like it.

Nine

BEN WATCHED SIR JONATHAN HACKBERRY THROUGH narrowed eyes as the man expounded on his most recent excavation along the Tigris prior to his return to England. His tales didn't interest Ben as much as the feverish gleam in Hackberry's eyes as he spoke. In Hackberry's excitement, he clipped the rim of his wineglass, but he snatched it before it toppled and soaked Lisette's table linens.

Ben was growing convinced the man's passion was not vested in becoming Eve's husband. He couldn't accept that Eve would choose Hackberry.

"The man is a windbag," Jake muttered.

Amelia, who sat between Ben and Jake, shushed him. "He will hear you," she whispered.

"Over the sound of his own blathering? Doubtful." Jake took his wife's hand beneath the tablecloth, and she very nearly glowed when she smiled back at him.

Women in love were lit from within, and that was the essence of what was missing between Eve and Sir Windbag. The man didn't make her glow.

Ben glanced around the table. Lisette's hand rested

lovingly on her stomach and a coy smile teased her lips when she met Daniel's unwavering gaze at the opposite end of the table. Lana's husband whispered in her ear and her eyes brightened. These unguarded moments between his siblings and their spouses strengthened Ben's resolve to get rid of Hackberry. He wanted what his siblings had found, and he wanted it with Eve, even if he must do something unforgivable to achieve his desire.

Bugger. Grabbing his glass, he drained it. The wine burned in his gut as Hackberry droned on, happily thinking he was an honored guest this evening. Ben tried to believe he was doing the man a favor by offering him a way out of his betrothal, or that Eve would be grateful for Ben's interference someday, but he had never been good at lying to himself.

When the last course was cleared, Lisette rose and everyone around the table followed suit. "Ladies, shall we retire to the drawing room?"

The women—Ben's sisters-in-law, his mother, his sister, and Lisette's cousin, Mrs. Serafine Tucker— exited the drawing room. Daniel set to the task of pouring brandy for the men and invited them to take a cheroot from the carved ebony box sitting on the sideboard.

Ben sized up the room. Other than Mr. Isaac Tucker and Hackberry, allies surrounded Ben. Now would likely be the best time to approach Eve's betrothed without gossip making the rounds tomorrow. He retrieved two cheroots, even though he'd never enjoyed them, and invited Hackberry to join him outside.

Margrave lifted his glass in a toast as Hackberry followed Ben to the glass doors leading to the terrace. Hackberry locked gazes with Ben's friend for a split second, then cleared his throat nervously. Margrave's brooding intensity could be intimidating to many, although Ben had known him too long to allow it to bother him.

Neither Ben nor Eve's betrothed bothered to light their cheroots, which made the moment suddenly awkward as they stood outside staring at each other. Sounds from the town house carried on the air, but didn't detract from the silence lurking on the terrace.

"Hmm…" Ben muttered, unsure how to begin.

Hackberry sat on the stone railing with his slender legs stretched out. "Yes, hmm…" He tucked the cheroot into his coat and crossed his arms. "Allow me to hazard a guess: this is about Eve."

Ben's nostrils flared at Hackberry's casual use of her name. It was irrational to feel such animosity toward the gent, but Hackberry enjoyed an intimacy with Eve that once belonged to Ben alone. Did Hackberry also kiss her? Ben's fingers coiled into a fist.

"She doesn't belong with you," he said with a dangerous growl to his voice.

Hackberry smiled gamely. "Yet she will be mine in a matter of weeks. How lucky am I to win the attentions of such a lovely young lady?"

Ben took a step forward, but Hackberry held up a hand, laughing. "No need to shed blood over the matter, Mr. Hillary. She might be promised to me, but her heart clearly belongs to someone else."

Ben dropped his fist, his brow wrinkling. "What is

this about her heart belonging to someone else? How do you know?"

"I saw the evidence myself today. She has not been the same since your return. If anyone should be inclined to violence, it should be me." Hackberry's mouth twisted into a smile that gave Ben the impression he wasn't completely happy despite his jovial tone.

Ben, on the other hand, experienced a lightening of his heart. Perhaps he wouldn't need to take measures to get rid of Hackberry. Eve might toss over the man and remedy the situation for him. "Has she hinted she might cry off?"

"Good Lord, no. What reason would she give? I cannot imagine her jilting me because she does not love me. This is a matter of duty, and Eve is determined to fulfill her responsibilities to make a marriage match."

How did Hackberry know what was important to Eve? He hadn't known her a month yet.

"We have talked, Hillary." Hackberry spoke with a droll quality to his tone, apparently reading his mind. "She has been refreshingly free with her thoughts up until now. She will become my wife even though I'm aware she prefers you, but I won't hold a grudge or punish her for what her heart wants." He dropped his arms to the railing beside him and shrugged his shoulders. "So tell me, what is it you wished to discuss with me?"

Ben's jaw tightened. It seemed pointless to make his offer now when it was clear Hackberry wouldn't be swayed. Ben had misjudged Eve's betrothed. Yet that flicker of determination inside Ben couldn't be snuffed. He squared his shoulders. "Five hundred pounds and the use of one of my ships bound for the destination of your choice. Take it or leave it."

Hackberry's mouth dropped open and a wheezy breath escaped.

The burn in Ben's gut returned as if the wine had festered. His words replayed in his head. He sullied Eve by treating her as if she were a commodity to buy. Hell, he degraded *himself*, but he couldn't retract his offer as long as there was a chance. "It is money to support your work, your studies. Intended as a philanthropic…" He trailed off when Hackberry's lip curled in disgust.

"You expect money will entice me to step aside. How very arrogant, Mr. Hillary. Honor cannot be bought."

"There is nothing honorable about holding a lady to a promise when you've said she prefers someone else. And what of your travels? Do you expect me to believe you are willing to give up your life's pursuit to settle for a domesticated existence? Eve would hate being left alone while you traipse off to God knows where, and if you even considered dragging her with you—"

"I wouldn't risk her welfare by taking her with me." Hackberry grimaced. "But I hadn't considered the dangers in leaving her alone either, not until this afternoon."

Ben couldn't believe what he was hearing. "Why would you ask for her hand if you plan to leave her?"

Hackberry cocked an eyebrow. "Why did *you*?"

"I didn't want to leave her. It—it was unavoidable."

Ben turned his back, refusing to discuss his problem with his opponent. "I never wanted to leave her." Sadness lingered in his words, despite his determination to give nothing away.

Hackberry didn't respond. The incessant trilling of a field cricket rang in Ben's ears as the moment stretched out, becoming unbearably long.

"Neither do I," Hackberry said quietly. "Want to leave her, that is. But I believe all parties would be best served by me accepting your offer."

So much for the man's honor not being for sale. Ben's gut clenched and he feared losing his meal on the terrace. He pivoted on his heel, a part of him hoping the man was mocking him.

Hackberry came forward with his arms out at his sides. "This is sudden, I know, but I was recently approached about an archaeological dig in Egypt, and now that you are making it possible—"

"You are choosing a bloody dig over Eve? What the hell is wrong with you?" Even though Ben was getting what he wanted, he couldn't fathom choosing anything over a lifetime with Eve.

Hackberry blew out an exasperated breath, lifting hair that had fallen forward on his forehead. "I know this sounds daft when I say it aloud, but I feel as if I have no choice in the matter. I am needed elsewhere. It is in Eve's best interests to be freed from her promise."

For a moment, Ben could focus on nothing else as Hackberry's words circled in his mind. *Eve's best interests.* Wasn't this how Ben had justified leaving her too? Only it hadn't been the right thing for Eve.

"You love her," Hackberry stated.

Ben glared in response. Of course he loved her.

Hackberry's off-kilter grin reappeared. Something sad about it gave Ben pause. "I know you love her, Hillary. You will see that she is well cared for and protected, which is more than I can do."

"Yes, always."

The man scratched his ear and slowly nodded. "Very well, then the matter is settled. I will deliver the news I cannot marry her tomorrow."

"No!" Ben's outburst caused Hackberry to jump.

The man sputtered until he found his tongue. "No? But how am I to relinquish my claim unless I speak with her?"

"*You* can't cry off. She must." Ben's blood began to simmer as he pictured the man jilting her—Eve's humiliation at being told Hackberry didn't want her. No, Ben would have no part in hurting her again. He jabbed a finger in Hackberry's direction. "She must make the decision to end your betrothal. That is the only way."

"I've already told you I have given her no reason."

"Then *give* her a reason." Ben spun away and stalked to the other side of the terrace lest he grab Hackberry and shake him senseless. He stood with his hands on his hips, dragging in deep breaths to calm his temper.

After a time, Hackberry cleared his throat. Ben still didn't look at him. "I don't know what you have in mind, Hillary, but I will not be unfaithful."

Ben snarled over his shoulder. "If you dared, I would run a blade through your heart."

"Remember, there is no call for violence. I am at your service. Simply tell me what I must do and I will do it. For Eve's sake."

Ben shook his head. "I don't know. Everything I think might work makes me want to punch someone."

Hackberry laughed, and Ben couldn't help smiling when he considered his ungentlemanly threats. Eve had a way of making him uncivilized.

Ben faced his rival turned temporary ally, his temper cooling marginally. "Perhaps if you annoy her enough, she will come to our way of thinking. Most unhappy couples seem to annoy the hell out of one another."

"That usually takes years. We haven't much time before we are to wed." Hackberry absently scratched his nose. "I cannot fathom Eve breaking her promise just because I annoy her. Besides, she has the patience of a saint."

Ben nearly snorted. Rarely had he seen evidence of this rumored saintly patience. Patience implied restraint, and even when she was younger, she had been unable to stifle her enthusiasm in most things. Her sincerity made her stand out from her fellow debutantes. Instead of practiced shy smiles and mundane compliments, Eve's responses had been genuine.

Hackberry was correct. Eve wouldn't break her promise over something insignificant, but they might be able to create doubts about Hackberry's suitability. Then Ben might have a chance.

"I've become a master at irritating the lady," Ben said. "And I am happy to tutor you in the finer points. As you pointed out, however, we haven't much time to spare. When will you see her next?"

"Tomorrow. I am to arrive for dance instruction in the afternoon." Hackberry ducked his head, and Ben was certain the man blushed. "I am hopelessly clumsy on the ballroom floor."

And off, Ben would say, given the report of his antics at the museum. "Splendid. I will collect you tomorrow afternoon, so we can arrive together. You will need to bring daisies." Ben headed for the town house.

"Wait," Hackberry called to him. "Wouldn't presenting flowers to a lady be the opposite of annoying?"

Ben kept walking, a smile on his face. "You have much to learn, my naive apprentice."

Ten

"Stop." Ben held up a hand as Hackberry descended the stairs of his own town house the next morning. "What are you wearing?"

Hackberry halted at the foot of the stairs, held his arms out to his sides—a brass-knobbed walking stick clutched in his right hand—and looked down at his attire. His brows dropped low. "Is something wrong? Too casual for dance lessons?"

Ben scowled as his gaze traveled over Hackberry. If the points of his collar were any stiffer, someone might lose an eye, and his gray trousers were cut to display his calves to their best advantage. Not even a hair was out of place. "Too bloody perfect, Hackberry. What are you thinking?"

The baronet inclined his head toward his manservant. "Thank you, Wilhelm, you may go."

"And that *waistcoat*." Ben curled his lip in disgust as he eyed the dark green embroidered piece. There wasn't a wrinkle in sight. Hackberry had been a rumpled mess the night of his and Eve's betrothal ball, but now that he was trying to earn her disapproval... "You look like a blasted dandy."

A laugh burst from Hackberry. "You are one to talk. Look at you, dressed as if you have an audience with Prinny."

"I am not the one trying to repel Miss Thorne." Ben had taken extra care with his appearance that morning, approving of his valet's choice of a cream silk waistcoat and black trousers. Now he wondered if he would appear too bland beside Hackberry in his colorful ensemble. For that matter, everything about Eve's betrothed was colorful, especially his unusual hobby.

Eve would view Hackberry's expeditions to exotic locations as grand adventures. Ben could just imagine her listening to Hackberry's tales, spellbound. She would lean forward, her eyes like polished rosewood, with her small yet prominent chin resting on her hand.

"I am dressed no different than usual," Hackberry said.

"Come here." Ben motioned to his rival with an impatient jerk of his hand. "There is nothing annoying about your appearance."

"And yet you seem put out with it." Hackberry's smile widened.

Ben clamped his mouth shut and refused to comment on Hackberry's observation. Once the man stood in front of him, Ben requested the cane and Hackberry surrendered it. "Now, unfasten your waistcoat, then misalign the buttons as you secure it again."

Hackberry shrugged and complied. "And this will repel Miss Thorne, misaligned buttons?"

"Perhaps." Eve had always shown a tendency toward needing to set everything back to rights: a crooked painting on the wall, a stray hair on Ben's coat, a smear of chocolate at the corner of his lips. His body tensed in memory of her touching him, her own lips parted while she concentrated on the task of pressing her lacy handkerchief to his mouth, her body lightly leaned against his for balance as she lifted to her toes.

Ben cleared his throat. "On second thought, align them again."

Hackberry rolled his eyes and snatched the walking stick from Ben. "We haven't the time for you to act like my mother. We will be late unless we leave now." He stalked out the front door.

When Ben joined him on the walkway, they moved at a decent clip toward Covent Garden. The neighborhood was quiet except for the occasional delivery cart traveling the narrow street, the incessant clack of Hackberry's walking stick striking the ground, and the grating call of a starling from the window ledge of a town house they passed. Neither Ben nor his companion spoke until they turned the corner onto Floral Street.

"Miss Thorne's brother isn't fond of you, you know," Hackberry said, slowing his pace.

Ben smiled wryly. "Whatever gave you that impression?"

"It's no secret. Everyone talks about your duel with gloves. I hear it was quite the spectacle and Thorne outsmarted—"

"Do you have a point?" he asked through clenched teeth.

"I do. Thorne will not welcome you into his home, so how do you suppose you will be part of today's dance instruction?"

Sebastian Thorne was the least of Ben's troubles. "He is a slave to his duties. It is a rare occurrence when he misses a meeting with the Lords." Ben was more concerned with Eve barring him from Thorne Place. After their encounter in the foundling hospital nursery, she had refused to look at, much less speak with him the remainder of the day. A real possibility existed that she would turn him away. "I need you to convince Miss Thorne you and I have become friendly, and that you requested my assistance."

Hackberry scoffed. "And why would I request assistance from her former beau? Even I cannot pretend to be that lamebrained."

"I am certain you are capable of rising to the occasion."

"God's blood," the man grumbled and shook his head as if questioning Ben's sanity.

Not that Ben blamed Hackberry. Ben hadn't considered how they would convince Eve to let him stay. He only knew he must be there, because the thought of Hackberry and Eve alone together left Ben's insides twisted in knots.

When Covent Garden came into view, they headed toward the crowd of vendors selling goods in the square. The first flowermonger they reached had a basket of white daisies with cheerful yellow centers.

"I will take a dozen," Hackberry said as he pulled a coin from his pocket.

After the exchange, the girl—no older than eleven, if that—performed an awkward curtsy and bid them a good day.

Ben arched his eyebrow at Hackberry. "May I?"

The man passed him the daisies with a puzzled frown. Plucking one from the bouquet, Ben returned it to the girl. "For you, miss."

Her face puckered in bewilderment, and she hesitantly accepted the flower when Ben continued to hold it out to her. She tried to return a penny, but he and Hackberry insisted she keep it.

Ben smiled at her. "That one is for you, miss."

A bright blush swept over her face as she placed the flower in her basket, then scurried to a spot several feet away.

"Now the bouquet looks"—Hackberry slanted his head to the side—"*lopsided*."

"Exactly." Ben thrust the flowers back into his hands.

Hackberry scratched his head and didn't press him for an answer. Ben was beginning to like that quality about him. Perhaps under different circumstances, they might become chums.

"Come this way. We have one more purchase to make." Ben headed toward a vegetable cart without waiting to see if Hackberry followed. He searched through the carrots, potatoes, and cabbages until he found what he wanted, then handed the old man a coin. Ben presented his offering to Hackberry. "Eat it."

Ben's companion balked. "An onion? I politely decline."

"I question your commitment to the cause, Hackberry." He held the white bulb higher, noting he'd probably chosen an unnecessarily large one.

Hackberry's eyes narrowed. "Very well, but you will owe me. This goes beyond the call of duty." He snatched the onion from Ben's hand and shoved the flowers against his chest. "Hold these."

After peeling off the outer skin, Hackberry grimaced then sank his teeth into the onion. Juice dribbled down his chin. The fumes from the onion formed tears in Hackberry's eyes. "Damnation, you really owe me, Hillary."

"Stop crying, you overgrown baby. I'm already paying you handsomely and tossing a ship into the pot."

The vendor cackled under his breath as they walked away. Hackberry only finished half the onion before he tossed it in the gutter. "Let me have those fla-howers," he said, purposefully breathing in Ben's face, then ducked to the side when Ben playfully swung at him.

Ben handed over the bouquet with a chuckle. He hated to admit it, but he could better understand the reason Eve would enjoy Hackberry's company. Hackberry seemed like a good-natured gent not afraid to laugh at himself.

As they continued their stroll to Savile Row, Hackberry buried his face in the flowers and inhaled. "They are a fragile little thing, but they haven't much scent."

"Unlike you," Ben drawled.

Hackberry ignored him. "Do you think this is the reason Miss Thorne doesn't like daisies?"

"I can't say." Eve had been adamant that there be no daisies in her wedding bouquet, and Ben hadn't questioned her. Their mothers had been under instruction to allow Eve whatever she wanted. The cost wasn't to be a deterrent. Perhaps another young lady would have taken advantage of his wealth, but Eve had always been sensible about those things.

Reaching Thorne Place at last, Hackberry grabbed for the knocker before Ben and rapped on the door. "Allow me to explain to Eve," Hackberry said. "Bringing you to our lesson might be just the thing to upset the apple cart."

"But I don't want to upset—" The door eased open, and Ben swallowed the rest of his reply. Upsetting Eve was not his goal, although now he feared that was exactly what his presence would do.

Thorne's butler stood at the threshold, his posture rigid and proper. The only sign of surprise was the slight widening of his eyes. "Sir Jonathan. Mr. Hillary. Miss Thorne did not inform me to expect both of you."

"Shh…" Hackberry flashed a dotty grin. "It is a surprise."

❧

Eve heard Jonathan's voice in the foyer and a trill of pleasure passed through her. She hadn't been confident he would come, for he had sent around several excuses lately bowing out of their plans. Nevertheless, today he was here, and Eve was willing to overlook his past inattentiveness so long as it didn't continue.

She was anxious to teach him the waltz. It was her favorite dance. Ben had introduced her to the joys of gliding around the ballroom as if clouds cushioned each step. It would be foolish to expect the same amount of grace from Jonathan. Yet she didn't wish to give up the dance entirely just because he had been traveling the world when the waltz came to London.

She hopped up from her perch on the settee in the drawing room to go greet her betrothed. Sweeping into the foyer, she stopped so abruptly it must have appeared she slammed into an invisible wall.

Ben. What in the blazes was he doing here? Her breathing became shallow and choppy. And with Jonathan?

"Ah, Miss Thorne. How exquisite you look today." Jonathan came forward, gushing with more compliments on her gown, her hair, and her healthy complexion. Her face burned at the extravagance of his flattery. This behavior was quite unlike him, although he'd never begrudged her a kind word.

He swooped down to kiss both of her cheeks one after the other, a horrible stench making her nose wrinkle before she could hide her reaction. He covered his mouth, muffling his sheepish chuckle. "Cook served onions earlier. I couldn't resist."

"Oh." He urged the bouquet into her hands. "Uh, th-thank—" Her nose tingled and she flicked her knuckle over it. "Thank you."

"Have you met Mr. Hillary?" Jonathan asked.

Eve blinked, bewildered by his short memory, then nodded.

"Oh, that is right. How could I have forgotten? You and he…and then he— Well, you both know what happened." Jonathan's smiled stretched across his face. "But it is all water under the bridge now, isn't it?" How casually he shrugged off his arriving with Eve's former betrothed, the man Jonathan knew had jilted her.

She puckered her lips in displeasure, but since her nose tingled again, she wiggled her lips side to side in an attempt to ease the itch.

Oblivious to her changing mood, Jonathan prattled on about crossing paths with Ben that morning and what an abysmal dancer Jonathan was. He spoke in rapid sentences she could barely follow, and he gestured wildly with his hands.

Her gaze locked on Ben's penetrating blue stare. His eyes, fringed with dark wispy lashes, conveyed an odd mixture of emotions. She thought she read hope and despair in their depths, but it could be nothing more than her fanciful imagination. And there was *longing*. She knew that look. *But is it for me?* Her heart ricocheted off her breastbone.

"Why, just the other day Lady Norwick was telling me how I needed to improve my footwork and suggested I learn to imitate the Hillary men, who are reportedly all fine dancers." Jonathan was still talking and she tried to focus on the sound of his voice to bring her back to him. "Apparently the ladies are very eager to attract Mr. Hillary's attention now that he has returned to London."

She jolted out of her trance. "Pardon?" She blinked again to ease the prickly burn invading her eyes. And her nose was itching like the dickens now.

Jonathan tossed a look back over his shoulder at Ben. "I figured I could do better than imitate Mr. Hillary. I asked for his help providing instruction."

"But I was planning to—achoo!"

"God bless you," Jonathan offered.

"Thank you. As I was saying—" She sneezed again.

"Bless you."

Then she sneezed twice more. Jonathan continued to bless her with each violent convulsing of her body before continuing his constant stream of chatter.

Ben came forward with a furrowed brow, handed her his handkerchief, and took the flowers. She looked at them for the first time. *Daisies? Oh, for heaven's sake.* No wonder her eyes and nose were running. She probably looked like a glowing red-nosed mess now.

Ben stalked over to Milo. "Take these away."

"Yes, sir." The butler abandoned his normally dignified pace to remove the offending flowers from the room.

She dabbed at her nose and smiled with gratitude at Ben. She couldn't very well ask him to leave now, could she? How had he known the daisies were the source of her sneezing? Worse, how had Jonathan failed to notice?

Her betrothed's smile was positively gleeful when she looked up at him. "Are we ready to begin?" he asked.

She offered a half smile of her own. When he bubbled with enthusiasm, he reminded her of an eager puppy. How was she to remain irritated with a puppy without feeling like an ogre?

"If you will follow me, gentlemen. The servants have pushed the furniture to the outer edges of the drawing room so we have ample space to move."

When Ben offered his arm, she was beyond tempted to accept his escort. Instead, she linked arms with Jonathan, offering an apologetic smile to Ben. He inclined his head in acceptance, then followed her and Jonathan to the drawing room.

Her maid looked up from her darning when Eve entered with the two men. Her thin gray eyebrows lifted, but she didn't make a sound. Since Helena was meeting with her solicitor, Eve had enlisted Alice to act as her chaperone this afternoon. Mama would have fulfilled the role if Eve had asked, but she hated to bother her mother when she rarely had a day when she felt well anymore.

"I'm afraid we have no music," Eve said, "but perhaps it will be easier to learn the steps without it first."

She moved to the center of the floor, lifted her arms into position, and took a deep breath to fortify herself for the hour ahead. Ben gestured for Jonathan to join her before selecting a spot close to the window where she couldn't help but see him. His gaze remained locked on her, making her stomach tumble over and over.

Her chin quivered the slightest little bit, and she clamped her jaw together to hide her nerves. When Jonathan stepped in front of her and blocked her view of Ben, it required all her willpower not to peer around her betrothed to see Ben again in spite of the way he made her shaky inside.

Jonathan's unexpected touch on her back made her gasp and jump. "Sorry," he mumbled.

"No, pardon me, sir." She stole a quick glance at his face to determine if he was insulted by her reaction, but he simply looked back with wide-eyed expectation. Her shoulders relaxed and she felt a smile tug at the corners of her mouth. She appreciated his easygoing nature. Even now, with her former love looking on, he maintained his cheerful countenance.

"Let us begin with the box step." Eve slowly went through the simple steps until Jonathan seemed to grow comfortable. "Splendid. You are performing superbly."

Ben was leaning with one hip against the wall and his thumb hooked in his trouser pocket. His oh-so-handsome face was devoid of expression, but his gaze burned into her.

"Step left, together. Side, together. Now right."

As Jonathan studied his feet and repeated the steps aloud, Eve's attention gravitated toward Ben. His blue eyes darkened when she held his gaze longer than proper. The corners of his mouth curved with a knowing smile. She glanced away quickly.

"Excellent. You are doing marvelously." Her voice came out high-pitched, and her praise was too lavish for Jonathan's performance. "Let's increase the tempo. I think you are ready."

His brows lowered dubiously over his serious eyes.

"Like this." She halted their dancing to clap out the rhythm. "Just move your feet in time with the tempo."

She stole a peek at Ben, who hadn't taken his eyes off her. A flash of heat swept through her as Jonathan took her hand to try the dance once again.

"On three we will move left. One, two, three." She bungled her own instructions, moved in the wrong direction, and came down awkwardly, rolling her ankle. A stabbing pain shot up her leg, and she cried out.

"Eve!" Ben pushed away from the wall.

"No," she blurted before he touched her. "I-I am all right." She lied. Her ankle throbbed with each beat of her heart, and she bit down on her lip to keep from whimpering.

Jonathan supported her as she balanced on one leg. He grimaced as if he too were in pain. "Miss Thorne, I am sorry. I should have paid better attention. Can you walk on it?"

It wasn't Jonathan's fault, but he was gallant to take responsibility. "I think so." Gingerly she touched her toes to the floor, but the slight pressure made her hiss.

"No, you can't." Ben lifted her in his arms, cradling her against his chest. She held herself stiff and fought the urge to melt against him as he carried her to the settee. The faint tones of his cologne teased her nose. She inhaled, savoring his scent: an exotic woodsy aroma with a hint of lemon.

"Oh dear," her maid said. Alice's mending had been abandoned on the floor, and she shifted her weight from foot to foot. "Oh dear. What should I do, miss?"

"Find a pillow, then send for the doctor." Ben's orders were spoken calmly, but it was clear he expected Eve's servant to comply.

Alice bustled over to the Chippendale chairs that had been shoved against the fireplace and retrieved two pillows. With great care, Ben placed Eve on the settee then crouched beside her. He took the pillows from Alice and arranged them under Eve's ankle as the maid left to carry out his instructions.

"Rest. The doctor will come soon." His voice was soothing and distracted her from the pain. "May I examine your ankle?"

He reached for her skirts, but she planted her hand against his chest. "No! And I don't need a doctor."

He covered her hand with his. Goose bumps rose along her arm. His heartbeat was strong and rapid, betraying his calm facade. "Evie," he murmured.

Jonathan cleared his throat, and they jerked apart. A furious heat seared her cheeks and she dropped her gaze to her lap. "Miss Thorne, please allow Mr. Hillary to check your injury. He only wishes to help."

When she glanced at Jonathan standing at the end of the settee, his long face and stooped shoulders stabbed at her heart. He appeared so defeated. She couldn't stomach the thought of hurting him.

"I will wait for the doctor." Her voice was firm, and Ben held his hands up in surrender. "Forgive me, Sir Jonathan," she said. "I only wanted a partner to waltz with me, and instead I've ruined our day with my clumsiness." And not just with her misstep on the dance floor. Her misstep with Ben was unforgivable.

Ben rocked back on his heels and sighed. He swung his head toward Jonathan. "We can't very well allow the entire day to be spoiled, can we? You brought me here for a reason, and I hate to see the lady disappointed."

A smile inched across Jonathan's face. "As do I. What do you propose?"

Ben rose and with a grimness befitting a condemned man, he held his hand out to Jonathan. "May I have this dance?"

"Ben," Eve blurted and laughed.

He winked at her, his eyes teasing. "Now, don't be jealous, Miss Thorne. I only mean to borrow your

betrothed. You may have him back as soon as he has
mastered the waltz."

Jonathan's good humor returned as well. "In other
words, she may never see me again."

"Exactly."

Eve's heart lifted as the men took position in the
center of the room.

"Am I the gentleman or lady?" Jonathan asked.

"I believe that is obvious, Hackberry. But for
the sake of learning, you may assume the role
of gentleman."

Their banter continued as Ben led Jonathan through
the steps.

"You are squeezing my hand," Ben complained. "If
I were a lady, you would crack the bones."

"If you were a *lady*, I wouldn't mind you holding
me so close," Jonathan shot back. "Give me a bit of
breathing room."

Eve chuckled as Ben purposefully tried to stomp
his partner's toes, and Jonathan danced and hopped to
avoid Ben's boots.

"That's better, more lively," Ben quipped. "Now
apply it to the waltz."

Given the chance to observe, Eve relaxed against
the cushion and rested her head along the back of
the settee. It was nice to see the men getting along,
although she didn't know what it meant. They seemed
the most unlikely of friends. Her eyes narrowed on
Jonathan's lovely green waistcoat as Ben wrangled him
on the dance floor when Jonathan made a misstep.

Oh, for pity's sake. The man couldn't even button
his waistcoat correctly. She suppressed a sigh. Poor

Jonathan needed a keeper, and she feared he would be lost without her.

The sight of two handsome men prancing around her brother's drawing room made her smile. They were both amiable gents, and she enjoyed their teasing with one another. After a quarter hour passed, she had to admit Ben was the superior instructor. Jonathan was already learning to travel and perform the promenade.

She applauded when Jonathan spun Ben under his arm. "Bravo!"

Milo walked in as they repeated the spin. His jaw dropped, and Eve giggled. Ben and Jonathan released each other and quickly moved to opposite sides of the drawing room. The staunch butler schooled his features, then announced the doctor had arrived.

Eleven

EVE'S ANKLE INJURY PROVED TO BE NOTHING MORE than a sprain, and six days later, she was well enough to resume her usual activities outside of the home. Only the occasional twinge reminded her to slow down and not overtax herself, but she was certainly well enough to attend one of Jonathan's lectures at the museum.

"Shall we?" Jonathan held out his arm to escort her to the door of Thorne Place.

When her maid donned a bonnet and nodded to Eve to signal she was ready, Eve linked arms with her betrothed.

Jonathan's eyes twinkled. "Did I ever mention the frame drum also could be traced to Greece and the goddess Athena?"

"Yes, I believe you have mentioned it a time or two." *Or fifty.* She squeezed his arm affectionately. His childlike enthusiasm made her smile, even if she was growing a bit tired of hearing the same information.

"I find it fascinating how diverse the ancient civilizations were, and yet universally they incorporated drums into their worship of their gods." He spoke in a rush of words. "Drums were used in war too, but most Continental empires only employ drums on the battlefield. There seems to be something terribly wrong with this practice."

"I never really thought about it, but I suppose that is true." Eve wrinkled her brow when they walked outside and there wasn't a hack waiting for them in the street. She tossed a look over her shoulder at Alice, who seemed just as puzzled. Jonathan whisked Eve along the walkway without explanation. She scanned the street for a carriage, but Jonathan kept moving when they reached the cross street. Her maid was lagging behind since she wasn't accustomed to a quick pace, nor was she a young woman any longer.

Eve politely cleared her throat to gain his attention. "Pardon me, sir, but where are we headed?"

He swung his head toward her as if startled. "Why, to the museum. Did you forget about my lecture today?"

"Of course I didn't, but it is across town. Surely you are not suggesting we go by foot."

He stopped short on the walkway, abruptly jerking her back. "Sorry," he mumbled. He rubbed his fingers over the deep creases between his eyebrows as he regarded her. "You enjoy walking and it is a pleasant day. I thought you would be pleased."

Her lips parted, but no sound came out. Was he truly oblivious to Alice's crimson face and the noisy huffing from trying to keep up? His preoccupation had seemed humorous and quirky before today; now it made her slightly queasy. She glanced at Alice, and his bewildered gaze slowly traveled toward her maid too.

"Ah," he uttered. "It is a bit far, I think." A deep blush flooded his face and her faith in him began to be restored. Perhaps he needed a nudge when it came to thinking of others, but he was not heartless. "We may need to walk a little farther to find a hack. Is that acceptable?"

She smiled, finding his compromise adequate. "Perhaps we could walk at a more leisurely pace as well."

"Agreed." Jonathan mirrored her smile then launched into happy chatter again. As they neared Piccadilly, they encountered more people out and about. "We should be able to locate a hack to hire ahead," he said. "Keep a lookout."

Eve checked on Alice and caught sight of a man several yards behind her maid. He stopped to pull his watch fob from his pocket as if checking the time, but she noticed his gaze straying toward them. He snapped his watch closed and turned around to walk in the opposite direction.

Unease trickled through her, but she tried to shake off the feeling. Her brother had always accused her of having an overactive imagination, and she knew it was true. Since she was a little girl, she had made up stories about gypsies, pirates, or enchanted forests where fairies lived among the ferns. In her imagination, everything was perfect: fathers didn't have fits of anger, throw valuable vases against walls, or barricade themselves in their chambers for days on end.

As the walkway became more crowded, Jonathan drew her to his side. They maneuvered around gentlemen, merchants, members of the servant class, and the occasional lady with her escort. Eve turned to motion Alice closer and caught another glimpse of the man with the watch. He met her eyes, then veered toward a vendor's cart, turning his back as he inspected the goods. There was nothing remarkable in his appearance, nothing familiar about him.

Jonathan urged her along. "I've spotted a hack at the next intersection."

Eve saw it too and hurried her step to keep up with him, but Alice fell behind again. "Sir Jonathan." She released his arm, intending to go back for her maid, and discovered the same man only several feet away. Was he following them? "Sir Jonathan, do you know that man? I think he is following us."

"Where?" Jonathan was searching straight ahead.

"Right there!"

The man grimaced when she pointed at him, then dashed into the street, darting between a carriage and wheeled cart crawling along the congested street.

"He *is* following us."

"Where is he?" Jonathan spun around, his shoulder knocking her bonnet askew.

"In the street. Dressed in gray." She reached to adjust the brim so she could see which way he went.

"I don't see him." Jonathan whirled again and sent her sprawling into Alice's arms. She and her maid hugged each other to keep from falling, and Eve's bonnet brim slipped lower over her eyes.

"Miss Thorne." Alice's voice trembled. "What is happening?"

"I don't know." Eve managed to right herself and

adjust her bonnet in time to see Jonathan spin again and nearly trip a soldier with his cane. The stout man stumbled forward and bumped into his fellow soldier. They hurled curses at Jonathan, clearly unhappy with him and his cane.

The larger soldier marched toward him, red-faced and almost foaming from the mouth. "Watch where you be swinging that blasted walking stick before I stick it up yer—"

"Oh dear!" Eve rushed forward to insert herself between the men, but in a flash, Jonathan had her behind him.

"A lady is present," Jonathan said with a snarl. "Stand down, mangold."

The note of danger in his tone made her shiver, even as his insult made her want to laugh. Wasn't a mangold a type of beet? She peeked around Jonathan to see the soldier's face did in fact border on purple like a beet, but the color was quickly draining from his cheeks.

"Yes, sir." Both men backed away, their postures submissive. They reminded her of hounds tucking tail.

"Apologize to the lady."

"Sorry, miss," the men mumbled before bolting away.

Jonathan turned to face her. "Are you all right? Did they frighten you?"

She blinked up at him, confused by the paradox he presented. Sweet bumbling man by day. Dangerous adversary by...well, also by day. "I was not frightened."

He blew out a breath. "Well, that makes one of us. I am still shaking. See?" He held out a trembling hand, then made a fist and pressed it against his thigh. "Please don't place yourself in danger again, Miss Thorne. It requires me to be brave, and I am not certain my nerves can handle it."

She bit down on her lip rather than blurt out she wouldn't have been in any danger if he were more careful with his cane. The poor man was shaken enough by the encounter. "I am sorry, but I wasn't thinking. I won't do it again." Although she didn't know how she would keep her promise if he continued to land them in situations not of her doing.

"Splendid." He sported a crooked grin. "Now, allow me to hail a hack." He stepped toward the street as a weathered carriage bumped along the rutted thoroughfare and waved his hand in the air to gain the driver's attention. After securing a ride and handing Eve and her maid into the carriage, he claimed the opposite seat.

Now that they were safely on their way, it was hard to believe they had been in danger moments earlier. Jonathan could have gotten himself severely injured or killed. She raised her eyebrows in his direction. "A beet, sir?"

"A *Beta vulgaris*, if we wish to employ the proper name." He chuckled and lifted his shoulders in a sheepish shrug. "I couldn't think of anything more fitting. I am not as quick-witted as some, I'm afraid."

No, she supposed he wasn't, but it was a rather disappointing discovery. He was intelligent and well-read. Usually witty went hand in hand with those characteristics. She sank against the seat back, her smile fading.

Three weeks earlier, she thought she knew everything she needed to know about Jonathan, but recently she felt as if she didn't know him at all. He had become even more absorbed in his work, less thoughtful, and now she was discovering he wasn't even as clever as she had assumed. It might seem like a petty thing to some, but she had always appreciated a man with superior wit. What if there were other things she hadn't learned about her betrothed? Perhaps more troubling habits or traits he kept hidden?

She tilted her head slightly to study him. He caught her eye and grinned, but there was something different about his smile. She couldn't quite put her finger on what it was, but he truly lit up again as soon as the hack rolled to a stop in front of the museum. As they strolled arm in arm past the fountains en route to the north entrance, he resumed his chattiness.

Alice gasped softly when they reached a nude statue.

"It is something to see, is it not?" Jonathan asked her maid.

"Aye, sir." A furious blush consumed Alice's face. "Never seen anything like it."

When they reached the foot of the stairs leading into the majestic Montagu House, Jonathan linked arms with Alice, too, and helped her navigate the steps. Eve warmed in response to his thoughtful gesture. Perhaps earlier she had just experienced a case of nerves. Their wedding was only a week and a half away. Surely it was common for some brides to have doubts.

Just inside the museum doors, Alice released a delighted cry as her head dropped back to view the ceiling, which had been painted like a blue sky. "I've never seen anything as grand. Where did they find a long enough paintbrush, do you suppose?"

As Jonathan gave his name to the porter, Eve tried to explain the process for creating murals on ceilings, citing what she knew about Michelangelo's Sistine Chapel. Eve hadn't seen the actual ceiling in Rome, but Sebastian had, and she'd read about how the masterpiece had been created.

A moment later, an under-librarian came down the stairwell to greet them. "Sir Jonathan, what an honor to have you and your guests with us today. Mr. Hillary has already arrived. Please, come this way."

Eve snapped her head toward Jonathan, her heart floundering. "Mr. Hillary is here?"

He took her hand to thread it through the crook of his elbow. "I mentioned the lecture when we left Thorne Place the other day. He expressed interest, so I thought it would be rude to exclude him." As they neared a small doorway, Jonathan said, "I find I like Mr. Hillary. Perhaps you should give him another chance."

Eve stopped in the corridor and frowned at him. "I do not understand you, sir."

He patted her hand. "I find that is most often the case with everyone. Do not let it trouble you." Without allowing her another word, he dropped her hand and entered the room ahead of her.

She exchanged a perplexed glance with Alice, then followed. Jonathan had already located Ben sitting in the back row and was whispering with him.

"I would be honored," Ben replied. Her insides quivered when he stood and graced her with a smile.

"Excellent." Jonathan slapped him on the back. "Miss Thorne, I have asked Mr. Hillary to provide you company while I prepare for my lecture. Come, there is room enough for you and your maid."

Ben's jaw hardened as his eyes narrowed at Jonathan. Her heart sank. Didn't Ben want to keep her company? Not that she wanted *his* companionship either. At least, not a great deal. "Hackberry, you forgot to ask Miss Thorne if she wishes to spend the afternoon in my company. Perhaps she would rather—"

"I don't mind."

The hint of a dimple appeared in Ben's right cheek. "That is a relief, Miss Thorne." He came forward to offer his arm. She hesitated, not certain touching him would be wise. After their brief contact when she twisted her ankle, she had been preoccupied with thoughts of him for days. It was unseemly for a betrothed young woman to ponder what it would be like to kiss her former love.

Would his lips be as soft as they once were?

Would he cradle her head with his strong yet gentle hands?

Would he angle her mouth just right, his kiss tasting slightly of mint?

"Miss Thorne?" Ben's voice jarred her from her memories. "Would you like to find a seat? The lecture will begin soon."

Jonathan's back was to them, and he was halfway to the lectern already.

Heat swept over her. "Please," she murmured and reached to touch Ben's arm, knowing every time she gave in to temptation, it would be that much harder to banish him from her dreams.

Twelve

BEN'S AWARENESS OF EVE ON THE SEAT BESIDE HIM eclipsed everything in the lecture room. He was in tune to every breath she took, the faint scent of her soap, the heat of her body filling the space between them even as she sat at the far edge of her chair to create distance.

He ached to touch her. Nothing too conspicuous. Just the casual brush of their arms or a surreptitious stroke of his finger against her inner wrist. But she was no longer his to touch. Ben reminded himself of this many times a day, but it didn't feel true no matter how often he repeated it. He folded his hands in his lap to keep from acting on the impulse.

Hackberry didn't believe he had made any progress with discouraging Eve. Ben was uncertain that was true. The way her pert nose wrinkled when Hackberry rushed off to the lectern without bidding her farewell spoke volumes. She was not pleased. Ben simply hoped her displeasure was directed at Hackberry only.

Encouraging Eve to toss over Hackberry was only half the battle, though. Ben needed to get back in her good graces if he hoped to win her heart again, and he needed to proceed carefully. If he overstepped his bounds, Eve would have nothing more to do with him. Her conscience wouldn't allow her to give in to temptation and make a cuckold of Hackberry, so until she cried off, Ben must practice patience.

There would be plenty of time to court Eve once Hackberry was no longer a threat. With only a week and a half left until the wedding, however, Hackberry needed to step up his efforts. Ben suspected he wasn't trying hard enough, or else Eve didn't want to see Hackberry's faults.

At the conclusion of the lecture, Hackberry chose a seat at the front of the room instead of joining them. A long stretch of quiet followed as another gentleman with slicked-down hair shuffled through his papers at the lectern, his lips moving as if he was mumbling to himself. Ben soon lost interest in the goings-on at the front of the room.

Eve turned her head and caught him staring at her. Her tentative smile made his pulse quicken. It had been too long since she had looked on him with anything resembling pleasure. She leaned to whisper in his ear. "I think Alice is getting antsy."

Peeking around Eve, Ben discovered the maid nibbling on her fingernails. He placed his mouth close to Eve's ear and whispered back, "I could arrange a tour if you think she would prefer to view the exhibits."

A slight quiver traveled through her. "Yes." Her voice had a wispy quality to it that made him smile. "I believe she would enjoy a tour. M-may I join you?"

His smile grew and he held out his hand. "Shall

we?" When she placed her hand in his, it required all his willpower not to gloat over this small victory.

The three of them slipped through the door as quietly as possible before the next lecturer began. He believed Hackberry would forgive their defection. In fact, he had been agreeable about the whole situation, which made him a bigger man than Ben. At first, Ben believed Hackberry's willingness to step aside was the act of a greedy man obsessed with his studies, but Ben didn't think that was true anymore. He seemed genuinely concerned for Eve's welfare and interested in her happiness, which only made Hackberry's decision more puzzling.

After their dance lesson, the poor man had looked miserable. He'd lamented giving Eve flowers that made her sneeze and causing her to become hurt during the waltz. Ben had tried to reassure him that despite being a horrid dancer, Hackberry wasn't responsible. Ben blamed himself. Even though he had known his presence made her uncomfortable, he had positioned himself where she couldn't avoid seeing him. Eve's injury was the result of being distracted and troubled by his presence. He was pleased she seemed more comfortable with him today.

"Wait here." Ben left Eve and her maid at the top of the stairs while he went to speak with the porter about locating a guide to show them around the museum. After they exchanged introductions with an older gentleman joining their group for the tour, the under-librarian led them to the upper floor where the insect exhibit was housed. Ben expected insects would hold little appeal for the women, but Alice seemed enraptured as their guide pointed out the different species and shared facts about the insect life cycle. When the under-librarian invited them to follow him to the worm exhibit, Alice was on his heels.

Ben and Eve hung back, walking at a sedate pace. She watched her maid with a soft smile, then linked her arm with his. "I've never seen Alice this excited about anything. I should allow her to accompany me on outings more often. Thank you for suggesting a tour."

"It was my pleasure." His voice sounded husky, and he cleared his throat. "Has she been to Vauxhall Gardens?"

Eve shook her head. "But that is a marvelous idea. I always loved dining outdoors and the orchestra. I haven't been in ages, not since—"

A becoming blush gave color to her cheeks and her freckles nearly disappeared. Not since their courtship two years earlier when Ben had taken her and stolen a kiss on one of the winding paths? That was the first time he'd said he loved her.

"I, too, have fond memories of the gardens," he murmured. Her blush deepened to a dark rose color, and she changed the subject.

"Did Amelia relay my thanks for the flowers?" she asked.

"She did. I hope it was acceptable to send them with my sister-in-law." Ben had felt awful about the daisies too, and he'd tried to erase the mistake with a dozen pink peonies and best wishes for a speedy recovery. Since he couldn't send flowers to a lady he wasn't allowed to court, he had requested Amelia's assistance in delivering them.

"It was a lovely gesture, but unnecessary," Eve said. "My injury was nothing serious, but the flowers lifted my spirits. Peonies have always been my favorite."

"I remembered."

She drew to a stop; a small crease appeared between her brows. "How is it we have been apart for two years and you recall my favorite flower, but Sir Jonathan—" She shook her head. "No, this is not an appropriate topic for conversation."

When she tried to walk away, Ben caught her hand. "Evie," he said softly. "You may talk to me." At one time, she had shared everything with him—her doubts, her dreams, her family secrets. He had shared everything with her as well. She was the only person he'd ever talked to about Charlotte's accident.

She worked her hand free and crossed her arms. "But I shouldn't. It is not proper to air dirty laundry in public."

He gestured to the empty room. "There is no one around to eavesdrop. If you need someone to listen... Once, we were friends too, were we not?"

"We were." Her lips turned down. "But we were also more, which makes it wrong that I should turn to you." Her protest sounded weak.

He suspected she wanted to confide in him, but pressing the issue would send her running again. He waited patiently while she wrestled with whether she could allow him to become her confidant again. She pressed her lips tightly together as if struggling to contain her words. Eventually, she lost the battle.

"Promise you will not assign this more meaning than it has. I am marrying Sir Jonathan. I have given my word; a contract exists between us. My course has been set."

"I know." He cleared his throat. "I promise to assign no unintended meaning to anything you confide in me."

"All right." She brushed a wisp of hair from her forehead, her gaze wary. "Lately I have begun to wonder how well I really know my betrothed, or how well he knows me."

"What do you mean?"

"*He* doesn't know my favorite flower, or what color I prefer, or even how I take my tea. And yet I suspect you do."

Ben smiled. "Emerald. Cream, no sugar."

Eve nodded, a soft glow emanating from her dark brown eyes. "I do not hold Sir Jonathan at fault. I do not know much about him either, other than he is uncommonly preoccupied with drums, and Athena lately. Oh, and his favorite ice, but I have a ten-year-old to thank for that information. He doesn't offer much without prompting." Her chuckle had a self-deprecating quality to it, and a pink blush dusted her cheeks. "I sound silly, don't I?"

"I've never thought you were silly, Evie." If that was all she truly knew about her betrothed, it wasn't much.

She threaded her fingers together and pressed her hands against her chest as if praying. "I realize how Sir Jonathan likes his steak or the title of his favorite book seem trivial, things I could discover once we are wed. Still, I cannot help wondering if we are walking down the aisle too soon. We don't know the smallest details about each other, which makes me worry there could be bigger, more important facts we don't know either."

Ben couldn't imagine Hackberry had any secrets to warrant her concern, and yet he didn't want to dismiss her outright, especially when she seemed to need a friend's ear. "What has he done to make you doubt him?"

Her head snapped up; her lips parted. "I-I never said I doubted him."

True, not with words, but she didn't have to say it aloud. The way she picked at her gloves and averted her gaze when she spoke of Hackberry revealed more than she realized. Ben held his tongue while she seemed to be sorting through her thoughts.

Her tongue darted over her lips and she looked away again. "I do not doubt *him*. I doubt myself and my judgment."

Because of what Ben had done. She didn't need to point a finger for him to know her reservations stemmed from his betrayal. "You have no reason to doubt yourself."

She shrugged. "Maybe not, but I think I might have been blind to his faults until recently. He can be so thoughtless at times, and woolly-headed and…and something else I cannot name. For instance, a man was following us earlier, and Sir Jonathan was oblivious. When I alerted him, he spun in circles—not noticing a thing—knocked me into Alice and then tripped a soldier, a *large* one. He nearly wound up in a fight, and I thought he would be killed, but the soldier seemed frightened. I saw a different side to Sir Jonathan. Just for a moment, but—"

"Wait." Ben shook his head to clear his confusion. "Someone followed you to the museum?"

"I'm not completely certain he was following us, but he ran away when I pointed him out."

"What did Hackberry say? Did he know the man?"

She wrinkled her nose. "That is what I was trying to tell you. He never saw him, because he was too busy bumping into me and instigating a fight."

"But you saw the man. Can you describe him?"

"I only had a brief view, but there was nothing remarkable about him. Light brown hair, skin tanned from the sun, I imagine. And his coat was a dull gray."

God's blood! She was describing Mr. Armstrong. The investigator had already been paid for his services. Why would he continue to follow Hackberry? Ben schooled his features so Eve couldn't detect his irritation, or culpability in the afternoon's events. "You said Hackberry nearly came to blows with a soldier on the walkway. How did that come about?"

Her eyebrows shot toward her hairline. "Good heavens, it was the most impressive display of clumsiness I've ever seen. He was fumbling about, his cane swinging this way and that." She linked arms with Ben and relayed the events in a flurry of whispers as they trailed after their tour group, her lively recitation making him laugh.

Thirteen

EVE HATED TO ADMIT IT, BUT SHE WASN'T EXACTLY upset when Jonathan invited Ben to join them at Gunter's after the lecture. She wouldn't go so far as to say she was pleased—that felt disloyal to Jonathan— but she would be lying if she denied enjoying Ben's companionship at the museum.

Unlike anyone else, he had a way of making her feel interesting and significant. He would lean toward her and look into her eyes any time she spoke, as if missing a single word would be reprehensible to him. And he asked questions—relevant ones—that showed he was truly listening.

At the museum, when she admitted to having misgivings about the swiftness with which she and Jonathan were marrying, Ben hadn't dismissed her concerns. And yet he hadn't used her doubts to his advantage either.

Of course, she didn't know what he wanted from her precisely. He claimed a desire to create a life with her, to have children and make a home together, but she had heard those same words two years ago. She might forgive easier than she should, but she didn't have a faulty memory.

She slanted a glance over her shoulder at Ben walking with Alice. Her maid hadn't stopped talking since they left the museum, but if Ben found her chatter unpleasant, one would never know from his attentiveness to her. Eve smiled as she returned her attention to the walkway.

"The Elgin Marbles were a sight," Alice said. "What do you suppose happened to the heads of the sculptures, Mr. Hillary?"

"That's a marvelous question. Perhaps they are shoved into the corner of an old attic, stored in a trunk."

"Mercy! I wouldn't want to be the one to find them. Can you imagine looking for your grandmother's wedding gown and discovering a trunk of heads staring up at you?"

"*I* can't imagine looking for my grandmother's wedding gown," Ben drawled.

Eve chuckled and noted Jonathan didn't join in. When he quickly glanced at her, his jaw was tight. Her merriment died away. His sudden change in mood caught her by surprise. He had been in good spirits when they left the museum, laughing and teasing with them. He had even commented on being pleased their party excused themselves early from the second lecture so Alice could enjoy the exhibits.

But now… She could feel the tension rolling off him, and the air around him crackled. His gaze darted across the street and narrowed. For a moment, she was afraid they were being followed again, but she couldn't see any sign of the man from earlier. In fact, everything appeared rather ordinary in Berkley Square with carriages clogging the street and people milling about in the park, but Jonathan's stiff posture made her uneasy.

"Something is wrong," she whispered. "What is it?"

"Nothing."

"It is the man again, isn't it? He is following us. Where? Behind us?" She swung around, looking for the man in the gray coat. "Mr. Hillary, we require your assist—"

"Julius Caesar!" Jonathan's sharp bark made her jump, and she dropped his arm. He drew to a halt, blinking at her. "Er... Sorry. I just recalled something I forgot to do before I left home this afternoon."

Ben clapped him on the shoulder, his smile looking a bit strained. "Is there a problem, Hackberry?"

"No problem." Jonathan removed his hat and tried to smooth down his wayward curls, but the move left his hair tousled instead. "Well, perhaps a slight one. I—I am afraid I am a bit lost. Does anyone know the way to the tea shop?"

"Oh, law," Alice mumbled under her breath.

Heat flooded Eve's face. When she had accepted Jonathan's proposal, she knew he could be absent-minded. Additionally, she had argued he was brilliant and interesting when others declared him too eccentric. Even his sense of direction being akin to that of a lemming's came as no surprise, but *this*—and every odd behavior he had shown today—left her speechless.

Ben raised his brows as if asking whether Eve wanted to tell Jonathan where they were or leave it to him. She supposed it would be best coming from her. Coughing delicately into her fist first, she pointedly flicked her gaze to the building across the street.

Jonathan swung his head to look over his shoulder. "Oh."

Ben offered his arm to Eve. "Shall we?" She didn't hesitate in accepting his escort, preferring to keep Jonathan at a distance, and very ashamed to admit it.

Jonathan seemed untroubled by Ben stepping into his place and assisted Eve's maid across the street. "What is your favorite ice cream, Alice?"

Alice shrugged. "I never had a dish before."

"Then I will surprise you," Jonathan said, his affable smile returning. "It appears crowded inside, Miss Thorne. Perhaps we should dine in the park. Would you like to find a shady spot while Mr. Hillary and I place our orders?"

Eve craned her neck to see through the shop window. As usual, every table was filled, and there was barely any room to stand. "That sounds lovely."

"We will not be long."

As soon as she and Alice crossed the street and couldn't be overheard, her maid clucked her tongue.

"He is likely tired," Eve said with a sigh. "I imagine he burned the midnight oil to prepare for today's lecture."

Alice shrugged, jostling her heavy bosom. "Perhaps."

Eve bit her bottom lip as a horrible possibility occurred to her. What if there was no explanation for his behavior today? Her stomach lurched. What if this was simply the real Sir Jonathan Hackberry he was allowing her to see?

Ben regarded Hackberry as they waited on the walkway for the waiter to reach them. "What was that little act? You got lost?" Ben scoffed. "No one is that harebrained."

Hackberry scowled. "I had to think of something," he hissed. "Besides, my little act should help settle the matter a little faster. At this rate, Miss Thorne and I will be welcoming our firstborn before she begs off."

A waiter exited the shop with a tray and hurried across the street.

Ben's smile likely resembled an animal baring his teeth. "Touch her and you'll be meeting Julius Caesar personally." His words were uttered under his breath for Hackberry's ears only.

Hackberry arched an eyebrow. "It's a wonder we have become friends with all the threats you make against me. I suppose I have low standards when it comes to friendship."

"As do I." Ben's fists relaxed at his sides, as he recalled they were on the same side, even if he didn't approve of Hackberry's tactics. Nevertheless, there were worse ways the man could discourage Eve. "I guess our low standards make us perfect for one another."

"You aren't going to ask me to dance again, are you?"

Ben didn't have a chance to offer a retort, since it was their turn to place their orders. Hackberry requested a dish of pineapple, nothing for himself, then turned to Ben. "What flavor does Miss Thorne like?"

"Vanilla."

"Should I order lavender then?"

Ben shooed him away. "Join the women. I will take care of it." After placing a request for two more dishes of ice cream to be brought to the park, he joined his party.

Eve offered a welcoming smile when she spotted him entering the grove of trees. Stray afternoon sunlight filtered through the lush branches of a maple and created a halo effect around her. Her thick lashes caught the light, making the ends wispy, and her brown eyes glimmered.

A knot formed in his throat. Did she realize how beautiful she was, or how much he'd missed her? Many nights in Delhi he had lain in bed with the image of her in his mind, looking just like this. Sometimes he would talk to her, imagining they had a connection that allowed her to hear his thoughts.

Loneliness wrecked a man's sanity.

Her smile slipped and the tip of her tongue darted across her full lips, but she didn't look away.

"Excellent. You are back," Hackberry said, reminding Ben that he and Eve were not alone. "I must go. Could you see Miss Thorne home?"

A soft squeak came from Eve's direction. Ben wasn't sure if it was a protest or simply an expression of surprise, but he didn't like being caught off guard any more than she did.

Eve's gaze had dropped to the ground, and she was picking at her glove again. Her embarrassment was like a thorn lodged in Ben's heart. If this was Hackberry's plan for driving her away, he should have first discussed it with Ben. Humiliating her was not part of their agreement.

Hackberry sighed, his shoulders drooping as the air left him. "Remember that thing I mentioned forgetting earlier, Miss Thorne? I really should see to it. I am sorry."

"Can it not wait until you've seen Miss Thorne home?" Ben asked.

"No, it cannot." Hackberry's jaw hardened, the muscles prominent and taut as he met Ben's glower without a trace of apprehension. "I'll trust you to see the lady home safely."

Suddenly, Ben saw the difference Eve had mentioned earlier. Hackberry was behaving in a damned strange manner. An unforgivably *rude* manner.

Ben squared off with Hackberry, not willing to ignore the slight on Eve. "I would be honored to provide escort for Miss Thorne," he bit out, "but perhaps she would prefer the company of her *betrothed*."

Eve cleared her throat, and they both turned toward her. A becoming blush added warmth to her normally pale complexion. "If Sir Jonathan has business requiring his attention, perhaps it is best he see to it. I do not wish to keep him from important matters."

Ben ground his teeth together. What was more important than seeing to Eve? He inclined his head toward her. "If you have no objection, I would be pleased to spend more time in your company."

"I have no objection."

Despite Hackberry's earlier rush to leave, he stayed until the waiter delivered their dishes of ice cream.

Eve accepted hers with a huge smile. "Did you order vanilla for me?"

"Hillary did. I failed to ask what flavor you liked."

"Oh." Her gaze cut to Ben as she took her first bite. Closing her eyes, she moaned with pleasure. "Pure heaven, Mr. Hillary. Thank you."

Her reaction was innocent but arousing as hell. Ben shoved a spoonful of ice cream into his mouth and tried to think of anything but the tiny drop of vanilla lingering on her bottom lip. Or how he wanted to lick away the sweetness for her. She upset his good intentions, however, when she stroked her tongue over her lips, leaving them moist. Ben suppressed his own groan of pleasure and looked away before he embarrassed himself.

Hackberry cleared his throat, his eyes narrowing on Ben for a moment. "Well, I must be off." He took Eve's hand and placed a kiss on her glove. "Until tomorrow evening, Miss Thorne."

"Until tomorrow, sir."

Hackberry looked back over his shoulder twice as he took his leave. When he disappeared into the crowd, Ben turned his attention back to Eve. "What do you have on your schedule tomorrow?"

"Lady Eldridge and Sir Jonathan are dining at Thorne Place tomorrow evening. Helena thought it prudent to entertain the countess before refusing her offer to host a wedding breakfast in my and Sir Jonathan's honor. Helena said her cousin can be quite insistent, but Sebastian and his wife support our decision to forgo another celebration."

"Hmm." Ben's ice cream lost its flavor, and he set down his spoon. He didn't want to think of Eve becoming another man's wife, and yet denying the truth didn't change anything. "Only nine more days until the momentous occasion."

"Yes, nine days." She focused intensely on her ice cream as she pushed it around with her spoon. "It feels as if time is rushing by."

For him too. In nine short days, he could lose her forever, but until she signed her name in the parish registry, he still had a chance.

When her ice cream resembled milky soup, Eve looked up with a rueful smile. "I've had enough. Once Alice is finished, we should probably find a hack to carry us home."

Alice's spoon scraped the bottom of her bowl as she pursued every drop of her treat. After her last bite, she sighed in satisfaction, pulled a handkerchief from her sleeve, and made a show of dabbing the corners of her mouth. "It has been a memorable afternoon thus far. I hate to see it end. Would it be acceptable if we walked back to Thorne Place, miss?"

Eve's eyes widened. "You wish to walk? It is a good distance."

"I will let you know if I tire, miss. Then Mr. Hillary can hail a hack for us." Her maid took the dish from Eve, stacked it in hers, then held her hand out for Ben's. "I will return these to the waiter and we may go."

Ben could have hugged the older woman. "It appears you must be burdened with my companionship a little longer, Miss Thorne."

Her smile when she took his arm and looked up at him through her lashes made his pulse quicken. "You are not too difficult to bear, Mr. Hillary. I will persevere."

Fourteen

WHEN ALICE BEGAN TO LAG BEHIND, EVE FEARED THE day had become too tiring for her. Eve stopped on the walkway to suggest they find a hack only to discover Alice craning to peer through the windows of a town house as she passed.

Eve grinned. Her maid had a reputation as a busybody among the other staff at Thorne Place, and it seemed rightly earned.

Ben had stopped when Eve did and was waiting. "Is everything all right? Should I hail a ride?"

Eve shook her head. She suspected Alice would deny being tired if asked, for it would mean less snooping on the neighbors. Eve linked her arm with Ben's, and they resumed their leisurely pace. "Amelia said you visited the foundling hospital again," she said. "Did you return to the nursery?"

"I did. I hadn't expected the experience to be as rewarding as it has been, and after speaking with several board members, I believe I could do more."

"Oh? What do you have in mind?"

"Apprenticeships at Hillary Shipping for the young

men. It is not easy, the life of a seaman, but neither is being a soldier in the army, which is where many end up."

"What a splendid idea. The work may be hard, but imagine all they would see sailing around the world." Of course, Ben didn't have to imagine. He had sailed many times with his grandfather as a young man and visited places she could only dream of seeing. "I've always wondered what it would be like to leave England. Sometimes I question why I had to be born a lady."

"For what it is worth, I am grateful you are a lady," he said with a wink. "Nevertheless, your sex shouldn't be a barrier to travel. Many ladies brave the unsavory conditions found onboard ship for the chance to see the world."

She shrugged one shoulder. "Perhaps their lives are different from mine. I expect a quiet life in the country is in my future, but I do not mind." *Too much.*

In actuality, living in the country wasn't a problem for her, but she didn't want to be there alone. She longed to have a husband by her side. She had seen how lonely Mama's life had been married to Papa. When he barricaded himself in his chambers and refused to let anyone inside, it was no different from deserting them in Eve's mind.

She had vowed to never marry a man like her father, and yet it appeared she was following her mother's example. Jonathan would abandon his wife and children just as her father had abandoned Mama, Sebastian, and her.

Ben slanted a frown in her direction. "I wouldn't

have pegged Hackberry for a gentleman farmer. He does not strike me as a man content to remain in one place for long."

"He isn't, but unfortunately he doesn't intend to take me with him on his adventures."

Ben came to a sudden stop, interrupting her progress as well. He turned to face her. "Did he say he intended to leave you behind?" His incredulous tone vindicated her hurt feelings. For a time, she had worried she was being unreasonable.

"He said it would be too dangerous." Jonathan had also sworn he didn't want to leave her, but she couldn't believe he intended to give up his pursuits either.

"Too dangerous? Balderdash." Fire burned in Ben's blue eyes. "Where do you want to go? Make a list. I will take you anywhere you like."

Eve's heart gave a tiny leap before reality set in. Ben wouldn't be taking her anywhere. She was engaged to another man. "What is this?" She wagged her finger back and forth between them. "Why are you offering to show me the world? Why has my betrothed burdened you with escorting me home? None of this makes sense."

"You are not a burden, Evie."

"Maybe not to you, but clearly Sir Jonathan thinks I am." As soon as the words left her mouth, she knew it was true. Something had happened between her and Jonathan over the last week. Something that should have distressed her, but instead caused a tiny spark of hope inside her to flicker to life. If Jonathan didn't want her anymore, perhaps her future was not cast in stone after all.

Jonathan paced the floors of Viscount Margrave's study; his bootfalls grew muffled when he reached the carpet. He hadn't been kept waiting very long, but any delay was unacceptable. Finally, the polished oak door swung inward with no sound. The well-oiled hinges of the viscount's door were a testament to his attention to detail. It had probably kept him alive all this time as a spy for the Regent's Consul.

"We were followed today," Jonathan blurted before Margrave could greet him.

The viscount sighed and sauntered to the sideboard to pour a drink. Margrave's training showed in the way he moved, like a large and dangerous cat on the prowl. "I told you, Armstrong is harmless. Ben won't keep the investigator on a retainer long if there is nothing to report, so continue to do nothing suspicious and the matter will take care of itself."

"It wasn't your friend's man, and I do not think you heard me correctly. *We* were followed. Miss Thorne, her maid, and me. Then again after the lecture."

"This isn't good." Margrave frowned before taking a sip of his drink.

"Really? You think it is a bad sign?" Jonathan rarely resorted to sarcasm to make a point, but this situation called for it. In fact, it called for a brandy. Or scotch. He wasn't fussy. Moving to the sideboard, he poured a drink for himself since the viscount hadn't volunteered to do it.

Margrave leaned an elbow against the sideboard, studying him with that unnerving intensity he had. "Do you know who followed you?"

"I didn't recognize the man, but he was not very accomplished. Miss Thorne spotted him with no difficulty. It's hard to believe he would be a member of the Home Office."

Occasionally, the Home Office mistook the group of elite spies, of which Jonathan was a member, for enemies, and even though the HO agents did not pose much threat to the Consul, they were not bunglers.

"I almost came to fisticuffs with a couple of soldiers today, thanks to the man's ineptitude." Admittedly, Jonathan's attempt to distract Miss Thorne would not go down in history as his most brilliant move. "I had to invoke the code word for submission. Otherwise, it came down to ruining my cover or taking a beating."

"Mangold." The viscount chuckled and sipped his drink.

A mangold beet was a member of the *Beta* plant genus. Beta was the second letter in the Greek alphabet, below Alpha. In the world of soldiers and spies, a beta was of a lower rank and expected to obey his superior. "Miss Thorne looked at me as if I belong in Bedlam," Jonathan said.

"Of course she did. What sane man shouts out random vegetables? If she was even familiar with the term."

"Unfortunately, she was." Heat seared his face and he moved away from his colleague before he made note of the blushing. The Prince and his cronies must have been foxed when they created their ridiculous codes.

"Huh." Margrave moved to a chair adjacent to the unlit fireplace and dropped into it. "Ben didn't say anything about hiring another man, but I agree he couldn't be from the Home Office if he was detected with no trouble."

Unless someone wanted to prove Jonathan was an easier target when he was out in Society. The night of his and Eve's betrothal ball, Farrin, his commander, had sent three men to waylay him in Covent Garden. They received their fair share of lumps in the process of surprising him, but Farrin's message was delivered. Jonathan had orders to travel to Egypt to eradicate an enemy to the Crown, orders he could not refuse.

Jonathan hadn't known what to do about Miss Thorne. He'd considered carrying through with the marriage, then setting her up in the country until his duties were fulfilled, but he had been worried about leaving her alone. Ben Hillary presented a more reasonable solution that Jonathan believed would make Miss Thorne happier in the end. Hillary's offer of a ship had helped keep Farrin at bay for a while too. Once Hillary and Miss Thorne were married, everyone would believe Jonathan left England to lick his wounds in private. His commander had agreed it was a perfect cover story, but perhaps Farrin was growing impatient.

Margrave drummed his slender fingers against his glass. "I could ask Ben if he hired a different investigator."

"I do not think Hillary had anything to do with it. He was with us after the lecture." Hoping to capture the man for questioning, Jonathan had followed Miss Thorne and Mr. Hillary after they left Gunter's, but there was no more sign of the man. Jonathan shook his head. "Besides, you know Hillary and I have reached an agreement where Miss Thorne is concerned."

"A wise choice given your profession." Margrave's frosty glare spoke volumes on his opinion of Jonathan's attempt to live a regular life. "Have you made progress with Miss Thorne?"

Jonathan shrugged before gulping his drink. The smoky liquid seared his tongue and throat, leaving them slightly numb and tingly. "I believe so, but it hasn't been difficult to discourage her and aim her in Hillary's direction. She holds a *tendre* for him still."

Margrave grinned. "You sound sulky."

"Sod off. I do not." Perhaps his pride suffered some bruising knowing his betrothed preferred another man, but it was for the best. "Aren't I allowed a moment to wallow?"

"Do whatever you like." Margrave pulled his watch from his pocket. "Just do it quickly. I have somewhere to be this evening."

"I returned to England with the intention of getting out of this business. Napoleon is no longer a threat, so why won't Farrin set me free? I have served my country."

Very well, perhaps he *was* whining a bit. Jonathan had known when he was recruited for the Prince's elite group of spies there would only ever be one way out.

Margrave smirked. "You don't want freedom any more than I do. It is what we know. What else would you do with your time?"

"I don't know. Marry the perfect lady, attend balls, fill a nursery. All the things normal gentlemen do."

When Margrave's brows lifted, Jonathan ignored the insinuation. He may not be normal, but he could still desire a conventional life.

"You cannot dance. Why would you care about attending balls?" The viscount's gaze ran up and down Jonathan, assessing. "You don't want out." His bald statement rankled.

"How the hell do you know what I want?"

"You did not abandon your cover. You have no friends or acquaintances, beyond a childhood association with Lady Norwick. You could have returned as your true self, but instead you chose to play the role of absentminded Sir Jonathan: drumming enthusiast, archaeologist, and clumsy oaf."

"I'm not that clumsy," Jonathan grumbled, then drained his glass.

"My point exactly." Margrave's shrewd eyes narrowed to slits. "What is it you want from me? I assume you came for a reason."

Jonathan had never asked the other man for anything. Beyond their early days training together, they'd had no contact until Margrave informed him Mr. Hillary had hired an investigator to follow him. Margrave wasn't his friend, but Jonathan needed him all the same. "Ask around at the head office. Find out if Farrin is having me followed, and why."

"And I should assist you because…"

"Mr. Hillary and Miss Thorne could be in danger, and I quite like them both."

Fifteen

THE NEXT MORNING EVE FOUND SEBASTIAN WITH Helena and her sister in the sitting room. Gracie was holding two fingers to her head like horns and hopping up and down. Ever since Eve taught her to play charades, the young girl never seemed to tire of making everyone in the household guess what animal she was pretending to be.

Dimples pierced Helena's cheeks when she caught Eve's eye, but she didn't interrupt the game to offer a greeting. "Is it a goat?"

Gracie's arms flapped against her sides and she sighed in exasperation. "I am *hopping*, Helena. Do goats hop?"

"It is a dancing goat," Sebastian piped up, all grins.

Gracie rolled her eyes. "Since when do goats dance? I've never seen one."

"You are too young to attend balls. Otherwise, you would know they do." He winked at Eve. She warmed at his teasing tone, reminded of many such instances when he'd teased her as a girl.

Gracie swung her head toward Eve as if seeking confirmation. Eve simply smiled and shrugged.

"Very well, Bastian." The girl's hands landed on her hips. "Show me how a goat dances."

She had begun using Eve's pet name for her brother not long ago, and from the way his eyes lit up, he loved it.

"Only if you join me," Sebastian said.

Gracie giggled, warming up to his game. She held out her hands in invitation. "You will have to teach it to me." Helena's sister was an eager one, full of enthusiasm for learning any new skills. She had taken to horseback riding as if she'd been born in the sidesaddle, even though she'd never sat a horse until a couple of weeks ago.

Eve slipped into a chair close to Helena, smiling. "Yes, give us a demonstration, Bastian. This should be enlightening."

His eyes twinkled with mischief as he rose from his place beside Helena on the settee and unbuttoned his jacket. He led Gracie to the middle of the room where they could move without hitting anything.

Eve's smile widened, knowing what would likely come next after years of living with her older brother.

He bowed to Gracie. She curtsied. He held out his hand. She readily clasped his with a blinding smile. And then he was spinning and flinging her as she stumbled around, tripping over her feet. He caught her before she fell, never pausing in his made-up, chaotic dance. She squealed as he lifted and swung her in a circle. Gracie was laughing so hard she could barely catch a breath, and when he began kicking up his heels and bleating like a goat, she dissolved on the floor in a fit of giggles. Helena and Eve were laughing too. Sebastian never failed to put on a good show for the ladies.

Gracie looked up at him with eyes shining. "I think I should like to go to a ball."

"Someday," Helena promised, "but we'll hire a *real* dance instructor to teach you before your coming out, although I daresay he will not be nearly as entertaining as our dear Sebastian."

Eve's brother and sister-in-law exchanged an affectionate glance that made Eve's heart ache. Her jovial smile slid from her face. Sir Jonathan never looked at her in such a way, nor did she think of him as her dear Jonathan. Perhaps if she didn't know what it felt like to be in love, or she wasn't faced with daily reminders of what a great love looked like, she could be content with what she and Jonathan had. Unfortunately, she *had* been in love once, and she couldn't forget how wonderful it felt. She didn't know what to do about her dilemma.

Helena, ever sensitive to others' moods, interrupted the lesson before Sebastian and Gracie could begin again. "I think Eve would like a moment of your time, darling."

Eve blinked in surprise. She hadn't come seeking an audience with Sebastian, but at the mention of it, she realized it was time to ask him about Ben's claim he had returned for her two years ago.

Surprisingly, Gracie didn't protest. Instead, she tipped her head to the side to study Eve, then gave one sharp nod of agreement. Helena put an arm around the girl's shoulders and ushered her from the room.

Once Eve and Sebastian were alone, he lowered

to the settee again. "Is Helena correct? Is something troubling you?"

She shrugged. It wasn't like her to be shy or with-hold information from Sebastian. He'd been her play-mate when they were children and her champion for as long as she could remember. She had always trusted him. If he had kept her and Ben apart, she didn't know how their relationship might change.

Sebastian cleared his throat to gain her attention, then smiled patiently when she still couldn't find the right words. "Does this have anything to do with Sir Jonathan?"

"Not directly, no." Taking a cleansing breath, Eve shifted toward him. She needed to see his face when she questioned him. She'd always been able to read her brother. "I need to ask you something. I do not mean any insult, but it has been eating at me. Ben said he came back for me on our wedding day and you turned him away. Is he telling the truth?"

The muscles in Sebastian's jaw shifted. Her mouth grew dry and her heart sped up. She recognized the haunted look in his eyes. He had been gazing at her the same way since Ben left. Suddenly, his drive to improve her standing in Society took on new mean-ing. He had a guilty conscience.

Sebastian found a piece of lint on his trousers and trapped it between his thumb and finger. "I encoun-tered Mr. Hillary near our street. He said he was headed to Thorne Place to beg an audience with you. I don't know if he was being truthful."

"What did you say to him?"

"It was three hours after he left you at the church.

The gossips had begun spreading tales about you. I'm afraid there were a good many things I said that I shouldn't repeat in a lady's presence."

"Sebastian." Her voice held a note of warning. She wouldn't settle for evasive maneuvering. They were not playing a game of chess. "Did you challenge him like he said?"

"I did." Red flooded his face. "I'm afraid my temper got the better of me that day. I should have told you about the encounter sooner, but I didn't see how telling you would change anything. Hillary was already gone. In retrospect, I'm sorry I kept it from you."

A trembling heat had begun to build as he spoke, making her quake. "You are sorry for *keeping* it from me? What about making decisions on my behalf and chasing away the man I loved? Or deciding my future without any consideration for what I wanted? Are you sorry for any of those things?"

"Of course I am. I made a mistake, but I was only trying to protect you."

"I didn't need protection." She could abide most anything except being treated like a shrinking violet. After living with their father's mercurial moods and being avoided like a leper over the last two years, Eve possessed more inner strength than many ladies her age. And more than some of her elders too. "I am not a weak-minded twit in need of smelling salts every time there is a crisis."

He pushed from the settee with a frustrated growl. "I know, but I do not feel any less responsible for you. You are my little sister. It is my duty to defend you."

"I didn't need—"

He held up a hand, interrupting. She bit her lip to keep from hurling unladylike words at him. "Maybe I misjudged the situation, although I daresay many gentlemen in similar circumstances would have challenged him too. After I'd gathered my wits about me, however, I realized I couldn't kill the mongrel. You loved him."

Her brother's account of events gave her pause. It didn't fit with Ben's version. "If you called off the duel, Ben wouldn't have sailed to India."

Sebastian sighed. "I didn't call off the duel, Evie. It doesn't work that way. There were witnesses, and our seconds had been chosen. I had to make an appearance as a matter of honor."

"Men and their honor," she said with a huff. "I think you use it as an excuse to behave like fools."

"Perhaps you are right, but I didn't create the rules and expectations. I simply abide by them."

His admission didn't come as a surprise. Sebastian had been trying to prove he belonged in the noble class as long as she could recall, all because their father hadn't been born a blue blood. His exemplary service during the Irish Rebellions had earned him a barony from the King.

Sebastian strode to the window, his movements jerky. "I planned to delope and end the matter. Mr. Hillary and I could have reopened negotiations afterward and repaired the damage, but the coward never showed up."

She shot to her feet too, hands landing on her hips. "He is not a coward." She couldn't allow her brother to insult Ben or believe he had acted out of cowardice.

"He didn't meet you, because he loved me in return. I would have been devastated if I lost either of you, but only he seemed capable of recognizing it."

"So did I. I swear I wouldn't have harmed him, and I never intended to chase him away." Her brother turned toward her with such a long face that her anger began to dissipate. Sebastian had made a grave mistake—one that caused her much misery—but she would never believe he'd meant to hurt her.

Besides, she had little in the way of family and couldn't afford to remain at odds with loved ones. If—God forbid—she never saw her brother again, she wouldn't want their last words between them to be harsh. She sank back into the chair with a grimace. "I suppose arguing will accomplish nothing. We cannot undo the past."

"No, we can't, although I wish I could." He stayed by the window, propping himself on the sill and drumming his fingers against his thigh. "It does not seem like a coincidence you have chosen to broach this topic now. Are you having second thoughts about marrying Hackberry? It wouldn't be unusual with your wedding day fast approaching."

Her head jerked up. "Did you have doubts about marrying Helena?"

"Ah… No, I didn't." He scratched his neck and smiled ruefully. "But I understand it is common for many people and nothing to be concerned about."

Her eyes narrowed on him. "If it is common, why *didn't* you have doubts?" Eve was happy for her brother and Helena, and she had supported their union. She just didn't understand why she would be afflicted with reservations when her brother hadn't been, unless he was fabricating the entire story about her feelings being commonplace.

Sebastian casually crossed his arms. "When I thought Helena would return to Scotland instead of marrying me, I found the prospect unbearable. She belonged with me, and it was as clear as the nose on my face. Once I'd convinced her to marry me, I was more concerned with making it down the aisle before *she* had doubts."

Eve nodded to show she understood his apprehension. Earlier in the Season, another young lady had jilted her brother and married his good friend. It was no wonder he'd been worried about Helena going through with their wedding.

Perhaps that was the source of Eve's anxiety too. She didn't want to be jilted again either.

"Has Sir Jonathan done something to upset you, Evie?"

She shook her head. Truly, Jonathan hadn't done anything unforgivable. He behaved oddly and was more absentminded than usual, but he had done nothing to warrant calling off the wedding. If anyone were guilty of wrongdoing, it was she. Ben was on her mind too often. She saw his face as she drifted to sleep at night, and his name was on her lips when she woke. When she should be looking forward to her new life with her betrothed, she was looking back at the one she'd almost had with Ben.

She fidgeted, drawing a figure eight with her finger around the embroidered violets dotting her ivory skirts. "I understand what it is like to find life unbearable without the person you love. I imagine it is clear that I still have feelings for Ben."

Sebastian's nostrils flared, and his face changed to bright red. She steeled herself for the tempest about to strike, prepared to go toe to toe with him again if necessary. "You do realize you are to marry Sir Jonathan in a week. You cannot afford to be swept up by nostalgia."

"I'm not." Her brother seemed to be suggesting her memories were all rosy, and that was far from accurate. She would never forget two years of snide comments aimed in her direction, the self-righteous noses lifted high when she passed ladies on Bond Street, or worse, the ones who looked through her as if she didn't exist. But neither could she forget the eagerness with which she had greeted each day before Ben left. How the sky was a richer shade of blue and the birdsongs had filled her with optimism and joy.

Sebastian was watching her with raised eyebrows, his expression challenging.

"I know my own mind, and I'm not being swept up by nostalgia."

"Good." Braced in the window, he seemed as immovable as a mountain. "Your head can't be full of wool when you have an important decision to make."

The small catch in her breath caused him to frown.

"Sir Jonathan might not be the husband I would have chosen for you, but he is a decent gent. Make your decision soon. I wouldn't like to see him go through what you and I endured."

Her pulse fluttered at the thought of hurting Jonathan the way she'd been hurt. She didn't think she could put another person through what she had gone through. She swallowed, her throat scratchy. "If I breach the contract…"

The lines around Sebastian's eyes softened, and his dark eyes shone with warmth as he came toward her. "I will not have you marry someone you don't want to wed for fear of the consequences. Joining your life with the wrong person is too large a price to pay."

Unfortunately, she *didn't* know if Jonathan was wrong for her; he just didn't feel quite right. Placing her brother at risk for being sued and providing more fodder for the gossips seemed a very steep price to pay when she couldn't be certain she wasn't just suffering from nerves.

Sebastian nudged her chin so she had to look at him. "I *will* stand by your decision. I want you to be as happy as I am with Helena. But if you haven't asked Mr. Hillary why he left you at the church, perhaps it would be wise to have that conversation before you consider severing ties with Sir Jonathan."

༄

Her brother's insinuation became a bee in her bonnet the remainder of the day. He obviously thought Ben had some dark secret that, once she learned the details, would send her dashing into Jonathan's embrace. The irritating notion that her brother might be right buzzed in her ears—that Ben had a secret, not that she would throw herself into Jonathan's arms. It wouldn't be fair to treat Jonathan as a spare in the event things couldn't be set to rights with Ben. A husband should be first in a wife's heart, and she was ashamed to admit Jonathan wasn't. She loved Ben, dark secrets and all, which was the reason she needed a moment alone with her betrothed that evening.

She didn't look forward to the task of crying off, but her decision had been made the moment she knew Ben was back. Unfortunately, it had taken her mind a bit longer to catch up with her heart, and for that, she was very sorry. She never would have accepted Jonathan's proposal if she had known their association would end in a broken betrothal.

"Lady Hackberry," she murmured to her reflection in the looking glass as Alice tied off the last of the tiny braids around her face. "Eve Hackberry."

Her maid swept the braids back on one side, pinned them, and coiled them to create a crown around her head. "It has a ring to it," Alice mumbled around the pins sticking from her mouth.

It sounded ill fitting and strange to Eve, but she kept her thoughts to herself.

Alice secured the last pin, then stood back to inspect her work. "Lovely," she said, as always. Eve never knew if her maid meant it as a compliment to Eve or herself, but she thanked her anyway.

With her toilette complete, Eve made her way to the drawing room to await their guests with Helena and Sebastian. The newlyweds were sitting together on the settee when she entered unnoticed. Sebastian brushed a stray strand of Helena's hair behind her ear and murmured something Eve couldn't hear. Helena's ivory skin glowed, and her pleased smile lit the room. Eve loved them both dearly, but in that moment, she was overcome with envy.

She longed for evenings snuggled together with her

husband on the settee while he whispered loving words in her ear. And she longed for that man to be Ben.

Milo cleared his throat behind her, startling her. Sebastian and Helena turned in time to catch her spying on them but pretended they hadn't noticed.

"Have our guests arrived?" Sebastian asked as he stood and offered a hand up to his wife.

"Yes, milord. Lady Eldridge and Sir Jonathan arrived at the same time."

Oh dear. She wouldn't have a moment alone with Jonathan before they dined as she'd hoped.

"Very good," Sebastian said. "We will come offer our greetings, then retire to the dining room. Have you notified Mother?"

"I sent a footman, my lord."

Eve allowed her brother and sister-in-law to lead the way, perhaps dragging her feet a little. She didn't want to sit through a meal pretending all was well when she knew her relationship with her betrothed wouldn't last much beyond dessert.

Jonathan greeted her with a kiss on her glove and complimented her gown before offering his arm. Mama met them in the dining room and exchanged a warm greeting with the countess and welcomed Jonathan.

Once everyone was seated and the first course was served, Lady Eldridge brought up the topic Eve had been dreading. "Helena tells me you've chosen a lovely gown and flowers for the church. We really must settle on a menu for the breakfast. Perhaps you, your mother, and Helena should come for tea tomorrow."

Eve looked helplessly toward Helena. Even if she were to marry Jonathan, she didn't want the attention a lavish wedding breakfast would bring. She wished to marry quietly and settle into married life without much ado.

Her sister-in-law set her spoon aside and delicately touched her napkin to the corners of her mouth. "Olive, you know we wish for a cozy family affair. A breakfast is not necessary."

The countess sniffed. "Even *family* must eat, Helena. Isn't that correct, Lady Thorne?"

Eve's mother smiled politely but didn't offer an opinion. The strategy discussed earlier in the week allowed for Helena to handle the countess, although Eve wasn't certain Lady Eldridge could be handled.

"Besides," the countess said, "the Dowager Duchess of Foxhaven plans to attend. What kind of impression would it leave if I were to host a wedding breakfast without serving breakfast?"

Helena wasn't prepared to surrender, much to Eve's admiration. "I believe we have a slight mis-understanding. Although Eve and Sir Jonathan are grateful for your kind offer, they don't wish to have a wedding breakfast."

Jonathan nodded his agreement.

"Oh, pish posh." Lady Eldridge leaned toward Eve, addressing her. "Dearest, the wedding breakfast is not for the bride. It is for her guests. There is no help for it. All you must do is smile prettily and accept everyone's best wishes. Do you like pastries?"

"Uh…" Eve glanced toward Helena for guidance, but her sister-in-law seemed as lost as Eve when it came to taking control of the conversation. "Pastries are nice, my lady, but—"

"Of course the gentlemen will want something heartier, so I was thinking an egg dish and ham." Lady Eldridge retrieved her spoon to finish her soup and pointed it toward Jonathan, who had been uncommonly silent during dinner, although talk of wedding breakfasts likely didn't interest him. "Do you like ham and eggs, Sir Jonathan?"

"I do, however—"

"Excellent!" The countess took a dainty sip of soup, but before Eve could gather her thoughts, Lady Eldridge barreled on. "I'm certain Lord and Lady Norwick will expect an invitation. And I suppose that means Lord Norwick's sister should be included as well. Lord and Lady Ellis are on the list, and if we invite Lady Ellis, we shouldn't exclude her siblings. You wouldn't want to offend the Duke of Foxhaven or his new bride."

"True," Eve murmured. She didn't wish to offend anyone, but there seemed no way to avoid it. As the guest list grew, her palms began to grow damp. There wouldn't be much time to cry off before Lady Eldridge had the invitations in the post. In fact, Eve wouldn't be surprised if the countess already had them written.

Eve caught Jonathan's eye across the table, but he didn't offer a smile as usual. Instead, he watched her with a gaze so intense, she worried he might be able to decipher her thoughts. She blinked and looked away.

By the end of the evening, Helena still hadn't convinced the countess a breakfast wasn't needed, despite her valiant efforts. "I will come by Eldridge

House tomorrow," Helena said as they walked their guests to the front door. "We can discuss the matter further then."

"Splendid." The countess flashed a brilliant smile, apparently believing she had won the argument.

The cousins exchanged hugs, and Sebastian escorted the countess to her carriage. Once Lady Eldridge was seen to, Sebastian, Helena, and Mama allowed Eve and Jonathan a moment alone to say good-bye.

Jonathan checked his watch. "It is late. I should be going. Thank you for a lovely evening, Miss Thorne." His grim expression said the evening had been anything but lovely. However, she couldn't very well call him out for being polite.

"We are pleased you came."

"As am I. Farewell for now." He took her hands in his and placed a dutiful kiss on her cheek. She would have asked him to stay except he was practically dashing for the door.

Milo opened the front door, and as Jonathan reached the threshold, Eve called out, "Sir Jonathan?"

He turned with an expectant smile, making her feel like the worst person on earth. She truly didn't want to hurt him.

"Would you have time to call on me tomorrow? There are things we should discuss." When he simply stared, heat rushed into her face. "A-about the wedding."

A small twitch of his eyebrow was the only sign he had heard her. "As you wish, Miss Thorne."

Sixteen

As soon as the door to Thorne Place closed behind Jonathan, he cursed under his breath. Miss Thorne wasn't going to cry off. There was but a week left before their nuptials, and she was planning a wedding breakfast—not entertaining ways to be rid of him.

The small surge of satisfaction at knowing she still wanted him ebbed as quickly as it came. She was better off without him. The kindest thing he could do for her would be to send her running into Ben Hillary's arms, but Jonathan had promised to allow her to make the choice.

He circled his palm over the dull ache in his chest. Even though letting Miss Thorne go would be in her best interest, it hurt to realize he was destined to be alone. There would be no one to mourn him when he was no more.

Forgoing a hack, Jonathan set off on foot for his town house. The gas lamps along Mayfair's streets illuminated the fog, creating a ghostly quality. He had nothing to fear from footpads or the like. The

Regent's Consul had seen to that. Jonathan was a man to be feared, but few people ever realized it when he played the role of a crackpot anthropology enthusiast.

Perhaps that was what had drawn him to Eve. She didn't dismiss him as simply a bumbling fool beneath her notice. She accepted him as he was with an open, loving heart. Eve *saw* him.

She doesn't see the real you.

"Sod off," he mumbled.

"You'll not get rid of me that easily," a voice replied from his right. An intruder entered the dim circle of light from a streetlamp.

In one fluid movement, Jonathan unsheathed the blade hidden in his walking stick and pressed the sharp tip beneath the man's chin before Jonathan recognized him. "Margrave."

A trickle of blood oozed down the viscount's neck, but he didn't so much as flinch.

Jonathan stepped back, dropping his blade. "What the hell are you doing sneaking up on me? I could have slit your throat."

Margrave's brow lifted. A flash of light caught on the knife in his hand as he sheathed it. "You were distracted. I shouldn't have gotten this close without you noticing. Mooning over a lady will only get you killed."

Jonathan didn't bother responding. His colleague was right. He couldn't walk around with his head in the clouds unless he was courting an early death. Perhaps he should take a cue from Margrave and abandon any hope of a normal existence.

Margrave fell into step with Jonathan as he continued toward his home. The streets of Mayfair were deserted at this time of night with partygoers attending balls that would last until the early morning hours.

"Farrin had you followed. Just as you suspected. A German seaman looking for coin. It was no wonder he was easy to spot."

Margrave's revelation came as no surprise. Jonathan knew Farrin had been trying to send a message.

"According to my source, Farrin has grown impatient," Margrave said. "You have a ship at your disposal, but you're still dallying with the chit."

Jonathan glared at him and Margrave held up his hands in submission. It was a trick. Farrin's men didn't submit to anyone.

"I am only repeating what I heard."

"God's blood. I am courting a *lady*, not dallying with a chit. Furthermore, what concern is it of his? I will leave London when I am damned ready."

Margrave regarded him with what appeared to be a measure of respect. "No one defies Farrin's orders."

"Well, it is about time someone stood his ground with the blighter."

"Hackberry." The viscount grabbed his arm, drawing him to a stop. "No one challenges the commander, because he tolerates no rebellion. Think carefully about what you are doing."

Farrin had a reputation for swift and merciless retribution, but what more could he do to Jonathan? He already had no family, no friends, and his chance for a happy life with Miss Thorne was being snatched away. "I don't fear Farrin."

"Then fear for your betrothed," Margrave said through gritted teeth. "You cannot guard her every moment. Our brothers are loyal to him, and she is vulnerable."

Jonathan rocked back on his heels, not believing what he'd heard. "He threatened her life?"

"If you do not take care of the problem delaying you, Farrin will. I know nothing about your assignment, but I would advise you to make haste."

Jonathan narrowed his eyes on his fellow spy. Did Margrave's loyalties lie with the organization? He gripped the handle of his walking stick. "And what are *your* orders?"

"Farrin can go to hell," Margrave spat. "A young lady is not an enemy of the Crown."

Jonathan's head spun, and he leaned on the cane for support. If Margrave had been ordered to eliminate Miss Thorne, how long did Jonathan have before another spy was sent for her? A string of curses flew from him, rising on the night air. "I will kill the bloody blackguard."

"You could, but another fat rat would happily scurry into his position. Fulfill your duties. Miss Thorne will be in no danger once you are gone. Nevertheless, if it brings you peace of mind, I will help Ben keep watch over her."

Jonathan growled low in his throat. He hated that he couldn't be the one to protect his betrothed—that he was the reason she was endangered.

"If you care about her," Margrave said, "take Ben's money and ship and leave."

"It is not that simple." And yet what choice did he have? There wasn't time to convince Miss Thorne to cry off. Tomorrow he must tell her their relationship was over.

✎

Eve hadn't slept a wink all night. Instead, she had rehearsed in her mind what she would say to Jonathan when he called on her today. She had altered the wording slightly each time until she thought she had prepared a sensitive and respectful parting speech. The problem lay with her, not him, but she fervently hoped they could remain on friendly terms. She found him amiable and enjoyed his company.

To show her sincerity, she had asked Cook to make Jonathan's favorite finger sandwiches—tarragon chicken salad with dried cherries—and those lovely little vanilla tea cakes he ate as if he might not see his next meal. Bohea tea filled her mother's precious Worcester teapot, and the best porcelain plates had been brought from the pantry. Eve had been as prepared as any lady could be to gently tell her betrothed she just couldn't marry him.

She never got the chance.

"What do you mean, *you* cannot marry *me*?" Shrillness broke through her words, shattering the illusion she could remain reasonable and calm under these circumstances. *This cannot be happening.*

She dug her fingers into the padded armrests to fight against dumping the sandwiches and cakes in his lap and crowning him with her mother's best silver tray. "Do you have any idea what this will do to me?" It was a miracle her reputation had been salvaged after Ben jilted her. She would never recover from a similar incident.

Jonathan sipped his tea, cool and collected, which only made her more crazed. "I think we both realize this is for the best. It is clear you still hold a *tendre* for Mr. Hillary. I am simply clearing the way for you to reunite."

She bolted from the settee and marched several paces away to place distance between them. "You cannot cry off and go around saying I hold a *tendre* for Mr. Hillary. I will be ruined. People will think we have engaged in an impropriety."

His smile was serene as he set his cup aside. The exquisite china piece clicked against the saucer. "Darling." If his placating tone was meant to calm her, it had the opposite effect.

She jutted her chin, her temper rising. "I am *not* your darling."

"You never were," he shot back, a ruddy shadow covering his suddenly hardened face.

Wonder of wonders. It seemed he was human after all. This was the first show of emotion he'd exhibited since their betrothal ball.

The ball. Her heart dropped to her stomach. Had he seen her dancing with Ben that night? Her indignation gave way to horror that he might believe she had been untrue to him.

"You cannot think I was unfaithful." Her voice cracked on the last word and tears welled in her eyes.

He sighed and pushed from the chair as if almost too weary to stand. "I could never believe anything unbecoming about you, Miss Thorne. You are a kind and decent young woman." He came to stand in front of her and raised his hand as if he might touch her before letting it drop to his side. "I will not repeat a word to anyone about what has occurred between us today. We will tell everyone it was your decision to end our betrothal. You may say I am too absorbed with my work and bad tempered when my attention is needed elsewhere. I believe this is the best solution to our dilemma. We are clearly not meant to be."

He saw their relationship as a dilemma? She couldn't say why, but it made her feel like crying. She didn't strive to be anyone's problem. She longed to be a helpmate, to stand beside her man in times of trouble.

With a sigh, she realized he was right. They did have a dilemma that could only be solved by parting ways. Jonathan was honorable and kind. He was the type of gentleman to allow himself to be maligned to protect her pride. But he *wasn't* her man. That didn't make him deserving of attacks on his character, however.

She frowned. "I will not spread tales about you."

"Then we will say nothing except it was your choice to cry off. The *ton* can make whatever assumptions about me they like."

While she appreciated his sacrifice, she could make no sense of it. "Why are you willing to fall on your sword for me?"

"I only want to see you safe and happy." His smile tugged at her heart. He appeared so sad and lonely in that moment. "Will you do that for me, Miss Thorne? Marry, have a family, and be happy?"

It sounded as if he was saying good-bye forever. "Only if…if you promise you will do the same."

"I would like that very much." He leaned to kiss her cheek one last time. "Take care of yourself, Eve."

She stood rooted to the middle of the drawing room floor as Jonathan walked away.

Seventeen

BEN WAS PREPARING TO VISIT THE DOCKS WHEN A SOFT knock sounded at his study door. He closed the logbook he'd just finished reviewing and placed it on a small stack of ships' logs he had already audited. His man of business would see them returned to the proper captains.

"Enter," he called as he stood to don his jacket.

His butler walked into the study bearing a small dish with a calling card.

Ben held up his hand to halt his progress. "I haven't time for callers. The *Sidony* docked this morning, and I am leaving to meet with her captain."

Dobbins didn't allow Ben's protest to alter his course. He came to stand at the edge of Ben's desk and held out the dish anyway. "Sir Jonathan Hackberry claims it is a matter of dire importance, sir."

Ben's heart lodged in his throat as possible calamities involving Eve raced through his mind. He rounded his desk and stalked for the door.

"Sir?" Dobbins's bemused voice barely penetrated his awareness.

He jerked open the door. Hackberry stood in the

foyer. The man's mouth was set in a straight line and his knuckles were white where he clutched his hat to his chest.

"Is Eve all right?" Ben was already moving toward the door.

"She will be fine."

That wasn't the reassurance Ben needed. He stormed past Hackberry on his way to the front door. "Where is she?"

"At Thorne Place where I left her. Probably telling her brother what a loathsome cur I am."

Ben skidded to a stop. His relief was so sudden, his body didn't know what to do with the adrenaline coursing through him, so fear transformed to anger. He turned on Hackberry, jabbing a finger in his direction. "In my study. *Now.*"

Hackberry sighed as Ben crossed the foyer again. Dobbins met him at the threshold of his study and scurried out of the way.

Ben was rarely in a temper, but when his anger made an appearance, it often left his servants hopping to please him. "Thank you, Dobbins. That will be all." He attempted to soften his tone to let his servant know he had done nothing wrong, although the words came out clipped.

Hackberry followed Ben into the study and closed the door with a firm click. "You will probably want to bloody my nose after I tell you what happened." He nonchalantly plopped into the chair in front of Ben's desk.

Ben crossed his arms. "Maybe I should plant a facer now and be done with it. Should save us both time."

"But I may be unable to speak intelligibly afterward, and you *did* ask me to tell you what happened."

He made a valid argument for patience. "Go on."

Hackberry's eyes narrowed in annoyance. "If you would cease yapping—"

"If you would quit stalling, I wouldn't be tempted—"

"Miss Thorne and I are no longer betrothed." Hackberry spoke over him, drowning out the last of his sentence.

Ben sputtered to a stop; his jaw hung slack.

Hackberry's smile lacked humor. "You heard me correctly. You may court the lady at your leisure."

Out of all the possible scenarios racing through Ben's mind, Eve calling off the wedding so soon hadn't been one of them. Hackberry had claimed he was making little progress toward that end. Ben laughed, his mood suddenly buoyant. "This calls for a drink."

Hackberry's grimace was understandable. Even though he had agreed to step aside, a man had his pride and being jilted was surely a blow to one's confidence. Ben would pour his friend three fingers to help ease his pain. Ben, however, was ecstatic and moved to the sideboard with a swagger to his step.

He returned with a single glass for Hackberry and lowered to the seat next to his. "Was it something you did last night at dinner? Did she cry off immediately, or did she deliver the news this morning?"

Hackberry's frown deepened. "Yes, well... I am afraid there was a change in plans. We agreed to tell everyone Miss Thorne chose to cry off, but in reality, I—"

"You broke your betrothal?" Ben was going to punch him after all. He lunged from his seat, but Hackberry was quicker.

Springing to his feet, Hackberry dodged under Ben's arm and slammed his walking stick against the backs of Ben's knees. Ben's legs buckled and he landed on the carpet with a thunderous thud.

Where the hell had Hackberry learned to move like that?

"My apologies, Hillary. It was an unfair blow, but I don't wish to fight you." Hackberry extended his hand. Ben eyed the man warily, calculating the odds of jerking him off balance to gain an advantage. "I need you to listen carefully, Ben. I haven't much time. We both want the same thing for Miss Thorne. She will be happy with you, and you can protect her."

"Protect her from what?" Against his better judgment, he accepted Hackberry's offer for a hand up.

"It isn't a what. It is a who. All I am at liberty to say is she is in danger as long as I remain in England. I need a ship tonight, the one you promised, and I need you to watch over Miss Thorne. Keep her safe."

Ben shook his head. Hackberry truly was a crackpot. "Who would want to hurt Eve, and why? She hasn't an enemy in the world."

"No one *wants* to hurt her, but there are men who will do it all the same. This is about controlling me, and Eve is only a pawn."

"A pawn?" Ben's heart skipped. Eve claimed someone had followed them to the museum. And then there was the incident between Hackberry and the soldiers. She'd witnessed another side to Hackberry, the one that had just thwarted Ben's attack with ease. Hackberry wasn't a clumsy, socially awkward anthropologist. He was a master of disguise. Perhaps an enemy to the Crown.

Ben's muscles tensed, and he eased closer to his desk. "You are not what you seem." He kept a firearm in the top drawer, but he would have to dive across the surface if there was any hope of reaching it.

Hackberry clamped a hand on Ben's shoulder, interrupting his plan. He leaned toward Ben, meeting his gaze. "I am your friend, and I care for Miss Thorne. That is the only truth that matters, the only real thing about me. Please, believe me."

Ben held Hackberry's gaze for several moments. The man's eyes were bloody earnest for a fraud and a liar.

Hackberry's eyebrows lifted in question as he awaited Ben's judgment.

"Bugger!" Ben might be a fool, but he believed him. Still, he couldn't lower his guard until he knew where Hackberry's loyalties lay. "Are you friend or foe to the Crown?"

A small twitch of Hackberry's mouth showed his amusement. "I couldn't very well keep Miss Thorne safe if I were set on destroying our motherland, now could I?"

"No, I suppose you couldn't." Ben pulled free from Hackberry's grasp. His mind was already preoccupied with where he could take Eve to ensure her safety. "I need to know who wishes her harm."

"It is best for you to remain in the dark. Miss Thorne will be in no danger once I leave England."

That wasn't good enough. He advanced on Hackberry until they were toe to toe. Now that he knew what the other man was capable of, he wouldn't catch Ben off guard. "I am not willing to gamble with her life."

"I know these men." Hackberry's eyes hardened. "They will lose interest in Miss Thorne once I am back in line, which I intend to be very quickly. I also have the promise of a trustworthy colleague that he will watch over you both until any danger has passed. If you can assist me, I will leave tonight. My belongings are packed, and I could have them delivered to the docks within the hour."

Ben nodded sharply. He wasn't inclined to leave Eve's safety in the hands of an unknown entity whether Hackberry trusted the man or not, but he agreed with putting distance between Eve and her former betrothed. "I have three ships ready to sail. Once the crew has delivered the cargo, the captain and ship will be at your disposal."

"Thank you." Hackberry clasped Ben's hand and pumped it twice. "I promise, once I am gone, you and Miss Thorne need not worry about anything. Just forget we had this conversation. Forget that I even exist, and everything will be all right."

Ben had his doubts that everything would be all right. Even if the threat to Eve went away, they would still have to deal with the fallout from Hackberry calling off the wedding. If no one else learned the truth about who cried off, Eve still knew, and Ben couldn't stomach the thought of her shedding another tear over him or Hackberry. Men were bastards.

✒

In an attempt to pretend nothing out of the ordinary had occurred that day, Eve retreated to the gardens with a book. Her brother and sister-in-law had taken the news of her broken betrothal better than she had anticipated. Of course, they believed the story she and Jonathan had agreed to give everyone. Sebastian and Helena thought the decision had been hers.

And it *had* been. Jonathan simply stole the moment from her. She gripped the spine of the book as heat washed over her. Being indignant didn't change anything, but she couldn't help revisiting those moments in the drawing room and feeling the rush of anger all over again.

At least there would be no legal consequences for the dissolution of their contract, but if anyone learned the truth, she would be ruined. Her reputation would suffer enough because she had cried off—or would have if she had been allowed to broach the subject first—but everything would be a thousand times worse if anyone found out Jonathan had tossed her aside. She prayed he would keep his word and tell no one.

A nagging sense that she was being watched made her glance up at the house. Sebastian was at his bed-chamber window, but he moved away when she met his gaze. Her brother was worried, even though he'd tried to hide it earlier. A heaviness weighed on her chest. Opening her family up to gossip and speculation again could have unpleasant consequences for them all. Sebastian and Helena had taken great pains to protect Helena's secret past, and any attention on the Thornes would naturally make Sebastian apprehensive.

Milo appeared at the French doors that opened onto the gardens. The butler maintained his stiff posture as he walked the pebbled path toward her, and not for the first time, she wondered if the servant ever took a moment to relax.

"Miss, you have a caller," he said when he reached her. He held out the small dish and calling card, but she didn't take the card. The identity of her caller was irrelevant.

"Could you please tell whomever that I am not receiving?"

"Might I beg you to reconsider?" a voice carried on the air.

Milo's face screwed up before he recovered his composure and turned toward the intruder, allowing her a clear view of the footpath. Ben was strolling toward them holding a white box tied with silver ribbon. Her pulse sputtered at the sight of him.

Milo drew himself up to his full height. "Mr. Hillary, I asked you to wait—"

"It is all right, Milo. Thank you, you may go." She rose to greet Ben, hugging her book against her chest like a shield. What was he doing here? Surely, word hadn't begun to travel social circles already.

"Shall I send a footman to stand attendance, miss?"

Eve opened her mouth to accept, but Ben answered for her. "That will not be necessary. I would like a moment to speak alone with the lady. It is a private matter."

He flashed a smile at the butler and received a sour frown in return. Milo looked to Eve for direction.

She would have to trust Ben in this instance. If he didn't think they needed an audience for what he had come to say, she was certain she didn't want anyone overhearing them. "There is no need to trouble a footman. Mr. Hillary won't be staying long."

Milo's forehead creased with doubt, but he left them alone in the garden.

Ben took her by the elbow, guided her back to the wooden bench, and then sat beside her. With a too cheerful smile, he offered her the white box on his palms as if serving her a tray. "I brought you lemon drops. Are they still your favorite?"

She placed her folded hands on the book in her lap as her stomach churned with uncertainty. It was improper for him to come bearing gifts to another man's betrothed, which likely meant he knew she had been jilted again. "W-What are you doing here?"

His smile fell and he lowered the box to the bench beside him with a pitying shake of his head. "Sir Jonathan came to see me. How are you, Evie?"

"Dear God. He told you what really happened." Her shoulders slumped from the weight of his revelation. "He promised to keep it a secret."

"He will not tell anyone else, and I will not tell a soul. You have no reason to be embarrassed or worried." Ben slid his arm around her shoulders, and she stiffened. She didn't want his sympathy or to pretend they shared the same intimacy they'd had before.

Hot tears of mortification built at the back of her throat, and she eased from his embrace. "Perhaps I did not want *you* to know." Old hurts rose to the surface, as raw as the day Ben left her. "I suppose you are pleased to have your opinion supported."

"What opinion?" He drew back with a puzzled frown. "I don't take your meaning."

She swallowed hard to keep her tears at bay. She refused to cry in front of him. Steeling herself, she boldly met his gaze. "You found something lacking in me two years ago, and now Sir Jonathan has as well. Congratulations. You have been vindicated."

"Balderdash!" His vehement denial made her flinch. "My leaving was a result of my own failings. Not yours. And you are not to blame for what Hackberry has done." He took her book, tossed it on the bench, then captured her hand before she could scoot away. "Do you truly think I came to gloat? I lost the best part of my life when I lost you. Not a day has passed that I haven't regretted my actions."

She rolled her eyes. For two years, he had never even written. She was no fool. His life had gone on as right as rain without her.

"It is true." He gently clasped her chin to make her look at him. His intense blue eyes held her entranced and caused a quiver deep in her belly. "I've been miserable without you, Evie. I would do anything to have you back again. I want what we had."

Her resolve to harden her heart toward him wavered. She wet her lips, distrustful of the small flicker of hope trying to ignite inside her. She would have to be mad to place her faith in him again.

"If what we had was so special, why did you leave the church?"

❧

Eve's voice was deadly calm and sent a frisson of panic to Ben's heart. He dropped his hand to his side.

"I—my nerves got the best of me," he said. This

was the closest he could come to the truth without humiliating himself, but he regretted his answer at once. The stricken look in her eyes ripped him apart.

"You doubted *us*? I always believed when one met his match, he knew it was right. I never once doubted you had been meant for me."

"I didn't doubt you, Evie. Or us."

"You did. You just admitted as much."

"No, it wasn't like that."

She wrapped her arms around herself and hugged tightly. Her gaze fixed on something across the garden. She wouldn't even look at him.

Damnation! Ben bent forward, propping his elbows on his thighs and cradling his head in his hands. He had known getting rid of Hackberry wouldn't win him a place in Eve's heart, but what if she never let him in again? The emptiness inside him grew more vast and bleak as silence stretched between them. His chest ached. He should probably go, but he didn't know how to say good-bye.

Eventually, he sat up, defeated. "I'm sorry, Evie. I never meant to hurt you."

She reached for his hand, cradling it between her palms. Her deep brown eyes shimmered in the afternoon sunlight. "Tell me what it *was* like. I want to understand. You can be honest with me. *Please*."

He closed his eyes and drew in a shaky breath. Experience told him she was sincere. She would listen without judgment, but he didn't know how to put what had happened on their wedding day into words.

He'd been unprepared for the onslaught of fear

that hit him. It had started with a small confession to his brother as they stood in the church vestibule, waiting for Eve's arrival. *I never thought I would be this happy again.*

The admission had unlocked his memories of Charlotte—memories of the day she died that he never allowed himself to remember. Suddenly, he'd become terrified of losing everything again. He feared his happiness would be snatched from him. If not now—or the next day or week or month—then someday Eve would die too. Or he would go first. The thought of their separation had made his heart squeeze painfully over and over until he couldn't breathe properly.

His pulse sped even now, and a tremor raced through him.

"Ben?" Eve pressed his hand between hers, her touch becoming an anchor to keep him from drifting too far into the past. "Tell me what happened on our wedding day."

He opened his eyes and exhaled. "I barely understand it myself. My chest felt like it was being crushed, and I couldn't catch my breath."

"Why didn't you tell anyone? We could have summoned the doctor."

He shook his head. "I don't know. I couldn't think properly. All I could think about was escaping."

She gasped softly.

"Not from you," he rushed to explain, "but from the horrible sense that I was dying. I'd finally found happiness and I was not going to be allowed to keep it."

"Ben." Tears filled her eyes and she brought his

hand to her lips. The warmth of her kiss seeped through his glove. "You could have told me. All this time…"

They had lost precious time because of him.

Eve reached out to caress his cheek, her fingers trailing along his jawline. "All this time I knew something had gone wrong. I believed you were coming back for so long. I regret giving up too soon. I'm so sorry."

She needn't say more. It was too late, just as he'd feared. Still, he couldn't leave without taking a chance and telling her what was in his heart. "I love you, Eve. I desire you for my wife. I long for a family with you, a home. I want to keep you safe and happy until we are gray and our backs are bent from old age. I want my last breath to be a promise to love you for all eternity, because I will. I will love you forever."

She covered her heart with both hands as tears fell on her cheeks. "I want a life with you too. That is all I have ever wanted."

Ben brushed his thumb over her cheek to wipe away her tears. "Still?"

She nodded, the tears coming more quickly.

His throat grew thick with emotion. He slid from the bench to kneel at her feet and held both of her hands. She smiled encouragingly. "Miss Thorne, would you do me the honor of becoming my wife?"

She pulled free of his hold to capture his face between her palms and leaned down so they were eye to eye. "Yes," she whispered.

Cupping her nape, he drew her toward him for a kiss. Warm, moist lips met his, and her breath hitched. Ben slid onto the bench beside her, his arms circling her waist. She melted against him as he gently explored her mouth with his tongue. When she sighed and opened for him, he groaned and dragged her closer.

A small thud brought them back to the garden. Their lips broke apart, but Ben didn't release her, and she didn't release him either.

He grinned. "I think we knocked over your box of sweets. You did not answer earlier. Do you still like lemon drops?"

"I rarely come to dislike something I've learned to love."

"Lucky for me."

Her smile lit him from within. "Lucky for me too."

He placed a featherlight kiss on her lips before retrieving the box from the grass.

As she accepted his gift, her gaze flicked toward the town house and a small line appeared between her brows.

"What is it?" Ben looked up to discover Sebastian Thorne at an upper window, glowering at them. Ben suppressed a sigh.

Eve's brother would not make things easy for him when they negotiated the marriage contract this time. He would want to ensure Ben received his lumps for breaking the first one, but Ben would endure as many awkward encounters as were required of him. As long as he had Eve by his side in the end, it was worth it.

"I believe your brother is requesting an audience. Shall we?" Standing, he offered his arm to lead her inside.

Eighteen

EVE THOUGHT HER BROTHER WAS SURPRISINGLY CALM considering he had just caught her and Ben in a compromising position. Sebastian's face was red and he spoke with a clenched jaw, but there wasn't murder burning in his dark gaze. She took that as a positive sign.

She and Ben sat side by side on the settee in the drawing room while Sebastian stood behind Helena's chair, gripping the back as if he wished to rip the cushion to pieces.

Helena had just returned from a visit to Lady Eldridge to inform her that Eve and Jonathan would not be marrying. Her round eyes were larger than usual. "My, I can barely stay abreast of the happenings around here today."

Mama sat in a chair closest to Eve. She rested her chin in her propped-up hand as if holding up her head required too much energy. A twinge of guilt vibrated through Eve. She hated that her mother had to bear up to one more scandal.

"You will marry by special license," Sebastian bit out. "We will not have a repeat of the last debacle."

Ben reached for Eve's hand and squeezed reassuringly. "As I mentioned a few moments ago, before I arrived I completed the application at the Doctors' Commons to expedite the process."

"Rather presumptuous of you," Sebastian said with an imperious lift to his brow.

"I was merely hopeful your sister would accept me. I thought it best to marry quickly rather than draw more attention to our unusual circumstances by having the banns cried."

"Based on observations, I have no doubt you are in a hurry." Sebastian's glower seemed to be a warning to keep his hands to himself until the vows were spoken. "Have you given any thought to how you will weather this latest scandal?"

"Now, Sebastian," Mama said, "you don't know how the *ton* will react. A love match is a rare enough occurrence to warrant some leeway. I imagine they will easily forgive our Evie for following her heart."

Eve smiled at her mother, knowing Mama would defend her or Sebastian no matter what wrong they had committed.

Sebastian nodded. "Perhaps, Mother. We will know soon enough, and if a retreat to the country is necessary, we can proceed with our plans to retire to Scotland as soon as Parliament adjourns. Eve and Mr. Hillary will join us."

Ben's hand tightened around hers and he met her gaze, his blue eyes earnest. "Eve and I will decide together how best to weather any scandal."

Not Sebastian deciding her fate. Not Ben alone, but she and Ben *together*. Whatever traces of wariness she'd held on to because of his past betrayal evaporated. "Perhaps an extended honeymoon on the Continent would be just the thing until the gossips become bored," she said.

Ben grinned. "I did promise to take you any place you like."

She hadn't thought a honeymoon trip would be possible as of yesterday, but now her life seemed filled with exciting possibilities. She couldn't help beaming at her husband-to-be.

The hardness in Sebastian's eyes faded, and the corners of his mouth turned up slightly. "I trust you will take good care of her on this trip, Hillary."

"We will take good care of each other," Eve piped up.

Ben nodded slightly, his smile widening. "And I will protect her with my life. She will want for nothing. You have my word."

"I will hold you to your promise." Sebastian circled the chair and came to stand in front of Eve. "Is this truly what you want? You needn't accept Hillary's offer out of concern that this may be your last chance to marry."

Ben's sudden fierce scowl made her laugh.

"Yes, Bastian. This is what I want. And subtlety is not your best quality."

"I never claimed it was." He winked at Eve. "Very well. Follow me, Mr. Hillary. We have a contract to discuss."

❧

The second time Ben and Eve's brother negotiated a contract, Ben agreed to every contingency Thorne added to the agreement. One might think the baron would soften toward him. He didn't.

"If you hurt her again," Thorne hissed through clenched teeth, "I will kill you."

Ben smiled politely. He didn't blame Eve's brother for not trusting him, nor would he begrudge the man the right to commit murder if Ben caused Eve more pain. "I will go say my good-byes to Miss Thorne until tomorrow."

A message from Ben's man of business had arrived half an hour earlier while he and Thorne were sequestered in the baron's study. The license had been granted quickly, thanks to his father's connections, and a response to Ben's inquiry had arrived from Mr. Cooper. The clergyman who'd supported Eve after Ben's departure agreed to wed them tomorrow.

The baron shook his hand and offered a "Congratulations" before dismissing him.

Ben had given the situation with Hackberry some thought in Thorne's study. There was a chance Eve might hear rumors of Hackberry leaving on one of Ben's ships, and he didn't want her learning about it from someone else. He hoped she could see he had acted out of desperation rather than any malicious intent.

Eve was alone in the drawing room. She closed the book she was reading and stared up at him with worry lines etched between her brows. "Did Sebastian behave?"

"He did as any good brother should." Ben joined her on the settee. "All the arrangements have been made for tomorrow. Are you certain you do not mind having the wedding at Hillary House?"

"The gardens are lovely. I am more than pleased with your father's offer to exchange our vows there."

"Splendid." He swept a lock of her dark hair behind her ear, his fingers tracing the gentle curve of the rim. "I wanted to talk a moment about Sir Jonathan."

She sat up straight and swiveled toward him. "Thank goodness. I wanted to introduce the topic, but I was uncertain how you would respond. Something he said has begun to concern me. You repeated the same words, which makes me think he said them to you as well."

"Oh?" Ben's stomach pitched. He couldn't fathom where the conversation was headed, but he feared he wouldn't like where it was going. "What did he say?"

"Several times he said he wanted me to be safe and happy. I understood his concern about my happiness. After all, he was jilting me. But I couldn't figure out why he seemed concerned about my safety or making sure I had a protector." She leaned toward him, her hand lightly gripping his arm. "Do you remember there was a man following us the other day?"

"Yes, why do you ask?" Wariness crept into his voice.

She bit her bottom lip and gazed at him as if considering whether she should proceed. "Do you think Sir Jonathan may be in trouble? I had the sense he thought he was protecting me by ending our association."

"Eve…"

"I know it sounds fanciful, but please hear me out. His strange behavior, his repeated wishes for my safety, the man following us." She ticked off each observation on her fingers. "It is all adding up. I feel certain he is in some kind of scrape and needs our help."

Neither of them had any business poking around in Hackberry's life. He'd warned Ben to forget he'd ever known him. "I am certain Sir Jonathan can handle any trouble he might have on his own. He does not require our help."

"So he *is* in trouble. What did he tell you? Is it gambling? Or perhaps he stole a valuable antiquity. Maybe someone is trying to steal an antiquity *he* uncovered." Her gestures grew more animated. "What if someone wants him to return to the Tigris and uncover something of value? Perhaps he is in someone's debt and feels honor bound to do his bidding. What are your thoughts?"

He chuckled under his breath. "I think you make trouble sound like a grand adventure. Sir Jonathan spoke very little about his personal life, other than he likes to keep it private. I think it would be wise for us to honor his wishes and stay out of his affairs."

She wrinkled her nose. "Well, if you did not want to meddle in his affairs, why did you bring up his name?"

Ah, yes. Here it was. The moment Ben must admit he'd behaved like a jackass, but it was better that she hear the truth from him. He captured her hand and held it against his lips, savoring the softness of her skin, stalling. "Please, don't hate me, Evie."

Her smile faded. "I've never liked conversations that begin with those words. And just to be clear, you might anger me sometimes, but I'm incapable of hating you."

He hoped that was true. "There is—" He cleared his throat. "I have done something distasteful for which I can offer no excuses, except to say I was desperate over the thought of losing you."

She froze, not even blinking. He could almost see the wheels turning in her head, her imagination creating all sorts of nefarious possibilities. Whether his action was better or worse than the imagined infraction remained to be seen.

"I meant what I said earlier about being bereft these last two years," he said. "I couldn't fathom spending a lifetime that way, so I bribed Hackberry to put an end to your betrothal. It was impulsive and I regretted it at once, but he accepted."

Color drained from her cheeks.

He rushed to explain. "I intended it as a test. I had no real thought that he would accept, although I should have realized. He seemed more interested in his studies than being a husband to you, and you deserve much more."

He held out a hand to her, but she backed away, fire snapping in her brown eyes. "You *bought* me? Like livestock?"

"No!" God, no! "Living without you has been hell. I wanted it to end."

She crossed her arms. "When did you make the offer to Sir Jonathan? Last night after the dinner party? I suppose he suspected I wanted to cry off."

Ben flinched. If Hackberry had suspected she wanted to end their association, surely he wouldn't have ended it himself. "He couldn't have known. That was our agreement. He was to make *you* want to cry off. I could not put you through any more embarrassment or hurt. This wasn't part of our plan."

Her lips pursed. "The day we had dance lessons. You were allies even then. I knew you were behind the sudden friendship with Sir Jonathan, but I never would have guessed you would stoop to bribery to make my fiancé leave me. This is beyond the pale."

"I know what I've done is despicable, and I would offer an apology, but it would be insincere. I wanted you. I *love* you." He reached for her, but she held up her hand, signaling him to stop.

"Don't."

"Evie, please." He didn't intend to sound plaintive, but he couldn't stop the wistfulness from seeping into his voice. They were so close to being together again. If he lost her now, he didn't know if he could bear it. "I am not proud of what I did, but I cannot change what I've done. Please tell me you are still willing to become my wife."

"Even if I was not, I haven't much choice now. My brother has negotiated a contract on my behalf. I will carry through on my word and marry you." She huffed when he reached for her again and gently captured her shoulders.

"I am not a duty to fulfill. I want you to *want* to marry me."

Eve's cool brown eyes bore into him. "Then make me feel confident in my decision. Act with some integrity."

She brushed his hands aside, hopped up from the settee, and tried to march for the door, but Ben caught her around the waist and pulled her onto his lap. Her lips parted and her eyes flared wide. Her fingers splayed on his chest, but she didn't push him away.

"You are right, Kitten. I didn't act with integrity, but I will not make the same mistake twice. Forgive me?"

She sighed. Her icy gaze began to thaw and she became supple in his arms. "I am uncertain it is prudent to offer forgiveness so easily, but I don't like being at odds with you. Especially the night before our wedding."

"I don't like being at odds with you either." When he smiled, she tentatively reciprocated. "If I promise to give you no more reasons to be angry with me, may I kiss you good night?"

Her smile reached her beautiful eyes, and the warmth of her loving gaze filled the emptiness he'd been carrying inside. "I suppose I can allow one kiss."

He placed a soft kiss on her lips, lingering longer than he should, given her brother's warnings, but he didn't care. He couldn't leave her with any doubts about how much he loved and wanted to please her. "I promise never to disappoint you again."

Nineteen

EVE WOKE THE NEXT MORNING WITH A SENSE OF OPTI-mism she hadn't experienced in a long time. Although she was still miffed over Ben paying Sir Jonathan to jilt her, she believed him when he said he had done it for her. For *them*. She had seen sincerity in his bright blue gaze and felt his love wrapping around her like armor, protective and substantial.

Some might label her a fool for trusting him again, but she trusted in destiny. From the first moment Ben had bowed over her hand after earning an introduction at the theater, she had known he was meant for her. The pull between them had been so powerful, she had waited two years for him to return, and just as she'd opened herself up to the possibility her destiny could lead elsewhere, Ben had come back.

Eve was not naive enough to believe second chances at love succeeded without effort from both parties, but as he had said yesterday, they would face their troubles together. This was exactly the type of marriage she wanted—the kind Sebastian and Helena had together, and Mama should have had with Papa.

Her bedchamber door creaked open, and Mama stuck her head inside. "The carriage is here, Evie, and your brother is anxious to leave. Are you ready?"

Eve smiled at her .mother, who had chosen to wear her finest silk gown and allowed Alice to place a sapphire clasp in her salt-and-pepper hair. Mama was overdressed for a garden wedding at Hillary House, but she looked stunning.

"I have been ready for a very long time, Mama." She linked arms with her mother to help steady her as they headed for the stairs.

"I know you have, dearest. I am pleased your wait is coming to an end, but I will miss you terribly."

As they reached the foyer, Eve kissed her mother's cheek. "I will miss you too, Mama." Her mother gave her a watery smile, and Eve's eyes filled with tears. Mama's unwavering support had helped her through her toughest days.

"For pity's sake," Sebastian piped up from the doorway, his wide grin teasing. "Are you going to stand around all morning getting soggy, or are you getting leg-shackled?"

"Both, if I wish it."

Her brother grabbed her in a rough hug when she reached him. "Helena and I will miss you too, poppet. You always have a place with us if you need it."

"I know." She kissed his cheek. "Thank you." Sebastian's offer was much appreciated, but she would never be returning home.

Outside, Helena's man Fergus was waiting beside the carriage to help her manage the steps. "You look verra pretty, lass. Mr. Hillary is a lucky man."

She blushed over the Scot's compliment and hurried into the carriage before he spotted the telltale signs of her embarrassment. Helena and Gracie had already claimed one of the benches, and Eve and Mama took the opposite seat. Once Sebastian joined them, the carriage pulled onto Savile Row for the short drive to Hillary House.

The Hillarys' butler offered a warm greeting upon their arrival and invited them to follow him. At the French doors leading to the gardens, the servant paused. "Mr. Cooper has arrived, and the guests are seated, Miss Thorne. If you would like a moment to prepare…"

She shook her head, a smile breaking across her face. "I am ready."

"Very good, miss." He returned to his station, allowing her another moment alone with her family.

Her mother gave her one last hug before she, Helena, and Gracie followed a footman outside where the other guests were waiting.

"It is not too late to come back home," Sebastian said as he offered his arm to Eve.

She wrinkled her nose at him. "I said I'm ready."

"*I* am not ready, but I suppose I'm expected to give you away regardless of my lack of enthusiasm over seeing you go." He placed a kiss on her hair. "I'll miss you, Eve, but your happiness eases my sorrow at losing you."

"You aren't losing me. You are gaining a brother-in-law to despise. Think what fun we will have during the holidays." She hugged his arm affectionately, sharing a chuckle with her brother. Sebastian had stepped

into their father's boots long before he'd passed away,
and he filled them nicely. "I couldn't ask for a better
older brother."

"You could, but you would still be saddled
with me."

A racket came from the front of the town house.
"Milady, please," a man implored. It sounded like the
Hillarys' butler.

"That is quite all right," a familiar voice sang out.
"We can find our way to the gardens."

The click of heels on marble moved quickly in
their direction. When Lady Norwick came into view,
Eve's heart stalled. She and the countess had grown
close over the Season, but Lady Norwick had known
Sir Jonathan Hackberry since childhood. She had been
responsible for pairing Eve and Jonathan together,
and Eve didn't expect the lady was pleased by the
latest development.

The countess's companion, Lady Banner, wasn't
far behind and wore a puckered expression. "*There*
she is," the baroness said, pointing in Eve's direction.
"We have arrived just in time, no thanks to your
dawdling, Bianca."

"Oh dear," Eve muttered under her breath as the
women marched toward them.

Sebastian squared his shoulders, readying for the
coming conflict, forever her champion. "Ladies, what
are you doing here?"

Her brother wasn't blessed with tact, but neither
the countess nor baroness seemed the least put off by
his question. Lady Norwick flashed a bright smile.
"We are here for the wedding, of course." She took

Eve's hands and held her arms out to her sides to gush over her dress. "You look marvelous, my dear. A lovelier bride has never existed. Mr. Hillary will not believe his good fortune."

Lady Banner eyed her as well. "Absolutely stunning. I am pleased we did not miss watching you walk down the aisle. I will just go find a seat."

With Eve still gawking at the newcomers, Lady Banner bustled out the glass doors to join the other guests.

Lady Norwick patted Eve's hand. "Sir Jonathan sent around a note yesterday explaining he is in support of your marriage to Mr. Hillary. He implored me to do the same." Her smile was kind. "He needn't have bothered. People might say many things about me, but I have never been accused of disloyalty to a friend, and you are one of my dearest. Fortunately, Amelia Hillary informed me of the date and time, since my invitation was lost en route to Norwick Place." Her thin eyebrows rose over clever brown eyes that sparkled with mischief.

Eve pressed her friend's hand between hers warmly. "Thank you for coming, milady."

"No thanks required." Short in stature, the countess had to stand on her toes to place kisses on both of Eve's cheeks. Then, with a jaunty wave, she swept outside.

Sebastian shook his head. "I always feel I've been in the presence of a hurricane after an encounter with Lady Norwick."

Eve chuckled. "Yes, she is a force of nature." And if one was fortunate enough to associate with a force of nature, it was lovely to remain in its good graces.

❦

Ben fidgeted with his cravat. It felt too blasted tight and he barely had breathing room. It wasn't well done of him to fidget, but it was taking Eve an awfully long time to walk down the aisle. When the door opened a second time, his head snapped up, eager to catch a first glimpse of his bride.

This time it was the Countess of Norwick. She hurried across the veranda, the loud clacking of her heels making everyone turn in their seats. When she flashed a smile and wiggled her fingers at everyone in greeting, he grimaced. Neither she nor her sister-in-law had been invited to the small ceremony, which made him suspicious of the reason she looked so blasted happy.

The longer he was kept waiting, the more his stomach churned. "Where is she?" he hissed to his brother, who was standing up with him.

Daniel shrugged.

What if Eve had changed her mind? He wouldn't put it past Lady Norwick to have dissuaded Eve and staged a distraction while his bride slipped away. It was no secret the countess wanted a match between Eve and Hackberry.

Damnation. He couldn't lose her again. He took a step down the aisle, and the doors opened again. Everything around him faded into nothingness as his gaze locked on Eve. She was the most beautiful vision he'd ever seen. Her ethereal ivory gown floated around her ankles as she moved toward him with purpose, and sunlight sparkled off the silver embroidery at the hem. Yet it wasn't her gown or the soft curls cascading down her back that made her breathtaking.

She radiated warmth, love, and goodness. His heart swelled with admiration, and his eyes misted as his bride walked with confidence toward their future together. Her full, pink lips curved into a beckoning smile as she neared—innocent and alluring all at once. He dashed away the moisture from his eyes before anyone noticed and caught Daniel's knowing smirk. He ignored his brother as Eve reached the end of the aisle on Thorne's arm.

The words were a blur as he waited for the moment the clergyman asked, "Who gives this bride?" Her brother answered on her family's behalf and relinquished her to join his own wife on the front row.

Ben took Eve's hand to lead her before Mr. Cooper, unable to take his eyes from her. She was a gift, but not from her brother or anyone present at the ceremony. Eve was a gift of fate, Ben's by design, and precious. So incredibly valued and wanted, he ached deep within, as if from this moment forward, his life would be ripped from him if she were taken away.

A dizzying fog invaded his head, and his heart began to beat heavily against his breastbone. A fine sheen of sweat blanketed his body. Eve's eyes grew round as she held tightly to his hand. "Ben…" Her concerned whisper sent a flood of heat through him as he realized everyone was watching him. Her family. Ladies Norwick and Banner. Eve herself.

Daniel nudged him gently and winked at Eve as he reached into his jacket pocket. "Stop fretting. I remembered the ring."

When Eve smiled and relaxed beside him, Ben's tension began to ease. He couldn't allow his thoughts to travel down that dark path. He wouldn't lose Eve. She was here beside him, safe. And he would keep her that way.

Mr. Cooper looked positively gleeful, presumably patting himself on the back for his part in their union. Ben was certainly grateful to the clergyman for taking matters in his own hands and writing to him in Delhi.

When Ben spoke his vows, he held Eve's gaze, taking her to be his wife and promising to love and cherish her for the rest of their lives. Eve's voice was strong and unwavering as she pledged her faithfulness, allaying his concerns that she had any reservations about becoming his bride.

Mr. Cooper held out the opened Book of Common Prayer to Daniel. "The ring?"

Ben's brother placed Eve's ring on the pages, and Mr. Cooper passed it to Ben. As instructed, Ben slid the ring on Eve's finger and echoed the minister's words. "With this ring I thee wed, with my body I thee worship, and with all my worldly goods I thee endow: In the name of the Father, and of the Son, and of the Holy Ghost. Amen."

Eve splayed her fingers close to her face to view the ring. He'd chosen an opal set in silver with two small rubies on either side. Her eyes sparkled when she looked up at him. "It is beautiful," she whispered. Her smile rivaled the sun and made his chest swell with pride for pleasing her. And because she was his at last.

When Mr. Cooper pronounced them man and wife, they were suddenly surrounded by well-wishers.

Ben good-naturedly endured his brothers' teasing as his mother, sister, and sisters-in-law embraced Eve as if she had always been part of their family.

"Somehow Mother managed to put together an impressive wedding breakfast on short notice," Jake said.

Ben frowned. "I suppose she would notice if Eve and I went missing." He was only partly jesting.

"At least allow your bride a meal before you ravish her," Daniel said with a smirk.

"Mind your own damned affairs."

Twenty

DESPITE ENCOURAGEMENT TO EAT HER FILL AT THE breakfast, Eve had only been able to pick at her food. Everything looked delicious, but she had been too anxious about Ben taking her home. She faced the prospect with a mixture of eagerness and trepidation.

She knew more than many young ladies about the goings-on between husbands and wives, because her mother had always been forthcoming when Eve asked questions. Knowledge did not alleviate her nerves, however.

Ben rubbed his thumb along her knuckles as they held hands in the carriage carrying them home after the wedding breakfast. "Why the small line between your brows, Kitten?"

"I am worried about undressing in front of you."

A short burst of laughter came from him. "I wasn't expecting such honesty."

"Why not? We are married now. If I cannot be honest with my husband, I don't know who I can trust with the truth."

His tender smile melted her heart. "You have

nothing to fret over, dearling. You needn't have an audience when you undress if you don't wish it." He lifted her hand to his lips and lightly kissed her sensitive skin. "But I am certain you are exquisite."

She wrinkled her nose. "I have freckles. Everywhere."

He sat up straighter and turned toward her. "Good God, *everywhere*? I will keep you up all night kissing each and every one." The wicked twinkle in his blue eyes as he pulled her into his arms made her stomach flutter. "I'd best start now."

He proceeded to rain kisses all over her cheeks, down her neck, and along her collarbone. She squealed and wiggled to escape his tickling. When he drew back, smiling, she settled in his arms with a contented sigh.

He snuggled her close and kissed her forehead. "You didn't eat much at breakfast. Perhaps we should plan an early dinner."

"If you like." She laid her head on his shoulder, closing her eyes and breathing in his scent. He smelled of cinnamon from the morning rolls and something exotic she didn't recognize. It was a surprisingly comforting combination.

She listened to the soothing clip-clop of the horses' hooves as the carriage traveled toward her new home in Marylebone. Ben's grandfather had acquired a town house near Cavendish Square after he made his riches, and Ben had inherited the property. The house held sentimental value for him, and because it was special to her husband, she would take extra care in managing their home. She would take extra care of him too.

"Ben, was something wrong this morning? You looked very pale all of a sudden."

His muscles twitched beneath her cheek. "I might have been in the sun longer than I should. I felt queasy for a moment, but it passed."

She pushed to an upright position to check his complexion once more. "Are you sure you are not ill?"

"I have never felt better, Evie."

His color had returned during the ceremony, and he appeared hearty and hale now. "You would tell me if you were not well, wouldn't you?"

"Of course." He laughed off her concern as he ducked his head to peer out the window. "We are almost home. Would you like to sit beside the window for a better view?"

"No, thank you." Instead, she leaned across him to ogle the neighbors' houses. Her maid would have a wonderful time scouting out the neighborhood and keeping abreast with the local gossip. When the carriage stopped in front of a Grecian-style town house, Eve nearly climbed into Ben's lap for a better look. She had seen the town house in passing, but it was much larger up close.

Ben chuckled. "Come inside before you smudge the glass with your nose."

She accepted his assistance from the carriage and linked arms with him before they climbed the steps leading to the front door.

The massive door swung open before they reached it, and a broad-shouldered man dressed in livery greeted them.

"Good afternoon, Dobbins. Have Mrs. Fitzhugh assemble the staff for an introduction to Mrs. Hillary."

"Yes, sir."

Eve couldn't help smiling at hearing her new address.

She and Ben passed through a narrow entry hall that opened onto a large circular foyer with several arched doorways leading to different parts of the house. "What would you like to see first?"

"Let's start there." She randomly pointed toward a doorway on the right.

"As you wish." Ben provided a brief tour of the rooms on the ground level—two drawing rooms, his study, the library, and a dining room—before returning to the foyer where a staff of eight had gathered. Ben rested his hand at the small of her back. "Please allow me to introduce my wife, Eve Hillary. I trust you will all make her feel welcome and answer any questions she might have as she assumes management of the household."

The servants offered tentative smiles and the proper greetings.

"Thank you," Eve said. "I can see what a splendid job you've done maintaining an efficient and lovely home. I do not anticipate many disruptions to your routines, so please, carry on as you have already been doing."

The servants dispersed with their heads held high, which was exactly as it should be. She didn't want to barge in, assert her authority, and throw the household into chaos. A slow transition seemed wisest.

Mrs. Fitzhugh remained behind when the others left. "Would you like me to show you to your chambers, ma'am? Your maid and belongings arrived earlier, so everything should be in order."

Ben clasped Eve's hand. "Allow me." He drew her toward the curved staircase. "Thank you, Mrs. Fitzhugh," he called over his shoulder.

The woman smiled fondly at him. "It is my pleasure, Mr. Hillary."

Above stairs, Ben led her to a doorway in the middle of the corridor. He paused with his hand on the handle. "You may change anything you do not like. The decor may not be fit for a lady's tastes."

Eve pursed her lips. "Are you trying to torture me? Open the door!"

He grinned, stole a quick kiss, and pushed open the door. Eve gasped. Never had she seen anything more beautiful. Rich green and crimson silk fabrics woven together with gold thread hung from the windows and puddled on the floor. An equally decadent coordinating fabric draped the carved bed, and a plush coverlet that Eve wanted to curl up in covered the thick mattress. A hand-painted cabinet held porcelain vases and silver candelabras with new candles.

She moved toward the intricately carved dressing table as if she was in a trance. Colorful bottles had been grouped together on the surface. "What are these?" She pulled the stopper out of one and held it under her nose for a tentative sniff. A woodsy lemon-like scent wafted on the air, and she sighed with pleasure.

Ben came up beside her and reached for a different bottle. "These are essential oils from Egypt. One of man's earliest forms of medicine, I've been told. I don't know what power they have to heal, but they have a lovely scent. This is origanum." He held the bottle out for her to sniff. It was a sweet and spicy scent and reminiscent of his cologne.

"I've never seen anything like this, Ben. I feel as if I've traveled to another world." She replaced the bottle and wandered to a small wardrobe to see what treasures were hidden inside. Long lengths of colorful cloth hung from the pegs. "Beautiful. Are these draperies too?"

He grinned. "No, this is called a sari. Women in India wear them."

She snatched the translucent cloth and held it up. "Ladies *wear* this? How?"

"They do not wear this alone." He reached for two satin pieces: a short corset-type garment that would come down to just beneath her breasts, and a colorful petticoat. "Once the blouse and petticoat are donned, the women drape the fabric around their waist and over the shoulder. You may use them however you see fit, though."

"Do you like how the women dress?" she asked as a flood of heat swept through her.

He hesitated, scratching the back of his neck. His blue eyes darkened as he held her gaze. "I do."

"Hmm." She didn't trust her voice not to crack. Replacing the fabric, she shut the wardrobe doors, ending the discussion of saris, and placed a bit of distance between herself and the slightly scandalous attire. "I do not see a thing I would change about my rooms. I will be quite comfortable here."

His relieved smile caused her heart to hitch. He'd truly been concerned she would not like her chambers, but she could not imagine a more perfect set of rooms.

After testing the fainting couch by lightly bouncing up and down while seated, she smiled up at him. "Where are your chambers?"

"Through the doors. Would you like a tour?"

She hesitated. It was on the tip of her tongue to say it would be inappropriate, before realizing a tour of a gentleman's private chambers—at least her husband's—was no longer forbidden. Her stomach tumbled at the thought of what was to come later. "Perhaps we could visit the gardens first?"

His eyebrows lowered over his eyes. "If you are certain you aren't too tired…"

"Not one bit."

Twenty-one

BEN HAD ENJOYED SHOWING EVE HER NEW HOME, AND the obvious pleasure she'd derived from her chambers was heartening. Furthermore, he had delighted in her company throughout the day. Even their dinner conversation had been stimulating and a break from his usual dull evenings at home. But, God's blood, lusting for his wife seemed to slow time to a near stop. Twilight had barely descended when he could no longer pretend he wasn't preoccupied with having her beneath him.

"Shall we ready for bed?"

Eve blinked, and a becoming blush swept across her cheeks. Eventually, she nodded. "I will summon my maid."

That had been an hour ago. Now crickets chirped outside his bedchamber window, and every time he heard Eve giggling with her maid through the adjoining door, he forced himself to the other side of the room rather than bursting in on her. Surely, brides frowned upon that sort of thing.

"Good night, ma'am. I will wait for you to ring for

me tomorrow." Her maid's muffled farewell drew him to the door.

"Good night, Alice."

As the outer door to her chamber closed, he secured the sash to his dressing gown and let himself into his wife's chambers. Eve was seated at her dressing table, pulling a brush through the curls falling to the middle of her back. Rich like mahogany, her hair glistened in the candlelight.

Her equally dark gaze locked with his in the looking glass. Her eyes glittered like obsidian stone, more black than rich brown in the muted light. She set the brush on the dressing table and smoothed her hands over her legs with a shy smile.

His blood scorched his veins when he saw what she had done. "You are wearing the sari." His voice sounded husky.

A rosy blush covered the exposed areas of her chest, neck, and face. Her lovely freckles faded. They weren't nearly as plentiful as she had promised, but he would still have fun searching every inch of her.

"Alice and I were uncertain if we draped it correctly," she said, her blush deepening, "but it hasn't fallen off."

A long length of fabric was bunched at her feet beneath the dressing table, and the precariously draped silk could easily slide from her shoulder with any movement.

"That wouldn't be the worst outcome," he said with a wink.

"Wouldn't that defeat the purpose?"

"Not mine." Ben came up behind her to place his

hands on her shoulders and leaned down to kiss her neck. "You look stunning." The scent of elemi—from the first bottle of oil she had selected earlier—wafted from her freshly bathed skin. He gently nipped her earlobe. "And you smell amazing."

She closed her eyes. Inky lashes fanned against her fair complexion to create a striking contrast, and a ragged exhale escaped her. When she opened her eyes, her wide-eyed gaze darted toward the bed reflected in the mirror.

"All right," she said in a much stronger voice than he'd expected, given her show of nerves. "I am ready."

He grinned. "Not quite yet, love."

His brave little bride was far from ready, but she would be keen for the marriage bed after he introduced her to the pleasures one could have there.

He slowly combed his fingers through the silky strands of her hair. The damp ends curled around his fingers, and he gently tugged until she tipped up her face. "I love you, Eve Lorraine Elizabeth Thorne Hillary." He kissed the end of her pert nose.

Her mouth curved into a tentative smile. "I love you too." He was happy to hear no hesitation in her profession.

"Come with me." He urged her to follow him and led her to stand beside the bed.

She averted her gaze as he reached for the sari and slowly unwrapped his gift. As the length of shimmering cloth coiled at her feet, a tremor shook her lush frame. She glanced at him from beneath her lashes. "I am sorry. I don't mean to be nervous."

Affection filled his heart until he felt it might burst.

He was hard and eager to be buried deep inside her, but he only had patience and tenderness for her. "You have no cause to be sorry. Nerves are to be expected, but I promise we will not do anything you don't want."

He drew her into his embrace, placing a kiss on her hair. She dissolved against him: warm, pliable, and so trusting he couldn't bear to betray her faith in him. Closing his eyes, he breathed in her sweet scent, contentment settling in his bones. Eve made him feel whole. She gave him peace, and he wanted to give her the same.

"Lie on the bed, sweetheart. I know how to make you more comfortable." He helped her climb onto the thick mattress and recline on the pillow. Her posture was as rigid as iron, as if the prospect of their joining was as enticing as a visit from the dentist.

He turned toward her dressing table to retrieve a bottle of scented oil before she saw his amused grin. As he returned to the bed, he unstoppered the bottle, poured several drops of oil into his palm, and placed the bottle on the side table. Climbing on the bed, he rubbed his hands together and gently lifted her foot. She rose to her elbows, her forehead wrinkling.

"I am only going to rub your foot now." He kissed her instep, then placed small pecks on each toe, erasing the tiny line between her elegant brows. "Lie back."

With the first stroke of his thumb across the arch of her foot, she released a breath and rested against the pillow, placing herself in his hands. He smiled and kissed her ankle before circling the delicate bone with his thumb. Slowly moving up her calf with long sweeps of his hands, he eased the hem of her petticoat higher on her legs, feasting on the sight. He'd often imagined what she would look like bared to him, and he wasn't disappointed. Divine ankles, well-sculpted calves, luscious thighs.

A strong urge to place his lips against her soft skin and nibble his way up her leg until he could taste her rushed over him. He held back, his muscles quivering. Much enjoyment could come from a slow seduction, and he wanted Eve as hungry for him as he was for her.

He concentrated on making long downward strokes over the plumper flesh of her inner thigh. Her chest rose and fell steadily, and a soft sigh slipped past her lips. Moving to her other leg, he repeated the gentle kneading and caresses, allowing his fingers to graze the dark curls between her legs. She shifted on the bed, her sigh closer to a moan.

When she opened her eyes, they were cloudy with desire. He smiled and stretched over her body to retrieve more oil. His shaft strained against the front of his robe, throbbing when he brushed her leg through the thin material. She lightly gripped the edge of his robe and pushed it down his shoulders to reveal his chest. She sucked in a breath, stroking his pride as he'd been stroking her body.

"Would you like me to remove my dressing gown?" he asked, teasing her. She wouldn't be ready yet.

She surprised him, however, by nodding. Returning to kneel between her legs, he untied the sash and shrugged off his robe. Her eyes flared wide for a brief moment.

He rested his hand on the gentle swell of her

stomach and cocked an eyebrow. "Do you like what you see?"

Her skin heated under his touch and she turned scarlet. "It is impolite to solicit compliments, sir."

A chuckle rumbled in his chest. "Forgive my rudeness." He didn't need compliments on his physique, although they would be arousing as hell to hear.

He smoothed his palms over her stomach, his thumbs caressing along the hem of her blouse, skimming just below her breasts. Her nipples hardened, but he resisted taking one in his mouth. He wanted her writhing on the bed, nearly mad with desire before he touched her in that way. She swallowed hard as he swept his hands slowly over her body, around her waist to the small of her back, and along the top of her buttocks. She moaned softly, her lips curving into a sensual smile.

God, she was beautiful, perfection. Strong in spirit, and yet so fragile when his hands spanned her waist. A swell of protectiveness built inside him.

She was his. His to cherish. His to love until... until *death* parted them. A sharp pain pierced his chest, making him want to wrap her tightly in his arms to keep her with him forever. Loving Eve made him more vulnerable than he'd been in a long time. He hated it. And yet he reveled in it as well. She made him feel alive again.

He swallowed hard, his throat suddenly tight and achy. "I would like you with less clothing, my dear. May I?"

Her eyes flickered open and she met his gaze without any signs of apprehension. "Yes."

❧

Eve's lower belly fluttered when Ben slid his hands under her blouse. His fingers skimmed the sides of her breasts before he pushed the fabric high on her chest. The fresh air on her bare breasts made them feel heavier and achy. She arched her back, seeking relief, but he rocked back on his knees, not touching her like she wanted. Unable to help herself, she brushed her hand across her nipple to ease her own need.

He uttered a mild curse as his heated gaze traveled over her, causing an unfamiliar pulse between her legs. "You are killing me, Kitten."

If that were true, he appeared happy to meet his death. His blue eyes were almost black and smoldering. She stole a glance at his cock, and then because it was a shocking sight, she looked again. In no way did he resemble the statues from the Elgin Marbles exhibit at the museum. His jutted long and powerfully from his body, and caused her a moment of trepidation. But then his hands slid to her back, soothing and gentle, and she became swept up in the lovely tingles raining over her.

He lifted her to a seated position and shimmied the blouse over her head. The decadent slip of satin over her skin elicited the most delightful shivers. He cupped her breast and smoothed his thumb along her flesh. Her nipple hardened even though he avoided touching it. "Beautiful," he murmured and covered her lips with his.

His mouth lightly played over hers with maddening slowness. His tongue flicked along the seam of her lips until she was panting.

"Kiss me," she pleaded.

His mouth came down harder against hers and his tongue swept between her lips, no longer teasing. He was taking possession of her—mind, body, heart—and she wanted nothing more than to be his forever. She startled slightly when her back made contact with the coverlet. While his kisses and the lovely feel of his fingers slipping through her hair had distracted her, she hadn't noticed he was stretching her out beneath him. His hot skin against hers branded her.

Ben pushed back to his knees and reached for her petticoat. She followed the flexing of his muscles with her eyes as he wrestled the petticoat over her derriere and tossed it on the floor. With nothing between them—both of them as bare as the day they'd been born—she didn't feel vulnerable or embarrassed as she had feared. It felt right and symbolic of their promise to one another. There were no barriers keeping them apart, no walking away from their troubles. From this moment forward, they would be one in facing whatever life gave them.

She covered his hand resting beneath her breast and entwined their fingers. Her eyes brimmed with tears. "I missed you so much."

He lifted her hand to his lips, closing his eyes as if struggling to maintain his composure. When he finally opened them again, his eyes shimmered in the candlelight. "I will never leave you again, Evie. I wouldn't survive."

He kissed her hand once more before cupping the soft underside of her breast and settling over her to lick a wide circle around her nipple. His tongue moved closer on each sweep until the tingling became too much. When he covered her nipple, his mouth hot and wet surrounding her, she cried out with relief. The gentle but firm pull of his mouth sent the ache to a new place. The pressure of his weight against her sex heightened her sensitivity. Deep inside, she throbbed.

His hand slid between their bodies to cup her, and the heat of his touch spread through her body. She bit her bottom lip to stop the unladylike groan building at the back of her throat from escaping. She hadn't expected this, the intensity and fire flowing through her veins.

He shifted to the bed beside her and gazed down at her. "Allow yourself to feel everything. Let the sensations carry you without worrying what will come next."

He kissed her tenderly once more before returning to her breast. Eve's eyes drifted shut when his lips closed around her, but they popped open again. The thrill of watching him kiss her so intimately was too tempting. She buried her hands in his golden brown hair, then trailed her fingers along his broad shoulders and down his back as far as she could reach. His skin was like satin stretched across granite.

When he stroked between her legs, she jumped. The sensation was odd, unfamiliar, and yet she wanted to feel it again. He didn't disappoint her. His fingers glided over her damp skin, circling and lightly feathering over a particularly pleasurable place. His lovely caresses drew husky moans from her, low and barely audible, but satisfying in a way she couldn't describe. He slowly inserted a finger inside her and her body clenched. As he slid in and out, the ache inside her intensified. She needed more, even though the thought of taking all of him made her heart slam against her ribs.

Releasing her breast, he positioned himself over her, cradling her face and smiling. His eyes were a soft blue and radiated with love. Her heart began to calm. Ben was her husband, and he would take care of her. He kissed her sweetly, his tongue caressing hers, their breath mingling. She arched into him, seeking, longing. He entered her slowly, stopping when she stiffened to kiss her until she began to dissolve against the bed. Between languorous kisses, he inched deeper until he filled her.

He closed his eyes and released a breath that was part sigh, part groan. His arms trembled as he supported his weight and held very still. The fullness of him inside her was foreign, and she shifted her hips to adjust to this new feeling. Ben's eyes flew open, worry etched in the lines on his forehead. She pulled him toward her to place a loving kiss on his lips.

"I love you," she murmured.

His worry lines faded and he kissed the tip of her nose. "I love you too."

As he moved slowly, she began to welcome the newness of their joining. She loved the closeness: the feel of his skin against hers; his breath on her neck. She stroked his back, following the curve and admiring how perfectly formed her husband was. And when he spilled his seed with several commanding thrusts and a low groan, she was content. At least mostly.

Ben kissed her once more before settling beside her

on the bed and pulling her into his arms. She rested her cheek on his chest, listening to his heart hammer and noting how it slowed in small measures.

He snuggled her, his mouth touching her temple. "Did I hurt you?"

She shook her head, surprised to realize there had been no excruciating pain. When she grew uncomfortable, Ben had distracted her with kisses. "It was nice," she mused.

His chest shook with laughter, jostling her.

She propped herself up on her arm to frown at him. "We just had a lovely moment together. I fail to see what is funny about it."

In a blink, she was flat on her back with her husband straddling her. He flashed a roguish grin. "Nice is a walk in the country or sipping lemonade on a warm afternoon. I don't settle for nice in the bedchamber, Kitten, and neither will you."

Before she could guess at his meaning, his mouth was at her breast and his fingers swept over that wondrous spot he'd discovered earlier. She moaned as heat filled her again. His touch was relentless, allowing her no rest and stoking a fire inside her until her body pleaded for relief. It came quickly, flaring and consuming her. Shocking cries ripped from her as he held her in a state of ecstasy—wave after wave of the most intense pleasure she had ever known—until she was at last depleted and collapsed against the bed.

Her limbs were too heavy to move. Even her eyelids refused to work properly. Ben lay beside her, stroking her hair from her face. She yawned.

Her husband chuckled. "Nice doesn't make you sleepy like this, does it, Evie?"

She shook her head, not bothering to open her eyes. "Stay with me," she mumbled as she rolled on her side away from him.

"I'm never leaving, remember?" Despite his promise, the mattress dipped as he climbed from bed, but he was gone only long enough to snuff the candles. When he returned, his strong body surrounded her. A drowsy smile pulled at her lips. She was sated, secure in the cocoon he created for her, and confident in their future as she succumbed to sleep.

Twenty-two

BEN WOKE ON A CHOKING GASP. HIS HEARTBEAT THUN-
dered in his ears. He stared into darkness, lost in the
space between nightmares and alertness. Charlotte's
trampled body weighed down his arms. The accusation in her eyes was slowly fading, leaving them glassy,
nearly vacant. Her last ragged breath sent a shiver
down his back.

The dream hung like a dense fog, slow to dissipate.
He knew he was at home—London. The sounds
outside were different from those in India. A soft body
was curled against his side, and warm, steady breaths
stirred the hair on his chest. An involuntary tremble
shook his body.

"Ben?" Eve's voice was groggy from sleep. Her
petite hand skimmed his damp skin. "Are you all right?"

Relief flooded through him. He wasn't in a dusty
lane holding Charlotte as she died. He was snug in bed
with his wife.

She stirred. "Ben, do you…need something?"

His pulse was slowing and the images from his
dream were starting to evaporate. "No, go back to

sleep, Evie. I didn't mean to wake you." He fought to keep distress from leaching into his voice.

"Are you certain?" she mumbled.

"Yes, dearling."

She turned her back to him, and Ben rolled on his side to tuck her against his chest. She wiggled until her derriere was well fitted to him. One deep sigh and she surrendered to sleep again.

Ben kissed her hair, breathing in her sweet scent. "I love you," he whispered.

He wished he could succumb to sleep as easily as she did. Instead, he lay in the dark with horrible images invading his mind. He didn't always recall his dreams, but waking up in the midst of one sometimes branded it into his memory.

Charlotte didn't speak in this dream. Just as she hadn't been able to say anything after the travel coach struck her. After the accident, he'd held her, telling her repeatedly that he loved her. He promised to do whatever she wished if only she would stay with him.

You are right. I can't allow Father to control me. We will marry like you want. We can leave tomorrow. Please, Char. Stay with me.

He had babbled about working in her father's bakery to support her until he received his inheritance, and promised her a house on the edge of the village. *The old Leabow place. You've always admired it.*

She had simply stared at him, her life slipping away. One moment they had been arguing about him needing to stand up to his father, and the next moment the girl he loved was gone. He'd still been pleading with her when her father arrived. Ben hadn't seen the rage on Mr. Tanney's face or anticipated his fist slamming into his cheek. Ben lay sprawled in the dirt, ears ringing, as the man hurled accusations of murder at him.

Nothing came of Mr. Tanney's indictment. When the magistrate made an inquest, the coach driver provided testimony that "the dotty chit ran into the lane." Furthermore, Ben refused to make a complaint over Mr. Tanney's treatment of him. He hadn't murdered Charlotte, but he was still responsible for her death. He had been the reason she was too upset to see the coach bearing down on her.

Fifteen was a tender age to learn a cruel truth: love could be lost in an instant. And he had sworn to never love again. Eve murmured in her sleep, and he hugged her close. Then along came this sweet and lively young woman, and his promise to never love again was broken. Eve held his heart and gave his life meaning. If he lost her, he would be lost too.

Those dreadful images flashed in his mind again, but this time he wasn't holding his childhood sweetheart. Eve's face stared up at him. A quiver originated from somewhere deep inside him, and the flood of impending doom that came with his spells bore down on him. He couldn't stop it.

Scrambling from bed, he tried not to wake Eve. She whimpered in her sleep, but he had no time to comfort her. His pulse tore through his veins as he reached his chambers and closed the door. Darkness was creeping up behind him. Breathing in through his nose and out through his mouth, he wrestled for control of his body and mind.

"The House of Hanover: George III, George II,

George I," he murmured. Working backward through the Kings and Queens of England required concentration and kept his despairing thoughts at bay. "The Stuarts: Queen Anne, William III and Queen Mary, James II, Charles II, Charles I, James I. The Tudors: Queen Elizabeth, Queen Mary, Edward VI, Henry VIII…" By the time he was reciting the Kings of the House of York, his heartbeat had slowed, and he was beginning to feel more like himself.

He hadn't experienced an episode this intense since his return to London. Raking his fingers through his hair, he released a shaky breath and went in search of the tinderbox kept on the mantel. He lit a candle and retrieved another dressing gown from his dressing room before settling in his chair to read.

Occupying his mind would calm him further, but he wouldn't return to Eve's bed. Waking in a cold sweat and trembling like a child was mortifying, and he never knew when a nightmare might strike. He didn't want his wife to see him when he was weak. Her father had been similarly tormented by his memories of war, and on more than one occasion, Lord Thorne had behaved like a madman out in Society before he'd become a hermit in his own home. Ben didn't want to burden her with his affliction. She deserved a normal life. *He* wanted a normal life.

In India, throwing himself into work had helped. There was comfort in routine, and any problems he encountered were solvable. He had an appointment with an investor at the docks tomorrow that he hadn't been able to cancel. He'd been irritated to be locked into a meeting the day after his wedding, but perhaps it would help clear his mind so he could concentrate on enjoying the remainder of the day with his wife.

Feeling a little more at ease, he got up to open the doors between his and Eve's chambers so he could hear her when she began stirring and slip back into bed before she realized he'd been missing.

❧

Eve squinted against bright sunlight pushing through the bedchamber window and smiled sleepily. A contented haze enveloped her as she spotted the colorful bed curtains and recalled where she was: in bed with her husband. Blindly, she reached for Ben and touched an empty place. She swept her arm across the sheets, searching for his warm body and only finding cool sheets. Her eyes popped open to discover he wasn't in bed with her, after all.

She sat up, hugging the sheet around her to cover her bareness, and looked around the room. The doors between their chambers stood open. "Ben?"

He didn't answer. Rubbing the sleep from her eyes, she slipped from bed and retrieved a robe from her dressing room. She took a moment to freshen up, then went in search of her husband. She found him slumped in a chair. His head hung forward, his chin resting on his chest, and he snored softly.

She moved to his side. He looked like an overgrown boy, oblivious to the world around him when he slept. Her smile widened as she leaned to place a gentle kiss on his cheek. As her lips touched his whiskered face, he startled, his arm flashing out and knocking her off balance. She grasped for the arm of the chair, but she grabbed air and landed on the plush carpet with an indelicate "Oof!"

Wild-eyed, Ben swung toward her where she was sprawled on the floor with her robe gaping. "God's blood! Did I hurt you?" He scrambled to haul her from the floor.

"I'm fine. I had a plush landing."

The rigidness in his shoulders melted and his eyes twinkled. He seized a handful of her bum and pulled her flush against him. "I see you've lots of cushioning back here."

"I meant the rug, silly man." Laughing, she swatted at his hands as he playfully squeezed both cheeks. "What are you doing asleep in your chair?"

He sat, pulled her into his lap, and nuzzled her neck. "Being bedeviled by a nymph, apparently."

"I wasn't bedeviling you. I was greeting you with a good morning kiss."

He planted a sound kiss on her lips. "Good morning." His seductive smile caused her heart to skip. His hand stole inside her robe to caress her breast, and her nipples puckered through the thin silk. "I intended to crawl back into bed with you before you woke. I'm sorry I missed my chance, or did I?"

His mouth glided along the gentle curve between her shoulder and neck, and she closed her eyes with a sigh. It felt so lovely when he touched her, and she would gladly crawl back into bed with him if not for the dull ache between her legs. She opened her mouth, but no sound came out. Her limited knowledge of husbands did not include how to dissuade them.

He flashed another heart-melting smile and extracted

his hand from her clothing. "I am teasing, Kitten. It's too soon. Perhaps you would like a warm hip-bath before breakfast?"

That actually sounded quite nice. "What are our plans today? So I might know how to dress?"

"I—uh…I have an appointment." His brows knitted. "I am sorry. It is too late to cancel now, but it is just one meeting at the docks and then I will be at your disposal."

Her heart fluttered at the mention of his destination, and her fingers tightened on his dressing gown before she realized what she was doing. Releasing him, she smoothed out the wrinkles with her hand. She couldn't meet his gaze. "I thought we would spend the day together."

He tilted her face up with a soft touch to her chin. "I am not leaving you, Eve. I would rather stay here with you, but I made the arrangement before I knew we would be married or that it would fall on the day after our wedding."

She sighed. He probably thought it was a ridiculous notion—ignoring his responsibilities and spending time with her—but she was only requesting a day. And they were *newly* wed.

He placed a tender kiss on her forehead. "We will do whatever you like this evening. Maybe dinner at the pleasure gardens or the theater? You choose where you would like us to go."

"Very well." His offer appeased her since she did enjoy Vauxhall Gardens. Furthermore, an evening of dining alfresco and then exploring the winding paths sounded like an amusing excursion. She lifted her eyebrows in mock sternness. "But I insist on a supper box."

"Anything you wish. I should summon my valet or I will be late. I promise to return as soon as I'm able." He scooted her from his lap and urged her back toward her chambers. "Allow me to ring for a footman so you can have that bath."

Eve pursed her lips as he dismissed her.

During her bath, he stopped by her rooms to bid her a good day and informed her the cook would send up a tray if she preferred breakfast in her chambers. "I won't be gone too long," he promised.

That was quite all right. No doubt she would wait for him as long as it took if the fact she had waited two years was any indication.

At the doorway, he turned back toward her. "Evie, I love you."

"I know. I love you too." After he strode out the door, she hugged her knees to her chest, feeling a little sorry for herself. She quickly tired of pouting, however, and made her own plans for the day.

First she would meet with the housekeeper Mrs. Fitzhugh for an overview of the running of the household, and then she would visit Mrs. Beardmore in the kitchen. That should occupy the better part of her day.

After Alice assisted her into a clean gown and her toilette was complete, Eve made her way below stairs to attend to her own duties as mistress of the house. She sadly underestimated the amount of time this would take, for an hour and a half later she was back in her chambers. No correspondence needed tending, and her maid had put away all her belongings yesterday, aside from a valise in her dressing room.

"I suppose I should unpack it," she mumbled to herself, less than thrilled with the mundane task. She carried it to the bed and released the fastenings to see what Alice had stashed inside.

The valise held a few books, a bundle of letters from her brother that he'd written while he was away at boarding school, her favorite pair of slippers, and a hand-carved jewel box inlaid with mother of pearl. She retrieved the box and lifted the lid, knowing she would find the necklace Ben had given her two years earlier. It was such a beautiful piece, and while she loved the ring he had chosen for their wedding, the symbolism of the necklace always had struck her as truly romantic.

She held it up to the light, admiring how the yellow diamonds sparkled. Did Ben even remember the necklace? Later, she would ask him about it and question why he'd wanted her to have it when he had believed they would never see each other again. She replaced the necklace and found a spot for the jewel box on her dressing table, then looked through the books to see if one enticed her to open it.

Two were gothic novels her sister-in-law had loaned her, and which sparked her interest a little, and the last was Jonathan's copy of *The Histories of Herodotus*. When she had asked him what had formed his love for ancient cultures, he talked at length about his love for this book. The next day he brought his copy to share with her. She had thanked him for his thoughtfulness and promised to read, and return,

Herodotus's writings with Godspeed. Her first promise was broken the moment she realized it was written
in Greek. She supposed she should at least keep her
promise to return his beloved book.

Inside her writing desk, she found a stack of foolscap. She would write a short note to Jonathan and send
a footman to deliver the book. But when she sat down
to compose the note, she didn't know what to say.
Should she rail at him for deceiving her? Ignore their
past and wish him the best? Perhaps she should forgo
a message altogether since they no longer claimed a
connection. She was sure her mother would advise
her to do that very thing, but Eve felt coldhearted for
even considering it.

No matter what Jonathan had done, she cared for
him. He hadn't judged her like so many others had in
the past, and she wouldn't judge him now. Truthfully,
she was worried for him. Something in Jonathan's
expression the day he cried off had been haunted.
Even though Ben thought they should mind their
own affairs, she couldn't reconcile herself to ignoring
someone she cared about when he was in trouble.

Perhaps all Jonathan needed was a listening ear, and
even though she could not fulfill the role, she could
encourage him to seek out Lady Norwick's counsel.

"Blast," she muttered. A brief visit to his town
house would be more effective than a note sent with a
footman. Fortunately, she had his book to provide an
excuse for calling on him without an invitation.

Twenty-three

EVE SCOOTED TO THE EDGE OF THE CARRIAGE BENCH and peered through the window as the young footman she'd chosen to accompany her to Jonathan's home approached his door with her calling card. She would need new ones printed with her married name, but her old one would have to suffice for now.

Her heart sped as the footman knocked. Calling on her former betrothed was bold—an action she would never consider under normal circumstances—but she couldn't escape the gnawing sense something wasn't right with him. In all likelihood, she should forget about Jonathan and settle happily into her new life with Ben. Nevertheless, she was here. It was too late to retreat.

The battered door to Jonathan's town house creaked open and a manservant appeared.

"Mrs. Benjamin Hillary requests an audience with Sir Jonathan Hackberry, sir," the footman said, handing over her card.

Jonathan's man read it aloud. "Miss Eve Thorne." He craned his neck to see around the brawny young man and met her gaze.

Her face heated in response to his impertinent stare. She'd had no occasion to visit Jonathan at his home, although it seemed clear his man knew of her. He would have, given she had almost become mistress of the house.

"Sir Jonathan is abroad, but I will record the lady's inquiry in the guest book for when he returns."

Her breath caught. Jonathan was gone already? It had only been two days since their wedding was canceled. His rush to quit England only strengthened her feeling that something was wrong.

The footman thanked Jonathan's manservant, then turned back as the carriage door flew open. Eve squeaked in surprise as Viscount Margrave stuck his head inside. "Why, Mrs. Hillary. It is *you*. I recognized Ben's carriage and thought to surprise him."

The calculated gleam in his hazel eyes said otherwise. He hadn't expected to find Ben any more than she expected Margrave to mind his own affairs. A married lady rarely had cause to call on an old love, especially when her marriage was so new. Most likely, he thought he'd caught her planning a tryst with her former fiancé. She should have considered how presenting herself at Jonathan's door might look to others, but she had only been concerned for him.

Not one to play games or allow others to intimidate her, she regarded Ben's longtime friend sternly. "Well, you have certainly surprised *me*, Lord Margrave. Do you make a habit of leaping out at ladies and frightening them, or are you playing spy on my husband's behalf?"

A corner of his mouth lifted in a wry smile.

"You are too clever for your own good, madam. You've discovered my secret. I do enjoy frightening young ladies."

When she wrinkled her nose, he laughed and climbed into the carriage.

The footman appeared in the doorway, his jaw set in a hard line. "Milord, please exit the carriage. I did not hear Mrs. Hillary extend an invitation to join her."

Lord Margrave flicked an insolent glance at the servant. "Mr. Hillary will thank me for seeing her home, pup. Close the door."

She bristled at the viscount's arrogance, but the hard edge to his voice elicited a frisson of apprehension for the young man's well-being. Forcing a calm smile, she reassured the footman Lord Margrave's escort was welcome, then handed the book to him. "Please deliver this to Sir Jonathan's door. It belongs to him, and I would like to return it."

"Yes, ma'am." The young man directed a scowl at Lord Margrave before closing the door and granting her request.

"Ben always had a talent for determining which men would be loyal to him," the viscount said. "The pup has done him proud today."

She pursed her lips. "I should have allowed him to toss you out."

"You are too gracious to do any such thing."

"We all have our faults, my lord." She settled against the seat back as the servant returned to his station and the carriage pulled into the street.

Margrave studied her from the opposite seat with an expectant lift of his eyebrows.

"Not that it is any of your concern," she said, "but I intend to tell my husband about calling on Sir Jonathan. We keep no secrets between us."

"Admirable. In the future, might I suggest you consult your husband before venturing out alone?"

She smiled sweetly. "You may not."

Ben and Lord Margrave had been friends for many years, and she'd spent time in the viscount's company during her longer betrothal to Ben. Her husband did have a talent for attracting the most loyal men, and Margrave clearly considered himself charged with protecting Ben's interests.

"My husband does not keep me on a tether, and I am certain he has not asked you to guard me. There is no need for your escort."

It was a moot argument given the carriage was already rattling over the cobblestones en route to her new home, but she wanted to send the message that his high-handed manner was unappreciated.

Margrave smirked. "Perhaps he should. Keep you on a tether, that is. A young woman about Town alone can land in all sorts of trouble."

"I see your point," she drawled. "You, sir, are definitely bothersome."

He tossed his head back with a hearty laugh. She'd never heard him sound anything close to merry or amused. The sound was disarming, and her shoulders lost their stiffness before she realized what was occurring.

"I also suspect you might be charming on occasion," she mused.

"You caught me on a good day." His smile faded, and he leaned slightly toward her. "I meant what I said about you being clever, so I must believe this slight lapse in judgment will not be repeated. Stay away from Sir Jonathan if you value your reputation."

A small huff escaped her. The man was right, but she didn't appreciate him drawing attention to her mistake. "I've returned his book. I see no reason to call on him again. And I assure you there is no cause to doubt my faithfulness. I love my husband."

"I would never question your regard for Ben. You waited longer than most ladies would have for him." Lord Margrave eased back against the seat, the iciness in his eyes melting away. "He needs you, madam. After what happened with Charlotte... Well, I'm not certain he would recover if he lost you. Please do not do anything that could place you in harm's way."

His concern was out of proportion to the situation, but she nodded to appease him. He had been a good friend to Ben after Charlotte's accident. She couldn't be too harsh with him for wanting to protect Ben from future heartache.

"Thank you." The viscount rapped on the roof. The driver pulled to the curb and stopped. Apparently, now that Lord Margrave had delivered his lecture, he was ready to make his escape. "Good day, Mrs. Hillary. It was a pleasure to see you again."

"The pleasure was all mine," she muttered as he exited.

She didn't have long to contemplate his odd visit, or Jonathan's quick departure for lands unknown, before arriving home.

Dobbins met her at the door and took her hat and

gloves. "Mr. Hillary would like you to see him in his study, ma'am."

Her stomach dropped. He couldn't have heard of her visit to Jonathan's already. Trying to brush off her worry as ridiculous, she strolled toward his study with an air of nonchalance. Ben was behind his desk when she entered, his head bent over a ledger. His grandfather's portrait hung above the fireplace behind him, and she took a moment to study it. He'd been a handsome man even in his later years. The thought of watching Ben age as gracefully made her smile. She cleared her throat to gain his attention.

Ben's blue eyes crinkled at the corners when he looked up. "There you are. I hadn't expected to find you gone when I returned." He replaced the quill and pushed up from the chair to round his desk. "Were you paying calls?"

The full force of his smile made her pulse flutter. She didn't want to anger him by revealing where she had been, but she had vowed to always be honest with him.

"I paid one call, which reminded me that I need new calling cards printed." She didn't mean to hesitate, but she wanted to feel his welcoming embrace while he was still pleased with her.

Ben wrapped her in his arms and she laid her head against him. She loved when he held her close: the spicy scent of his cologne, the strong beat of his heart, the hard planes of his chest. He made her feel protected and cherished, which only served to make her feel rotten for having slipped off to see Jonathan without discussing it with him. She hadn't been in any physical danger—the notion was quite ludicrous, really—but Ben would see it as his duty to protect her reputation as well as her person, and she hadn't allowed him the opportunity to have his say in the matter.

"Mr. Davis will see to your cards," he said, "and you should provide him with a list of shops where you would like an account."

"I will." She eased from his embrace and sighed. "I've something to tell you, and I am uncertain how you will receive the news."

"Oh?" He leaned against his desk, crossing his legs at the ankles. "From your dire expression, I take it you expect I will be unhappy."

"There is no reason you should be, but I expect you might." She lowered into the chair in front of him and glanced up at him with a flirtatious tilt of her head. Her interest was in him alone, and she needed to let him know her excursion wasn't motivated by unresolved feelings for her former betrothed. "I went to see Sir Jonathan today."

A scowl appeared on Ben's handsome face. He crossed his arms and said nothing. The silence hung on the air, finally weighing on her until she couldn't bear it.

"Only to return a book he loaned me."

Ben's eyebrows lowered over his stormy blue eyes. His lips pressed together in a thin line, and he still didn't speak.

Eve clutched her hands in her lap, her heart beating ferociously. She would prefer a rant to this unnerving silence. "You might be pleased to know he wasn't home. He has already traveled abroad. It seems rather sudden, don't you agree?"

"I could have told you Sir Jonathan set sail already if you had asked." He sounded much calmer than she'd expected given his stern countenance. "I thought we agreed to allow Sir Jonathan his privacy."

She frowned. Her husband seemed to be purposefully obtuse when it came to Jonathan. Why couldn't he admit the circumstances surrounding Jonathan's departure were peculiar? "I am not convinced he truly wants us to stay out of his affairs. If he has fallen on hard times, he needs someone on his side. He has no family. I wish you would look into the matter."

Blood rose in his cheeks. "You seem uncommonly concerned for the man you *didn't* marry. I am beginning to wonder if you truly planned to end your betrothal with him after all."

"I did!" She shot to her feet. "I invited him to tea because I wanted to end our betrothal, and I would have if he had given me a chance." Her chin quivered as she fought to keep her composure. She was close to tears. Hot, angry ones.

"Lord, Evie. I don't want to quarrel with you." Ben pushed from the desk and opened his arms, but she shook her head and swiped at the traitorous tears as they slipped onto her cheeks.

"I do not want to argue either."

"I am allowing my jealousy to get the better of me. Forgive me?" When she didn't come to him, he came to her instead to gather her against him. "Please don't cry, love. It breaks my heart to know I am the cause."

She slid her arms around his waist and sank against

his chest. "You have no reason to feel jealous of anyone. You never have. I've loved you and no one else almost from the moment we met."

Tipping her chin up, he placed a soft kiss on her lips. "Likewise."

She scrunched her nose and glared at him.

"What did I say to earn that look?"

"Likewise?"

"Yes, Mrs. Hillary. Likewise." He dipped her backward so fast, she squealed. Cradling her back to support her weight, he leaned down until they were nose to nose. "I love you madly, deeply, and with every beat of my heart," he whispered, sending *her* heart into a gallop. "Is that better?"

"Y-yes," she said breathlessly. "It was very nearly perfect."

"So are you." And then he kissed her until she forgot why they were at odds.

Twenty-four

BEN FOUND IT DIFFICULT TO TAKE HIS EYES FROM EVE that evening at the pleasure gardens. Her skin glowed from the fresh air, and her smile dazzled. She was a vision in a rose silk gown that bordered on risqué for her. As they strolled through the Triumphal Arches with arms entwined, it seemed he wasn't alone in his admiration. He glowered at any man he caught ogling her, but he didn't dare make a comment about the scoundrels. He had depleted his quota for jealous snits earlier that day.

It was true her persistent concern for Sir Jonathan roused his envy, but her choice to visit his home was alarming. Even if Sir Jonathan was correct about Eve no longer being in danger now that he'd left England, Ben didn't want Eve to be discovered snooping. Nor did he want his wife moving about London without a proper escort, and the young footman Parker was not equipped to provide adequate protection against Sir Jonathan's unsavory associates.

"I don't want you leaving home without me until I have hired a man to watch over you. I will place an advertisement tomorrow."

"You want to place me under guard?" She halted in the middle of the path and turned to him in wide-eyed shock. "Because of today?"

Ben flinched as passersby slowed their steps and shot curious glances in their direction. "Lower your voice, dearling. Everyone does not need to know of our affairs."

She, too, seemed to notice they were drawing attention. "Then why bring it up now?" she asked in a fierce whisper. What a picture she presented: pert chin lifted in challenge, a spark of ire in her brown eyes.

A slow grin crossed his face. "Excellent point, my love. Shall we resume our conversation at a more appropriate time?" He offered his arm to suggest they continue their stroll, and she linked arms, her good-natured smile returning.

"I hope no one answers the advertisement for at least a fortnight. Then I will have you all to myself."

"You will always have me all to yourself, Evie." There would never be anyone else to turn his head. For two years, his feelings for her had only grown stronger, and now that she was his, he loved her with an intensity that frightened him. It made him yearn for her when they were apart and caused a physical ache deep in his bones. Uncomfortable with this newfound vulnerability, he changed the subject. "There are matters I need to see to, however, before we leave on a honeymoon trip."

She released a tiny squeak of excitement. "I cannot believe we are going to see the world."

"*Parts* of it." He chuckled, her enthusiasm pleasing

him to no end. "There are some places I'd rather not revisit, but I promised to take you wherever you like. Have you begun your list?"

"No, not yet. Have you?"

"I have destinations in mind, but I am most interested in fulfilling your wishes. We'll need to decide our final destinations soon so I can complete the necessary forms. You should plan to come with me to the ship to determine what items will be needed to make our quarters more comfortable. We can visit the docks this week."

He had already chosen his most seaworthy vessel and skilled captain for the voyage.

"Perhaps Amelia has suggestions," she said.

"I am certain Lisette could be of assistance too." Both of Ben's sisters-in-law had traveled with his brothers and would know how to help Eve prepare for life onboard ship. "You should invite them to tea. They will know what a lady's needs are onboard. I am afraid I will be of little help."

She beamed at him.

"What is it?" he asked. "What have I done to earn such a bright smile?"

"It sounds as if you've never traveled with a lady companion."

"I haven't. You, dearling, are my first."

Her cheeks glowed and she snuggled closer to his side. "And that is the reason you've earned my smile."

As they neared the supper boxes, Ben spotted Jake with his wife Amelia and Lord and Lady Norwick. He'd invited his brother, the earl, and their wives to join them for dinner, thinking Eve might appreciate the company of other ladies. She'd had no one to talk to besides her maid and him since the wedding breakfast.

"I see our guests have arrived," he said, gesturing toward the couples.

Eve flashed a smile at him. "I am so glad you thought to invite them."

The ladies greeted each other with kisses on the cheek before Amelia and Lady Norwick pulled Eve to a safe distance so as not to be overheard.

Jake crossed his arms and grinned. "You do realize they are talking about you."

"Yes, old boy," Norwick said with a chuckle, his stocky frame jostling. "Bianca leaves no stone unturned. Before the orchestra takes the stage, my wife will know every detail of the last twenty-four hours of your life."

Ben smirked. "If you think you two are being spared, you are fools. I'd wager they are comparing notes as we speak. Best of luck, gents."

"The best of…? Oh, hell." Norwick's round face turned crimson. "Must B discuss such things with her friends?"

Jake simply cocked an eyebrow, clearly unconcerned about the ladies' hushed conversation, then waved to someone behind Ben. "Here comes Margrave. I am surprised to see him here. The gardens seem too tame for a bachelor's tastes."

"I invited him." Ben spun on his heel to find Viscount Margrave sauntering their way. "He offered to make inquiries into Lord Wellham's whereabouts at the House of Lords today. It appears as if the earl vanished, but someone must know where he is."

"Is the blackguard still dodging you?" Norwick asked as he extracted a handkerchief from his jacket and wiped his sweaty forehead. "I told Bianca it would be too warm for the gardens tonight."

Ben frowned at the earl. "How do you know about Wellham?"

"I played hazard with him at the Den a few weeks ago. He said you were just back from Delhi and looking for him. He was three sheets to the wind and as chatty as an old crow. Said you were probably trying to call in his vowels. I haven't seen him since."

"He is avoiding me because of an old gambling debt?" Ben couldn't be certain he could even find any of the IOUs he'd collected when he used to frequent the gaming hells. He hadn't played for the money so much as the challenge. "I should thrash the unscrupulous bugger just for the principle of it when I find him."

Norwick shrugged. "You might have to wait your turn. It seems Wellham has fallen on hard times. I heard the duns have been sniffing around his town house, and he auctioned his best horse at Tattersall's last month. Bianca heard he left Town in the middle of the night to avoid everyone he owes money, but his sisters have no idea where he has gone. Apparently, he isn't staying at any of his properties."

Jake clapped Norwick on the shoulder. "Nice work."

"I still don't know where to find Wellham," Ben said.

"True, but you know why he has been hiding from you."

Margrave joined the group and without preamble

addressed Ben. "Take a walk with me? I'd like a word alone."

His friend had always been a private sort, but Ben had no objections to speaking in front of his brother and Lord Norwick. Nevertheless, he humored Margrave and fell into step with him on the path he and Eve had traveled earlier. The walkway was nearly deserted this time, and the sky had transformed into a series of orange brushstrokes on a faded gray canvas. A few bright stars pierced the sky.

"We shouldn't take long," Ben said. "Supper will be served soon." He had already spent enough time away from Eve that day. "Norwick just revealed Wellham has gone into hiding. Apparently he is avoiding collectors and thinks I am trying to speak with him about an old gambling debt he owes me that I couldn't care less about."

His friend nodded. "I see. Unfortunately, I wasn't able to attend the Lords today, so I have no leads on where he might be hiding. However, I wish to speak with you about Mrs. Hillary."

"What does my mother have to do with Wellham?"

Margrave ground to a stop and nailed him with an incredulous stare. "Mrs. Hillary, your *wife* of one day. Remember her? The pretty one with silky hair, sultry eyes, and curves that make a man—"

"Of course I remember my wife," he snapped. And he didn't like his friend noticing her finer qualities. "I'd suggest you forget about her eyes, and any other body parts you find appealing, unless you want to go a few rounds at Gentleman Jack's."

Margrave snorted. "We have been friends since

Eton. I have no designs on your wife, you fool. That doesn't mean I am blind, however, and neither are all the other men in Town, which is the reason you need to take her in hand."

"Take her in hand?" Fists formed at Ben's sides. He had never come to blows with his friend except in good fun, but Margrave was crossing a line. "You are the last person I would expect to dole out marriage advice. You've never had an affair lasting more than a night."

Margrave's chest puffed up like an officious toad, and he ignored Ben's jibe. "Do you have any idea where she was today?"

"She called on Sir Jonathan Hackberry and learned he has left England. What concern is it of yours?"

"Oh." The viscount blinked, his indignation leaving him in a rush of breath. "She told you."

"Of course she told me. I don't know what type of ladies you keep company with, but Eve does not hide things from me. She is aboveboard and always has been. How do you know she was there?"

"I saw your carriage on the street and stopped to chat with you, but your wife was alone. It isn't safe for her to move about Town without an escort, Ben."

The last thing Ben needed was Margrave's disapproving glower and lecture. He felt rotten enough about leaving his wife to her own devices when he should have been by her side today.

"I hope you will discourage her from venturing out on her own again," Margrave said.

"I already have. Now, if you are finished telling me how to be a good husband, I would like to return to the supper boxes and be one." Ben didn't wait to see if his friend agreed. He'd taken several steps down the path when Margrave called to him.

"I am only trying to help you see there are dangers lurking about."

Ben's heart stalled. He didn't need a reminder of all the horrible things that could befall her. Forgetting them so he could enjoy a moment of sanity was the challenge.

❧

Eve had been rather relieved when Lord Margrave didn't stay for supper. There was something unnerving about the man, and she could see the tension in Ben's face when he had returned from walking with the viscount. She assumed they had exchanged words. Probably about her.

Eve glanced at her husband's reflection in the looking glass of her dressing table. He was perched on the side of her bed, hands resting on his knees, distracted.

Opening a jar of lotion, she extracted a dollop and rubbed her hands together. "Did Lord Margrave tell you we ran into each other today?"

"Pardon?" Ben looked up, his blue gaze cloudy for a moment. "Oh. Yes, he mentioned seeing you."

When he said no more about it, she abandoned the topic. No need to stir up trouble where none existed. Something was preoccupying him, though. She rose from the dressing table and joined him on the side of the bed. "Is everything all right?"

He slanted a smile at her, but it didn't light his eyes like usual. "I have a few things on my mind. Business matters."

"I see. Is there any way I can help?"

He slipped his arm around her waist and shifted toward her. "You already are. I've quite lost my interest in business with you near." The wicked twinkle in his eyes caused a fluttering in her lower belly.

"Is…is that truly helpful? I thought it would be a hindrance."

He buried his fingers in her hair, cradling her nape. "You are never a hindrance, Evie. Sometimes I need to get away from my thoughts."

She closed her eyes as he kneaded her neck and reveled in the warmth spreading through her. "I know your thoughts trouble you sometimes. What is it that bothers you so?"

When he began to withdraw his hands, she opened her eyes. His puckered brow caused her heart to skip.

"Did I say something wrong?"

He shook his head, but leaned slightly away so there was space between their bodies. "I never said I was troubled by my thoughts."

"You didn't need to say it. I can see it in the lines of your face and the way you grind your teeth sometimes."

He drew back. "I do *not* grind my teeth."

The affronted pucker of his mouth made her chuckle. "Yes, you do. You've done it as long as I have known you."

"No one has ever said a word about it to me, and I've certainly never noticed."

"I notice most things about you. I find I cannot keep my eyes off you." She reached out to caress the muscles shifting along his jaw even now, and he leaned into her touch. "I'm afraid you are too handsome by half. It is a curse, really."

A laugh rumbled in his chest. He covered her hand with his. "A curse? How so?"

"Well," she said with a teasing smile, "it must be incredibly difficult to accomplish anything with ladies clamoring for your attention all the time and finding excuses to touch you."

Slipping her hand inside his satin robe, she demonstrated just how distracting it could be. She explored the hard contours of his muscles, her fingers playing with the light sprinkle of brown hair across his chest.

He captured her hand and brought it to his lips to place a kiss in her palm. His eyes had turned to that lovely smoky blue color they had been last night. "You are the only lady I want touching me."

She eased her hand free and slid it along his trim stomach. "Well, if I'm allowed to touch you, I want to touch you *now*."

"Oh, bother!" He rolled his eyes. "It's the bloody curse again." Grabbing her around the waist, he fell backward and dragged her on top of him.

She sat astride him and pushed the robe off his shoulders to marvel at his perfection. It wasn't that he was without blemish—he had two moles above his collarbone and a thick crimson scar on his bicep where a rope had burned the skin once onboard ship—but he was wonderfully formed, unlike other gentlemen who found work vulgar.

He propped his hands behind his head, his position submissive. His lazy grin invited her to explore at her leisure. It was hard to believe this amazing man was

hers to love, to care for and cherish forever. She had
seen the shadow of hurt in his eyes a moment ago, and
she wanted to ease his suffering.

Last night he had called out for Charlotte. Losing
her had to be one of the most painful moments in his
life, and yet he had only spoken of her once in Eve's
presence. He had recited the facts of her accident as
if reading an account in the newssheet. Then he had
thanked Eve for her expression of sympathy before
shrugging off the effect his first love's death must have
had on him.

If his memories of Charlotte were haunting him,
she wished he would confide in her. But she didn't
know how to broach the subject without causing him
more distress if that wasn't the source of his pain.

Cupping his face, she leaned close to kiss him softly.
She poured tenderness into the kiss, communicating
with him in a way words never could. She offered him
compassion, healing, or peaceful oblivion if only for a
moment. Anything he needed was his.

He moaned against her mouth. "Evie."

Rolling her beneath him, he took his time undressing her. Their lovemaking was slow and beautiful,
made up of lingering caresses and whispered oaths to
love one another forever.

Twenty-five

BEN WAS SHRUGGING INTO HIS JACKET WHEN THE doors between his and Eve's chambers flew open. His wife's glower didn't surprise him, but her grumpiness struck him as rather adorable when paired with her mussed hair and drowsy eyes.

"You left my bed again."

The accusation in her tone didn't catch him off guard either. In spite of her sweet nature, he had expected her to kick up a fuss.

She yawned, rubbing the sleep from her eyes with her fist while clutching her dressing gown closed. "Why did you sneak off?"

"I couldn't sleep." He turned his back to retrieve his watch from a side table so she wouldn't see the evidence of the blush rushing into his face. Last night, he couldn't stop Margrave's words from echoing in his head: *There are dangers lurking about.*

Catastrophic possibilities had plagued him the moment he'd snuffed the candles and her fragile body snuggled against his. Dangers were *everywhere*: the stairway, a kitchen fire, a fall from her horse, ne'er-do-wells on the streets. When he thought of her leaving the protection of his arms, nausea welled up inside him, leaving a sour taste at the back of his tongue. It was insanity. He knew it, but he had been powerless to stop the thoughts that bombarded him in the dark. It was humiliating to admit he'd needed to light a lamp before he could corral his worries.

Tucking his watch into a waistcoat pocket, he faced her again. "I didn't want to wake you, so I retired to my room."

"You *should* have woken me." She came forward to wrap her arms around his waist, laying her head on his shoulder. "I would have sat up with you."

Ben hugged her close. "But you shouldn't have to. If you sat up with me every time I can't sleep, you would never feel rested."

She pulled back enough to see his face. "Is that how you feel? Never rested?"

"I have learned to adjust."

"Hmm… I suspect I will adjust too." Her smile warmed his heart. She would likely be a welcome source of comfort, but he wouldn't wake her. "What keeps you from being able to sleep?"

He shrugged. This morning his worries seemed silly. "Different things."

"Very well. What kept you awake *last* night?"

"I don't know. I'm sure it was nothing." He smiled gamely, hoping she would not pursue it any further.

"Good Lord!" Her eyes widened in horror. "Do I snore?" This last was whispered as if it would bring shame on her entire family line if it were true.

He chuckled. "No, but you kick." That was not a lie. Even when asleep, she had boundless energy.

She wrinkled her nose. "Oh, that is not well done of me, is it?"

"You don't kick hard. Just enough to get my attention." Smoothing back her riotous hair, he kissed her forehead.

"I'm sorry," she said. "In the future, I will try to be more aware."

He eased her from his embrace. "Maybe it would be best if we stayed in separate bedchambers until I am sleeping better. Then I won't disturb you."

"I see." Her tone did not imply consent, but they could talk about it later. She stepped back, looked him over from head to toe, and pursed her lips. "You are already dressed for the day. Am I to assume you have a morning appointment?"

"Perhaps," he said with a teasing smile. "If you agree to join me for breakfast and a ride through the park."

Eve's forehead smoothed out and her mouth turned up at the corners. "That sounds lovely. I will ring for Alice."

"Very good. Come find me in my study when you are ready to go to the breakfast room."

When Eve joined him below stairs, she wore a smart yellow walking gown that was overshadowed by her sunny smile. Warmth expanded in his chest when she linked arms with him and chattered all the way to the breakfast room.

As instructed, the footman had placed her close to his end of the table, and the newssheet was waiting beside his plate. Eve snatched it before moving to her seat.

Ben pushed in her chair and leaned over her shoulder. "You stole my paper, dearest."

She slanted a glance in his direction, her brown eyes big and guileless. "Oh, I did not see your name on it. Would you like to share it?"

"Don't play innocent with me, Kitten." He tweaked her nose, then retrieved the newssheet before sitting in his chair. "What part would you like to read first?"

"The gossip, of course," she said.

"I thought you abhorred gossipmongers."

"I do, but I would like to know when they are talking about me so I'm not caught unaware."

Ben frowned as he opened the newssheet and turned to the gossip pages. He didn't like the reminder that he had dragged her name through the muck in the past. Other than a tidbit about his and Eve's marriage the day after their wedding, there had been nothing else printed about them in the gossip rags. He scanned the pages. "Not one mention of you today. I hate to admit it, but I expected more attention for our sudden marriage. I am a little disappointed we are not considered important enough." He closed the newssheet and returned it to the table with a wink for her.

Eve smiled and unfolded her napkin. "Sebastian said he has a new contact that will keep our names out of the papers. I thought he was trying to make me feel better, but it seems he was telling the truth."

"Bravo, Lord Thorne." He nodded to the footman to begin serving them.

"What parts do you like to read?" she asked.

"I follow the arrival and departure of ships. What

cargo they are carrying. The captain responsible for seeing it safely into port. The list of passengers."

She lifted her fork and gingerly poked at the soft-boiled egg in the eggcup. "I was thinking about what you said regarding needing to know our destinations to file the appropriate papers. Does that mean you know Sir Jonathan's destination?"

Her question slammed into his gut. Her insistent inquiries about the man rubbed him the wrong way. "The ship will deliver her cargo to Morocco, then it is Sir Jonathan's decision where he travels next." He shot a glance toward the footman. "You are dismissed, Parker."

"Yes, sir." The young man made a hasty exit, perhaps sensing Ben's mounting aggravation.

Eve, however, seemed oblivious. "But how can he travel without the proper documents?"

"The captain will see to everything." Tightness spread along his jawline, but it didn't keep him from voicing his frustrations. "Must you bring up your former betrothed at every opportunity? How would you like me speaking of a past love to you?"

She set her fork on her plate and folded her hands in her lap. "Sir Jonathan was never my love. He was a kind man who wished to marry me, and I agreed because he was pleasant and I want a family someday. But most significantly, I had given up hope of you coming back. *You* were my first choice, and if I'd had any clue you were on a ship headed for England, I wouldn't have encouraged his attentions. Furthermore, if you want to talk about Charlotte, I will listen with the utmost patience. Your feelings for her have never threatened me."

He flinched at hearing Charlotte's name. No one spoke of her to him anymore. Not his family. Not even his closest friend acknowledged her. It was as if everyone thought Ben might crumple into a pathetic heap on the ground if they did, or else they had forgotten she ever lived. It seemed Eve was the only one to believe he had the strength to remember her.

His wife stared back at him, waiting. Her eyes overflowed with compassion.

He swallowed around the lump in his throat. "Thank you, but it was long ago. I would rather not talk about her—Charlotte." Opening the paper to block his view of Eve's disappointed face, he tried to lose himself in a familiar routine, but the print jumbled together so he couldn't make sense of the words.

Her sigh was pregnant with resignation, and his spine began to lose its rigidness. She was abandoning the topic. As he sank against the seat back, she stood. Her fingers curled around the edge of the newssheet and slowly drew it down. The paper rustled as the top half buckled under the pressure of her hand. "Pardon me," she said ever so politely. "Please forgive my interruption, but I had hoped we might continue our conversation."

His sigh came out as more of a growl, but she merely batted her lashes and smiled. He folded the newssheet and placed it on the table. "Do you truly want to listen to me speak about another woman? A girl, really. We were both children."

"Seventeen and fifteen. On the cusp of adulthood, and certainly capable of love." She lowered to her chair, her gaze searching.

His face heated under her scrutiny. Did she know about his nightmares?

"As you say, a young man can love," he said, halting to sip his tea and gather his thoughts. "In my youth, love was a quickening of my heart or a rush of joy upon seeing Charlotte's face. It was thrilling and consuming. It made me believe forever was a real possibility, as if Charlotte and I would stay the same always."

Eve's gaze lowered and he could hear her swallow. He shifted toward her, worried he'd said something to hurt her. "I remember," she murmured. "I thought the same about you and me."

He reached for her hand and she looked up, lacing her fingers with his. "My heart still pounds when I see you, Evie. You thrill me and consume my thoughts, but my love for you is different. At fifteen, I barely knew myself. I couldn't see that a part of me was missing, much less what I would need to make me feel whole once I became a man. But I found it. I need *you*."

Fat tears clung to her lashes. She smiled and squeezed his hand. "I need you too."

"Perhaps you can understand the reason I don't want to dwell on the past—yours or mine. I finally have you, and I don't want anything interfering with our life together."

"Neither do I." She dabbed at her eyes with her napkin. "Very well. No more talking of Sir Jonathan or Charlotte. Besides, I would rather focus on our future, starting with our honeymoon. Sebastian enjoyed Lisbon. Would that be a good place to start?"

"I think it would be a perfect spot. I've always been

fond of Toulon, so we should plan a stay there as well. Then we could dock in Naples next."

"What about Rome? Since we will be in the vicinity…"

Ben happily returned to his breakfast as they exchanged thoughts on their trip. "Most definitely a visit to Rome is in order. It would be a crime to miss out on the history the city has to offer."

❧

Eve tried to be a gracious hostess to Ben's sisters-in-law the next day, but she found her mind wandering as they spoke about a previous voyage they had shared from America. Lisette could boast the most experience onboard ship since her husband was a captain—or Daniel had been before he'd settled into a more domesticated life—and Eve was sure she should take note of the woman's suggestions, but all she could think on was Ben.

After their candid conversation at breakfast and a lovely turn around the park in the curricle yesterday, she had expected he would wake her if he had another difficult night, but he didn't. This morning she woke to blinding sunlight streaming through the windows and no husband in her bed.

She'd confronted him on his failure to wake her, and he insisted he did not intend to bother her in the middle of the night. She had never realized how headstrong he could be. Worse than not waking her, he'd brought up sleeping in separate rooms again.

"Sweet Mary," Lisette said in her thick Creole accent. "What has he done?"

Eve blinked. "Pardon? What has who done?"

Amelia smiled kindly, her most unusual blue eyes sympathetic. "She means Ben, dearest."

Lisette and Amelia exchanged a knowing glance.

Eve looked from one lady to the other. "What did that look mean? You seem to know something I do not."

"You seem flustered this afternoon," Amelia said. "And any time Lisette or I find ourselves in a bewildered state, usually a Hillary man is responsible."

Eve sat up straight. "Is that true? Do you have trouble understanding Ben's brothers?"

The ladies laughed.

Amelia winked over the rim of her teacup. "They are a complicated lot, aren't they?"

"And mulish," Lisette piped up. "Once Daniel gets an idea in his head, it would be easier to change the position of the North Star than to change his mind." She grinned. "Of course, he would say I am twice as stubborn, and he might be right."

It was difficult to believe either lady had trying moments with their husbands. They both seemed very content, and Eve had seen their husbands dote on them. In fact, Jake seemed uncommonly attentive to Amelia any time Eve had been in their presence. Her worries receded a bit.

Perhaps Amelia and Lisette faced similar issues as new brides and had either found ways to adjust or bring their husbands around to their way of thinking. Eve hoped for the latter. Her gaze shot back and forth between her visitors as she debated the wisdom in broaching such a personal topic. She needed to talk with someone, however, and confiding in her brother's wife would be too mortifying to bear, even if Helena was a dear friend.

Amelia set her cup and saucer on the low table in front of the settee. "You needn't be afraid to speak freely, Eve."

Her reassurance didn't keep Eve's stomach from churning. Lisette regarded her kindly with her exotic green eyes.

Eve took a cleansing breath then blurted, "Ben thinks we should sleep in separate beds." She winced. It was twice as embarrassing saying it aloud.

When she glanced up, her companions' regarded her in stunned silence. Lisette's jaw had dropped. Fire engulfed her and a light dampness blanketed her body.

"He suffers from insomnia," Eve said, "and he doesn't want to disturb me. And I'm certain he has bad dreams. I realize he is trying to be courteous, but I am his *wife*. I want to help him, even though he thinks he doesn't need it. Have you dealt with anything similar in your marriages?"

Amelia blinked several times then looked toward Lisette with her elegant eyebrows raised in question. Lisette's head shake was nearly imperceptible.

Splendid. Absolutely wonderful. Eve was alone in this one. "I am likely making too much of a small matter. Perhaps I should just allow him what he wants. I don't like quarreling with him."

"Oh, Eve." Amelia left her seat to perch on the arm of Eve's chair and hugged her. "You know Ben better than either of us. If your intuition is telling you he needs your help, you must trust it. Please be patient with him, though, and do not give up. It might take some time for him to realize he isn't alone anymore and doesn't have to face his troubles alone."

Eve saw no choice but to keep trying. She had learned from watching her parents attempt to cope with Papa's problems that loneliness and despair were the result of going it alone. She hoped Ben would come to realize they were stronger and more capable of overcoming obstacles together. And if he couldn't reach this conclusion on his own, she did not mind giving him a gentle push. In fact, he might need a nudge in that direction tonight.

Twenty-six

BEN FOLDED THE LETTER HE'D RECEIVED FROM
Charlotte's brother that afternoon and dropped it
on the side table as he began to prepare for bed. Mr.
Davis, his man of business, had composed a letter on
Ben's behalf last week, while he had been focused
on courting Eve, requesting Ben be allowed to pay
the Tanneys' rent before they were evicted. Ben had
already written twice since his return to England
with similar offers, and her brother politely declined
each time.

When Ben learned Charlotte's brother was on the
verge of losing the bakery in Eton and that Robert
Tanney and Charlotte's mother might be evicted,
he'd wanted to help. If he and Charlotte had success-
fully eloped as they'd planned, the Tanneys would be
his kin, and he wouldn't allow any of his family to
go without their basic needs being met. In fact, he
preferred the Tanneys do more than just survive. He
wanted to see them enjoy a certain level of comfort he
could easily provide.

Since he hadn't been able to purchase the building

from Wellham like he'd wanted, he thought perhaps an appeal from a stranger would make it easier for Robert to save his pride and accept help. Unfortunately, Ben's man of business hadn't been any more successful than he had.

Robert had returned the banknote with a strongly worded refusal. *With all due respect, Mr. Hillary's assistance is neither wanted nor required.* Ben could hear the disdain in the man's letter. It had the same scornful tone Charlotte's father had used when Ben tried to pay his respects at their home after her death.

A soft knock sounded at the doors between his and Eve's chambers. He turned with an expectant smile as his wife entered in her night rail. It was a sweet cotton ensemble with a high collar and lacy ruffles made for sleeping rather than seduction. "Come to say good night, love?" he asked. He expected he wouldn't be able to fall asleep any time soon since he would be wrestling with what to do about Charlotte's family now. He was pleased Eve had agreed to sleep in separate chambers.

She approached and lifted to her toes to kiss him. Her hands rested lightly on his shoulders as her lips pressed to his. Her mouth was moist, warm, and inviting. He encircled her waist and held her close when she would have pulled away. Deepening the kiss, he teased her lips with the tip of his tongue. She eagerly opened to him, entwining her arms around his neck and pressing her body against his. He delighted in her sweet sighs and the shivers running down his back where she played with the hair brushing the collar of his dressing gown. When he pulled away, they both were slightly breathless.

"Stay with me?" he whispered.

A dazzling smile swept across her full lips. "That is why I am here, dear husband." She dropped her arms from around his neck and eased from his embrace. Tossing another flirtatious smile over her shoulder, she moved toward the bed. She kicked off her slippers, climbed under the covers, and leaned against the pillows. Her chin lifted in challenge. "I am staying the night with you. The whole night, as in *sleeping* in your bed."

His body tensed. That wasn't his meaning, and she knew it. "We already had this discussion. For now, it is best for you to sleep in your chambers, and I will sleep in mine. There is no sense in you losing sleep too."

"No, you had this conversation while I listened. It is my turn to talk. While you might think you are showing me a kindness, in reality you are creating distance between us. I realize you don't see it yet, but I do. Amelia advised me to be patient and persistent, so I—"

"God's blood, Eve! Don't tell me you spoke with Amelia and Lisette about this." His brothers would give him hell once they heard he'd suggested separate bedchambers. He drove his shaky fingers through his hair and stormed to the other side of the room to put distance between them. "I cannot believe you would humiliate me that way."

"If it is any comfort, I humiliated myself too." When he turned to argue, he expected to find her glowering or at least with her hands on her hips, but she wasn't. Her head was tilted at a contemplative angle, as if trying to sort him out. "I didn't intend to embarrass either of us," she said in a small voice. "I only wanted to talk with someone, and I didn't know where else to go."

Splendid. He'd brought this on himself. And now he wouldn't be able to look Daniel or Jake in the eye. "If you wanted to talk, you could have come to me."

"Could I? I get the sense you would prefer I not."

He sighed in exasperation toward the ceiling. He didn't have the wherewithal to reason with her. "Tomorrow," he said, looking at her. "We will discuss it tomorrow. Is that acceptable?"

"Yes, tomorrow sounds reasonable." Lifting the covers, she wiggled down in the bed until her head was on the pillow and the counterpane reached her neck.

"What are you doing?"

"Going to sleep." She closed her eyes with a self-satisfied smile.

His tension doubled. He approached, tossing his hands in the air for emphasis. "You are in *my* bed."

She opened one eye. "We will discuss it tomorrow, remember?"

"Eve."

She yawned, loudly. "Excuse me, but I'm done in to a cow's thumb. Forgive me if I am asleep before you crawl in."

She closed her eyes while Ben stood beside the bed, befuddled. When had his sweet, amenable wife become so tenacious?

As he stood there waiting for her to respond to his hovering, her chest began to rise and fall with steady regularity. Her face took on a soft innocence that chipped at his frustration. She was asleep already. And she looked so warm and inviting. Longing tugged at his heart. If he couldn't sleep, he supposed he could retreat to his study below stairs or her chambers where he wouldn't disturb her. Would he ever be able to maintain his resolve when it came to her?

Making a decision, he ripped off his dressing gown and climbed under the covers, turning on his side facing away from her. It wasn't well done of him, but he was annoyed with himself for giving in so easily. She rolled toward him to fit her smaller frame to his and snaked her hand under his arm to rest it on his chest.

"I am still in a temper," he lied, not even feeling as irritated with himself anymore now that her comforting softness was pressed against him.

"I know," she murmured. "I'm sorry."

Her answer made him smile. She wasn't sorry to have him wrapped around her finger. No more sorry than he was to be driven to please her. Raising her hand to his lips, he placed a kiss on her warm fingers. "Good night, Kitten."

Then, to his surprise, oblivion was claiming him as well.

                             *

Eve was jerked out of sleep by a gut-wrenching keen. She bolted upright in bed, her heart battering her ribs. Ben thrashed beside her. The sound was coming from him.

"Ben, wake up." She grabbed his shoulder and

tried to shake him awake, but he remained lost in his dreams. "Wake up, love. You are dreaming."

His wail quieted to an occasional whimper that tore her heart to pieces.

She smoothed the hair from his damp forehead as tears sprang to her eyes. "It's all right, my love. It is only a dream." The mournful sound eventually died away, but he remained restless. Stretching out beside him, she continued to whisper soothing words and doling out caresses until he began to settle. His dream didn't wake him as it had on their wedding night, and he didn't call out this time, but she couldn't help wondering if he dreamed about Charlotte again.

Even after his breathing returned to normal and he rested peacefully, she stroked his head and placed loving kisses at his temple. "I love you," she whispered. "So very much."

She couldn't bear knowing he suffered in any way. She would carry the burden for him if it were possible rather than endure the sense of helplessness she experienced.

He was lying on his back, and she snuggled against his chest, placing his arm around her. Her hand splayed over his heart to feel its steady, robust rhythm. She could feel the strength of his heartbeat and the firmness of his chest beneath her cheek. Her husband was a strong man, built of brawn, but there was a vulnerability to him she hadn't suspected. And she loved him more than ever in that moment.

Perhaps these nightmares were the true reason he left her bed at night, but why would he feel he had to keep this locked away and hidden?

Whatever his motive, she wouldn't mention tonight's incident. She was afraid if he knew, he would use it as an excuse to push her away, and truth be told, she couldn't stand any more distance between them. His self-imposed exile to India had been brutal for Eve, but nothing was lonelier than having the man she loved within arm's length and still being unable to reach the place of exile in his mind.

Early morning light had begun to filter through the sheer curtains at the window before she fell asleep again. It seemed only moments had passed when Ben gently jostled her awake, but the room was aglow. She squinted against the brightness. "What time is it?" She sounded like an old toad.

Ben smiled and kissed her cheek. She caught a whiff of tooth powder on his breath. "It's early still," he said, "but I did not want to leave without saying good-bye."

She groaned, rolled on her side, and pulled the covers over her head. Another long day at home dragged out before her.

He chuckled and patted her bottom. "I won't be going far—only to my study. I am interviewing footmen, and then I have an appointment. This afternoon we will take a trip to the docks so you can see where we will be living for the next few months."

Eve tossed the covers aside in her excitement. "Ben, why didn't you say something last night? Alice will be in a dither if she hasn't enough time to make everything perfect. She says it is a reflection on her."

She scrambled from bed and swept toward her chambers to ring for her maid.

"You may extend my apologies to Alice," he called after her. "Tell her to choose something sensible, for it is likely to get dirty at the docks."

She paused at the adjoining doors and aimed a cheeky grin at him. "A small tip about women, my love. Telling them what to do is an exercise in futility."

"Yes, I have firsthand knowledge," he drawled. It was nice to see his good humor had returned this morning. He gave her a little wave, and she disappeared into her chambers.

After having breakfast in her chambers and attending to her correspondence, Eve decided to wait for Ben in the library below stairs.

Dobbins exited Ben's study as she reached the ground floor. "Mr. Hillary will see you now," he said.

She startled at his formal manner until she realized a man was standing in the foyer. Curious, she took his measure as he crossed to Ben's study. The man was certainly tall enough to be a footman—over six feet—but he was willowy like a woman, although his weathered face was far from feminine. How odd that a man his age would answer the advertisement for a fourth footman. Surely if he had been in service long, he would have been promoted. He disappeared into the study.

"Dobbins, is that man here for the footman position?"

"No, ma'am. Mr. Gilroy is from Bow Street." Her shock must have shown on her face, because the butler rushed to explain. "There is not a problem. Mr. Hillary is hiring him to look into a matter for him. That is all."

Ben was hiring an investigator from Bow Street? "What matter would that be, Dobbins?"

The servant's craggy face blazed red. "I am afraid I cannot say, ma'am. Mr. Hillary does not make me privy to his business."

"Of course, I was not thinking." She offered an apologetic smile. She hadn't meant to make Dobbins feel uncomfortable. "Please inform my husband that I am waiting for him in the library once his meetings are finished."

She could think of only one reason Ben was hiring an investigator. He was looking into matters with Jonathan as she'd requested. Her step was livelier as she retired to the library. Despite her husband's protests that they mind their own affairs, he thought there was something strange about Jonathan too. Well, she could rest easier knowing everything was in his hands now.

Twenty-seven

EVE HAD NEVER BEEN TO THE DOCKS. SHE GAWKED AT everything, not knowing which way to look next. She swung her head toward the massive rows of warehouses lined up like disciplined soldiers on her right then back to the enormous ships moored to her left until she felt a little dizzy. She counted eight of the floating giants on this stretch of the river, although Ben said the docks could accommodate three hundred ships. That many ships in one area were inconceivable to her.

The docks were much more orderly than she had anticipated. When she had first heard about the ruffians and thieves who frequented this seedy area of London, she had been sufficiently frightened, which she supposed was her mother's intention. Mama had warned her away from visiting Ben at the docks when they were betrothed. Eve had never been one to take unnecessary risks, so the lecture had been senseless, but it made Mama feel better.

Dock laborers—rough-looking men with faces tanned and weathered like animal hides—cut in front of them with creaky carts headed toward a warehouse. Ben pulled her to a stop.

She glanced around while they waited for the men to pass. "Where is Hillary Shipping?"

"In Wapping, close to the Pool," Ben said, smiling down at her. "Our grandfather started his business there. Even though most of Daniel's ships arrive and depart from the West India docks, and the bulk of mine must go through the East docks, we never moved the office. Daniel thought it would be bad luck."

"Is it far? I would like to see it."

"I'm afraid it is no place for a lady."

She refrained from rolling her eyes. "I am with my overprotective husband. I'll be perfectly safe. I want to see your office."

He slanted a long-suffering glance at her. "Lord save me if you refused to take no for an answer."

"What is that supposed to mean?" She faced him with her hands on her hips.

He grinned and tweaked her nose. "It means I'm almost powerless to deny you anything."

"*Almost?* It sounds like I need to work harder," she teased.

Once the path was clear, they continued along the quay, joking with one another and chatting about this part of Ben's life she wanted to know better.

"You share Hillary Shipping with Jake too," she said. "Does he keep ships?"

Ben shook his head and drew her protectively under his arm to wait as another set of men rolled barrels down a gangplank. "Jake advises us on legal issues that arise, and he plays nice with members of

Parliament who start squawking about sponsoring legislation that could interfere with business."

"It sounds as if he was saddled with the least desirable tasks."

"Out of necessity. He is the only one of us with enough patience to deal with the windbags."

She smiled. Jake had likely developed the ability to navigate strong personalities at a young age. How else was he to survive his three older brothers?

Through a gap between ships, she spotted a rowboat with five men in the main channel of the Thames. They pushed the oars through the murky water with brute strength to make the boat inch up river. The River Thames was always in motion—a living entity that slithered through London like a cunning serpent. She shivered and returned her attention to the ships.

"Are you cold?" Ben drew them to a stop to shrug off his jacket.

"No, I'm fine."

Despite her reassurance, he draped the garment over her shoulders. She grabbed for her bonnet, holding it down as the breeze along the quay jerked at the brim. Ben brushed aside a strand of hair that flew in her eyes.

"I have never been fond of the river," she admitted.

"You are not afraid of the water, are you? Many people are. We will be at sea for days on end. Will it bother you?"

She scrunched her nose and laughed at herself again. "I'm not afraid of the water. I can swim, at least a little. It is the river. It reminds me of a giant snake."

Ben lifted an eyebrow and his lips twitched in mirth. "My, you *are* fanciful today, Mrs. Hillary."

"I am fanciful every day, Mr. Hillary, but I typically keep my thoughts to myself."

"Well, I do hope you plan to abandon the habit of keeping your thoughts a secret. I love the way your mind works. Here she is." He swept a hand toward the gangplank the men had used to disembark the ship. "My pride and joy, the *Eve Lorraine*."

Her eyes flew open wide. "You named a ship for me?"

"Of course I did. Every gentleman christens at least one ship for his beloved."

The sight of his loving smile paired with the most romantic gesture she could have imagined caused her heart to nearly burst with happiness.

"I'm anxious for you to see her." He stepped onto the gangplank and held out his hand. "Shall we?"

She nodded, too overcome to speak. Placing her hand in his, she allowed him to lead her onboard ship—her *namesake*. Chills raced down her back.

Ben identified different parts of the ship as they crossed the deck. "The cabin under the half deck serves as temporary accommodations for important guests," he said as they reached a solid door with an iron handle.

"Will important passengers be traveling with us?"

He grinned. "None as important as the owner's wife. This will be our cabin during the voyage." Tugging the door, he directed her inside to a space larger than she had expected.

Eve looked around with an assessing eye. It had small windows along the sides of the cabin, which kept it from feeling like a tomb, and it boasted a plush bed, but she would want the coverlet from her bedchamber at home and extra pillows. There was also a small space for a dressing table to be placed next to the washstand, which she would need. "The cabin is already well appointed. I cannot think of much more we should need." She spun toward him to find him watching her with twinkling eyes. "You have been busy, Mr. Hillary."

He shrugged in a modest gesture that endeared him to her. "It is only the basics. We won't set sail for another two weeks. That should give you enough time to outfit our cabin to your specifications. The lighting is fair, but if you prefer more for reading, you may visit the great cabin during the day."

"What a lovely suggestion. I will visit the book-shop before we leave." She pulled a piece of foolscap from her reticule and helped herself to the quill and ink on a desk in the corner before scribbling "books" on her list. "Where will my maid sleep?" Alice had surprised and pleased Eve by expressing her wish to travel with them. At once, Eve had abandoned plans to hire a younger lady's maid to accompany her on the trip.

"There is a cabin on the deck below where she should be comfortable if you would like to see it."

"Yes, I want to make her quarters as comfortable as possible." Her loyal maid deserved a few comforts at her age and after her unwavering kindness during Ben's absence.

Once they had toured Alice's cabin and the great room, they returned to their cabin so Eve could look around once again and add more items to her list. Ben lounged at the desk with his foot propped over his knee and allowed her as much time as she liked.

Once she felt confident she hadn't missed anything, she folded the foolscap, tucked it into her reticule, and issued a contented sigh. "I'm eager for our trip. Are you certain we must wait two weeks?"

He flinched. "Yes, about that… I have something I would like to discuss with you." Standing, he waved toward the chair. "Would you like to sit?"

Her heart gave a little flip when he regarded her with such a grim expression. She did as he requested, settling her skirts around her, but she didn't know what to do with her hands all of a sudden. They fluttered for a moment before she forced them to be still, folded them on her lap, and tipped up her head to meet his gaze. "What is it you would like to discuss?"

She hoped it wasn't more of that nonsense about sleeping alone. They hadn't discussed anything further this morning, and she would rather they forget about the entire affair. She certainly had no plans to sleep alone onboard ship.

∼

Ben propped on the edge of the desk, wondering if he was doing the right thing by considering delaying their departure until he had settled things with Charlotte's family. He didn't want her misinterpreting his need to help the Tanneys, but it felt wrong to leave England without seeing to their welfare. Eve had sworn she never felt threatened by Charlotte, but he didn't want her believing he hadn't let go of his first love. His heart belonged to Eve and had for a very long time.

Nibbling her bottom lip, she lifted her gaze and his heart expanded until it felt too full for his chest. He leaned forward to kiss away her worries. Her plump mouth moved in unison with his, and he was tempted to abandon the topic for another time, but he wouldn't. It was best to have the matter in the open.

He reluctantly broke the kiss and sat up. "At breakfast the other day, you invited me to talk about Charlotte. Although there is nothing more to say about our time together, I must do something for her family before we travel abroad."

"Very well." Eve's open expression and unquestioning acceptance eased his concern that she might misunderstand his motivations. "What can I do to assist?"

A relieved smile spread across his face. "Nothing at the moment, but I might need to travel to Eton before we set sail. There is a chance it won't be necessary if I can connect with the Earl of Wellham, but he has been a hard man to find."

Because he could see the confusion in the furrowing of her brow, he started telling his story from the beginning of his campaign to save the Tanneys' bakery. "When I returned to London, I sent a man to inquire after Charlotte's family. I've kept abreast of them over the years. It is just something I felt I needed to do."

Eve reached for his hand and threaded their fingers together. "You still care about the Tanneys."

He shook his head. "It has never been like that for us. Charlotte's family was pleased when I started showing interest in her, but after her death, her father blamed me. I doubt they care if I live or die, but I made promises to Charlotte. I promised to take care of her and her family, and I need to keep my word."

Eve rose from the chair, then sat on the edge of the desk beside him. She stroked his back, her nails lightly scratching through his waistcoat. "Mr. Tanney was wrong. You didn't cause her death. You realize this, don't you?"

"I do." On some level, this was true. He hadn't caused Charlotte's accident directly, but he bore some responsibility. "Come here."

He widened his stance, and Eve moved to stand between his legs. She twined her arms around his neck and pressed a sweet kiss to his cheek.

His hands spanned her waist and instead of the past flashing through his mind, he saw his future—the children Eve would bear him, the happy home they would have together, a lifetime of laughter and love. He needed to do this one thing for Charlotte's family, so he could embrace the life he had been given with Eve.

"What did your man learn about the Tanneys?" she asked.

"Her father died while I was in Delhi. Pneumonia. Charlotte's brother inherited the bakery, but it seems his father had fallen on hard times and Robert Tanney hasn't been able to make a go of it. He is behind on rent, and the Tanneys will be evicted by the end of the month."

"Couldn't you settle the debt for Charlotte's brother?" There was no hesitation in her response. To Eve, it was natural that he would pay the Tanneys' debts, even if it possibly meant less in the coffers for her.

Pulling her close, he brushed a kiss across her cheek. "God, I love you. How is it you can be kind and understanding about this?"

"It is easy when I have everything. My life is rich. I can afford to show a little kindness to others."

He held on, resting his cheek lightly on the top of her bonnet. His life was richer than he had ever hoped, but he constantly wrestled with the fear he could lose it all in a blink. He should embrace happiness as easily as his wife, but he didn't know how.

"I tried to assist Mr. Tanney as you suggested, but he has refused every offer of assistance," he said. "I understand that he has his pride, but I can't allow him to lose the bakery and end up on the streets. Charlotte's mother is already in poor health. My second thought was to purchase the property from Lord Wellham and forgive the debt, but as I said, he has taken off to regions unknown. I met with an investigator this morning to make one last attempt to find the earl, but I am not counting on success."

Eve played with the hair at his nape, and he closed his eyes to savor the tingles generated by her touch. "That explains the Runner I saw earlier. I thought you were hiring him to look into the situation with Sir Jonathan." When his eyes widened, she held up a hand to stop his chastisement. "I will not say anything more about it, I promise. If he said he wants to keep us out of his private affairs, who am I to argue? Perhaps Lady Norwick knows why he was behaving so oddly before he left. Maybe she knows some of his associates and could question them."

He couldn't allow her to involve Lady Norwick

or pursue this any further, no matter what Hackberry said about forgetting their conversation. "Eve, your curiosity and good intentions will do more harm than good. You must leave well enough alone. Our lives could be in jeopardy if you begin meddling in his affairs."

"In jeopardy how? That is ridiculous." She dropped her arms from around his neck and tried to step back, but he drew her closer. Her hands rested against his chest, and he wondered if she could feel the pounding of his heart. Her complexion drained of color as she appeared to comprehend he was serious. "W-what has Sir Jonathan gotten involved in?"

His throat grew tight when he looked into her fearful eyes. "I didn't intend to scare you, dearling. I promise, you are safe as long as you abandon this fascination with uncovering Sir Jonathan's secrets."

She shook her head, denying her fear, but her eyes were misty and her bottom lip trembled. "Are you in danger too?"

"No, and neither are you." He caressed her cheek with his thumb. "We are both safe as long as we forget about Sir Jonathan. I don't know what he has gotten into exactly, but he can take care of himself. I saw how capable he is of self-defense, and he doesn't require help from either of us. Promise you will never go to his town house again or make inquiries about him. I need to know you are safe."

"I promise." As she eased from his hold, her eyelashes flickered, seemingly working out everything in her mind. "Why didn't you tell me? I never would have gone to his house if I had known."

"I should have told you. I'm sorry, but Sir Jonathan warned me not to share our conversation with anyone."

Her brows formed a V, and she issued a small sigh of frustration. "I am not just *anyone*. I am your wife. It is commonly accepted that a gentleman tells his wife everything, so unless one truly means no one else should know, he shouldn't spill his secrets to a married man."

Ben blinked. There was much logic in her argument. He was certain his brothers' wives knew every embarrassing detail about him.

"And as long as we are discussing secrets," Eve said, "I know you dream about Charlotte's accident. I heard you call out for her on our wedding night, and last night you had a nightmare. You don't have to keep it a secret. My father used to dream of the war. His screams would wake me at night."

Ben opened and closed his mouth without uttering a sound. His throat was too dry to speak. Were his dreams as bad as that? Did he cry out and wake his household? The possibility made him queasy.

"Papa's nightmares wouldn't leave him alone." She reached to cradle his face, acceptance shining in her soulful eyes. "Have you been having bad dreams since the accident?"

"No," he managed to utter. "A few times afterward and occasionally throughout the years. Not as often as I've been having them lately." He covered her hand on his cheek. "I'm sorry for putting you through this again. I do not want to be a burden."

"You could never be a burden, Ben, but I would gladly bear anything to be with you."

Her bright smile rekindled his hope. Perhaps it was possible to break free of his fears and accept that in this moment, they were happy, in love, and had a promising future together. He held his arms open, and she walked into his embrace. "I missed you, Kitten."

She glanced at him from beneath her thick lashes. "Likewise, Mr. Hillary."

Twenty-eight

IN THE END, BEN CAVED TO EVE'S WISHES TO SEE Hillary Shipping. The Pool of London was a world apart from the East India docks, and he questioned his good sense now that they had arrived. He tucked Eve under his arm close to his side as the raucous sea of merchants, dock laborers, watermen, and sailors swallowed them. Every few yards, a lightskirt was offering her wares, and if Eve's round eyes were any indication, she wasn't missing a single sight.

"I shouldn't have brought you here," he shouted above the noise.

"I never would have forgiven you if you hadn't. Are we getting close?" She beamed up at him, and the guilt of exposing her to this part of his life lifted. He was proud to show off his grandfather's operation, and the empire he and Daniel had built, even if some gentlemen of better ilk looked down on him for his ties to trade. It didn't stop them from trying to take a piece of his fortune at the gaming tables.

The roof of the shipping office came into view, and he shouldered through the crowd, sweeping Eve along with him. As he'd come to expect, a queue had formed outside the doors as men waited to be hired on to one of their ships. They cleared a path for him and Eve; a few nodded in greeting, and he reciprocated.

Inside, the manager was sitting in his usual place behind a sturdy table interviewing a man. He glanced up, his expression solemn. "Good afternoon, Mr. Hillary."

Ben took a moment to introduce Eve before showing her into one of the back offices. "This was my grandfather's office. Not much has changed, other than you'll find Daniel behind the big desk every morning instead of Grandfather. The lazy cur is too distracted by his family to burn the midnight oil. It's rare to see him here past noon anymore."

They kept a smaller desk in the corner that Ben used before he left for India, but Daniel's young brother-in-law liked to come to the docks with him and had taken it over. Ben didn't mind. He preferred his study at home.

She wandered to the large desk to inspect a miniature of Lisette that Daniel had commissioned an artist to paint. "And where would I find you most mornings?"

He knew she was asking where he kept an office, but all he could think about was how scrumptious she'd looked this morning when he had woken her. Her mussed hair had made her look as if she'd been well shagged, but she hadn't. "In bed with you, love."

She glanced back over her shoulder, pink sweeping across her cheeks. "Are you implying we will continue sleeping together?"

Last night he had been aggravated with her for barging in and insisting on sharing his bed, but it was the first night he'd slept without waking in a long time. "I cannot promise there will be much sleep occurring."

She replaced the miniature and slowly spun around. When she propped her hands on the desk behind her, her breasts jutted forward and the most depraved images flooded his mind.

He should have lingered in bed this morning and gotten his fill, but he hadn't. Blood pounded through his veins as he imagined filling her here on the desk.

She must have recognized his desire, because her skin flushed all over and her breathing changed.

Shutters across the window allowed thin slices of light to fall on the plank floor. No one could see inside and no one would interrupt. He turned the key in the lock and raised his eyebrows in question.

Her skin flushed crimson. "In here? What if someone comes in?"

He pulled the key from the lock and dangled it in front of him. "No chance of that happening, love." When he crossed the floor, she pressed back against the desk as if trying to escape, her eyes growing larger the closer he came.

"But won't they hear us?" she hissed.

Reaching her, he slid his hand down to her waist and leaned close to whisper in her ear. "Not if you are quiet when I bring you to climax." He blew a slow stream of air across the rim of her ear. She shivered and he hugged her to bury his face in her neck. She was wearing the scent she'd chosen for their wedding night, and it sparked the most decadent memories.

She pressed her hands against his chest and looked up at him with a slight tip of her head. After a moment of studying him, she lifted to her toes to place her mouth at his ear. "Do you promise to be quiet too?"

His grin widened. "I promise no one will have a clue as to what we are doing." The challenge of making love to his wife while keeping anyone beyond the door ignorant was one he couldn't resist.

She leaned against the desk. Her brown eyes glittered in the dim light. A small nod was all the encouragement he needed.

Grasping one end of the ribbon holding her bonnet in place, he untied the bow and removed it. Wispy rich brown hair fell around her face where the wind had wrestled it loose earlier.

She was so beautiful. He loved her full mouth and the dusting of freckles across the bridge of her sweet little nose. He loved the warmth of her expressive eyes and smile. "I am the luckiest man alive for being allowed to love you."

She skimmed her fingers up and down his arms, creating currents racing through his body. "We are both blessed."

He captured her hand to release the tiny buttons on her glove before sliding the kid leather from her fingers. When both gloves were removed and discarded on the desk, she grasped the lapels of his jacket and eased it off his shoulders. He let it fall to the floor. She moved to his cravat; her lips parted as she concentrated on untying the elaborate knot. He grazed a kiss against her furrowed brow. "Would you like my help?"

She shook her head.

He'd known she wouldn't accept. She had always been determined when it came to figuring out puzzles. Just as she had been determined to unravel him last night when she climbed into his bed. As she untied the first knot, he captured her hands. "Evie."

She froze with her ear cocked toward the door. "Is someone coming?" she whispered.

There was movement in the front room. "I believe Mr. Cullip is gathering his belongings."

"Good day, Mr. Hillary. I'm closing up shop." The manager's muffled voice carried through the office door.

"Good day," Ben called back to him, but he sounded distracted. His gaze was locked on her. Once the outer door slammed shut, he cupped Eve's bottom and pulled her flush against him. Heat seared her cheeks as his thick shaft pressed against her belly.

"Do you think he knows what we are doing?" It was unnecessary to whisper now, but she couldn't help herself.

"No," he whispered in return, but the cocky grin on his face said otherwise.

"You are proud of yourself, aren't you? I suppose you will be crowing about your prowess next time you strut through the door."

He laughed. "I do not strut, nor do I crow. What do you take me for, a rooster?"

She smiled, because she was teasing and he knew it.

Ben had always read her correctly. He watched her with such intensity in his blue eyes that her blood began to simmer. "But I am proud of myself for winning you," he said.

She fumbled with the buttons on Ben's waistcoat, but he didn't brush her hands away to take over. Instead, he kneaded her bottom and nibbled her neck. His mouth created the most delicious sensations and distracted her to no end. When her clumsy fingers released the last button, he lifted her and spun around to plop her bottom on the desk.

"Ben!"

He smiled. "Did I surprise you?"

She laughed and loosened her grip on his waistcoat. Never knowing what to expect made life with him thrilling. "I like surprises."

"I like *you*." He slid his fingers into her hair, and a hairpin pinged against the desk. "A lot," he murmured, his mouth hovering only a fraction from hers. She leaned toward him, but he pulled back with a teasing grin. When he did kiss her, he rained playful pecks all over her cheeks, the tip of her nose, her lips.

She groaned in protest and captured his face, pulling him toward her until their mouths collided. The contact ignited a fire in both of them, and they tugged at each other's clothes in their haste. She shoved his waistcoat from his broad shoulders and grabbed for his cravat. Her fingers worked adeptly this time, and she threw it aside as soon as the last knot released. A triangle of smooth skin showed where his lawn shirt gaped. She placed her lips to his chest, the soft hair tickling her nose, as she dragged the tail of his shirt from his trousers. Tunneling her fingers beneath the shirt, she followed the contours of his muscles and brushed his nipples. They hardened, and she pinched them lightly as he often did to her. He sucked in a breath, encouraging her exploration. She smiled up at him before closing her mouth over the bud and wetting his shirt.

With a soft growl, he shoved her skirts high on her thighs and kneaded the plump part of her legs. "Blasted drawers," he grumbled.

She released his nipple to offer to remove them, but he pulled her from the desk in one quick motion then untied the ribbon around her waist. They fell in a heap at her feet.

Before she could catch her breath, he whipped her around to loosen the fastenings down the back of her gown and untied her corset. He shoved her skirts and petticoat to her waist, baring her bottom, and bent her over the desk. Her hand slammed into the miniature and knocked it to the floor.

She peered back over her shoulder, her lips parted in surprise. His eyes glimmered as he held two fingers to his mouth and licked them. With his hand trapping her skirts at her lower back, he slid his fingers between her legs and found her sensitive place. She closed her eyes on a sigh and turned back toward the desk. Legs spread and lying across the oak surface, she'd never felt so vulnerable. Or excited. Her heart knocked so hard against her ribs, she fancied he could hear it.

He stroked her front to back, back to front slowly over and over before circling the now pulsing bud eager for his touch. She ached deep in her core. He wasn't taking her fast enough. She tried to stand, but he gently pushed her back down. "I'm not finished with you, Kitten."

She whimpered, not caring if she sounded wanton

and desperate. He slid a finger inside her, then two to ease her ache. She gripped the edge of the desk, her heart slamming harder. Several featherlight flicks over her spot made her climax hard, and she cried out. Far from the quiet she had promised.

As he caressed her inner thighs and bottom, she sank on top of the desk. Tingles filtered through her, and the warmth of Ben's hand on her back seeped through her gown, comforting and welcome. When her breathing began to slow, he slid his hand around to her stomach and helped her stand. She pressed back against him, her head reclining on his shoulder. He kissed her reverently as he caressed from her waist to beneath her breast and back again. "I love you," he whispered.

When his knuckles brushed over her nipple, it jutted through the fabric of her gown. She hooked her fingers in the neckline and uncovered herself. He tweaked the tip of her breast and buried his face into her neck. Groping between their bodies, she fondled him through his trousers. He moaned under his breath and pressed into her palm. Four strokes finally broke his restraint, and he tore at the fastenings of his trousers. He entered her from behind, his body cradling hers. With a hand on her hip and another holding her breast, he thrust into her as if desperate to have her, to make her his. She *was* his and had been from the moment she'd laid eyes on him. He needn't ever worry about losing her.

His mouth grazed her ear, his breath ragged and hot. Holding her tightly, he filled her, and when he came, his pleasure seemed to hit him just as hard, and he released a satisfying moan. His arms cradled her against him as his chest rose and fell. He kissed her shoulder then the back of her neck before he released her long enough to turn her within his arms.

Neither of them spoke as they held each other's gazes. Words were inadequate anyway. No word existed to describe the strength of her love for him. It was invincible and it made her feel the same. They were invincible *together*.

He swept the hair from her temple and kissed her lips softly. "Evie," he murmured.

"Me too."

He smiled, reluctantly releasing her. "I will help set you back to rights, then we should return home."

A lovely fog had settled over her, and she went through the motions of dressing while humming a happy tune. When they both looked presentable again, Ben offered his arm and led her from the office. Outside the main building, he stopped to lock the door before they continued to the quay. The crowd had thinned a bit, but it was still an overwhelming sight. She and Ben strolled arm in arm, her admiring the ships while he guided them in the direction of the carriage.

"Mr. Hillary!"

Ben stopped and swung around at the sound of his name. It was Mr. Cullip, Hillary Shipping's manager, bustling toward them. He'd said he was going home for the day. Eve's face flooded with heat as she realized he'd likely been making an excuse to allow her and her husband privacy. She released Ben's arm to pretend fascination with the ships and river, walking a little closer to watch a steamer surge up the river with a cloud of smoke pouring from the stack. To see a barge moving at such a speed was dizzying and quite amazing. She rarely had the privilege.

Looking over her shoulder, she caught Ben keeping watch over her while Mr. Cullip continued his discourse. She smiled reassuringly and resumed studying the steamer until it had moved too far upriver to see. Backing up, she bumped into someone.

"Excuse me," she said and swung around to offer a proper apology. Her eyes flared wide as she found herself standing toe to toe with the man who had followed her and Sir Jonathan to the museum. "It is *you*."

His mouth gaped for a moment before he blurted something in a language she couldn't understand.

"I beg your pardon?" She looked for her husband and called out to him. "Ben, this is—"

The man shoved her out of the way and dashed into the crowd.

Eve stumbled backward. Her heel hit something solid, and then she was falling. She heard Ben shouting her name before she crashed into the cold river.

Twenty-nine

THE WORLD AROUND BEN FROZE. HIS GAZE LOCKED TO the place where Eve had disappeared over the quay. He ran to the edge, ripping his coat off.

Her head bobbed to the surface. She started coughing. Her mouth filled with water as her petticoats and gown dragged her under again.

Ben tugged off his boots in seconds. Spotting the muted light blue of her skirts through the muddy water, he plunged into the Thames feet first as close to her as possible. The river burned his eyes, but he kept them open. He couldn't let her out of his sight.

He'd judged the distance correctly, and she was within his reach. Wrapping his arms around her waist, he kicked them toward the surface with Eve limp in his embrace. They broke through the water with shouts of "man overboard" echoing on the air. Someone jumped into the river, splashing him in the face and blinding him for a moment. Turning Eve in his hold, he cradled her back against his chest to keep her face from falling back in the water.

"Evie, wake up." He tried to jostle her awake, but

her head lolled to the side. "Please, Kitten. Wake up. Talk to me." He couldn't feel her chest moving. She wasn't breathing. A rushing sound filled his ears.

A man grabbed his shoulder. "Give her to me."

"No! I have her." Ben wouldn't entrust her to anyone else. Tightening his hold around her chest, he jerked her against him as the man reached for her. He couldn't let her go. She lurched and began sputtering, coughing up water. Ben held her as violent coughs shook her body repeatedly. A sob built up in his chest, but he held it inside. He had to keep his wits about him to get her to safety. "Help me get her out of the water. She needs a doctor."

The man held up the end of a rope. "Let's get you both on land."

Ben nodded and allowed him to tie the rope around Eve's chest. He checked the knot twice before kissing her cheek. "Raise her up," he barked.

Three men standing on the quay heaved on the line, and she began to rise from the river as Ben tried to lift from below. Rivulets of vile water ran from her stockings. She had lost a boot.

"Ben," she croaked and reached a hand for him.

"I'm coming too, Evie. Hold on to the rope."

She tried, but her grip was too weak and slipped off.

A man on the dock tossed another line to Ben, and he secured it around his middle. Now that Eve was being lifted over the side of the quay, he couldn't get out of the water fast enough. Once a group of sailors pulled him to safety, he crawled the short distance to where Eve lay crumpled on her side in a puddle. Her eyes were closed, but her chest was moving.

"Eve." He tugged her into his arms and buried his face in her soaked hair. A tremor shook him. He could have lost her. He still could if she became ill.

Mr. Cullip knelt beside him, handing him a blanket. "We should get her to your carriage."

"Yes." Ben draped the blanket around her and tried to stand with her in his arms, but his knees buckled.

One of the men who had rescued them stepped forward. "Let me help, Mr. Hillary." He had been in the queue outside Hillary Shipping earlier.

Ben allowed him to take Eve. Mr. Cullip draped a second blanket over Ben's shoulders and handed his boots to him. Ben shoved them on his feet and accepted Mr. Cullip's hand up. "Send for Dr. Portier to meet us at the town house."

"Yes, sir." Mr. Cullip stayed long enough to see if Ben's shaky legs would hold him, then bustled away, disappearing into the crowd.

Ben led the man carrying Eve to the carriage and climbed inside so he could reach down for her. Once they were settled on the bench with Eve on his lap, the man closed the door and his driver pulled away from the docks.

Eve rested her head on his shoulder. "Are you hurt?" Her voice was barely above a whisper.

"Am *I* hurt? Good God, Evie. You weren't breathing." The sob he'd held inside burst from him like the howl of a wounded animal. A horrid shaking overtook his body, and all he could see was Eve's lifeless body in his arms, her lips blue. Suddenly *he* couldn't breathe. He clawed at the wet cravat around his neck.

Eve sat up. "I will get it."

He unintentionally slapped at her hands in his desperation to loosen the knot. His fingers fumbled as panic welled in the back of his throat. A loud pounding filled his head, resounding in his ears.

"Ben, let me." She reached for him, but he was already choking.

Black dots shrouded his vision, and a pressure intense enough to crack his ribs pressed on his chest. "Oh, God!" He hadn't seen this coming and now he couldn't stop it. Bucking against the weight holding him down—smothering him—he braced for the onslaught.

❧

Eve landed on the carriage floor, stunned by the jarring impact. Ben stiffened on the bench, his arms jammed against the sides of the carriage. His breath left him in rapid, shallow huffs. Deep in his throat, there was a low moan. A hazy memory filtered into her awareness.

A strange noise came from Papa's study; his door stood ajar. Hugging her doll, she inched toward the crack, hoping she wouldn't find her brother inside. No one was allowed inside Papa's study except Papa, and she hated when Papa made her stand at attention while Sebastian received raps on his knuckles or lashes against his backside. She would rather be the one punished.

Sitting by helplessly while someone she loved suffered was the worst sort of pain. "Ben." She shifted to her knees to pull herself back onto the seat beside him—to offer him comfort.

"Stay!" The whip-crack command made her jump.

Sinking back to the floor, tears filled Eve's eyes. She rested her hands on her knees, desperate to touch her husband while he fought against whatever had him in its grip. But she wouldn't. She had learned to keep her distance that day in her father's study.

Papa was sitting on the floor slumped against his desk, his face buried in his hands. Muffled sobs came from him.

"Oh, Papa." She dropped her doll and went to throw her arms around his shoulders. He bellowed and swung out, his face frightening. His blow sent her flying into a pedestal, and a vase came crashing down on her. Her cheek bore the brunt of the hit. Eve didn't mean to do it, but she wailed.

"Evie!" Her mother's panicked voice and running footsteps sounded in the corridor. Mama burst into the study. Eve pushed to a seated position and cried harder. Mama dropped to her knees to gather her to her bosom. Eve sagged against her, feeling safe again. And then the worst happened.

"You hurt your daughter." Mama shook in her rage. "What is wrong with you?"

The horrified look on Papa's face caused Eve's heart to stop.

That was the day he had exiled himself to his chambers. She would never forget that look. Ben wore the same tortured expression now.

He scrubbed a hand down his face. Defeat latched on to him and made his body slump forward. He wouldn't meet her eyes. "Eve, what did I do to you?"

She shook her head. "Nothing." Her throat had grown tight, and she feared crying in front of him. They were on shaky ground. One misstep, and she might drive him away.

Reaching for her, he drew her up on the seat beside

him, then backed into the corner of the carriage as if he didn't trust himself with her. "D-Did I hurt you?"

"No!" She scooted toward him, ignoring the wariness in his eyes, and threw her arms around his neck. "You saved my life." She felt his arms tighten around her, and she melted against him, absorbing the slight tremors still traveling through his body.

"I want to hear what Dr. Portier thinks after he examines you," he said.

Eve didn't feel a doctor visit was necessary, but she wouldn't argue. If he needed reassurance from Dr. Portier, he would get it. She would agree to anything to keep him from withdrawing from her.

The carriage rolled to a slow stop in front of their home. Ben helped her inside, calling out orders as they moved toward the stairs. "My wife needs a hot bath, and have Mrs. Beardmore prepare a pot of tea."

"There's no need to put anyone out," she said, but Dobbins was already headed for the kitchen.

She caught a whiff of the river on her hair and thought perhaps a bath might be wise after all, especially when Dr. Portier was expected.

Upstairs in her chambers, Ben rang for her maid. When Alice appeared, he ordered her to strip Eve of her wet clothes and retrieve a wrapper.

"Yes, sir." Alice hurried forward to work loose the fastenings of Eve's gown while Ben stood there as if he had to oversee Alice's duties.

His damp clothes clung to his still-quivering muscles. The shaking had slowed considerably, but the aftereffects of his attack were still evident.

The terror in his voice when he had realized she

was falling still echoed in Eve's ears. Knowing she had caused him pain like he'd experienced with Charlotte tore her heart in two. Eve bit her trembling bottom lip and willed herself not to cry. When tears welled in her eyes anyway, she turned her back to him. She needed a moment alone to collect herself.

"You should change too," she said quietly. "I don't want you to catch a chill."

He hesitated but eventually spun on his heel and entered his chambers through the adjoining door.

When the lock tumbled, she burst into tears.

◈

Ben was composing a letter in his study while he waited for the doctor. He couldn't bear to look into Eve's fearful eyes again. The sound of her sobbing in her chambers had shaken him.

Self-loathing was a bitter taste coating his tongue. He'd knocked her to the floor of the carriage during his attack. What type of ghastly fiend raised a hand against a lady? He'd been horrified when he'd injured his brother at the church, but this... How was he to live with the knowledge he had so little control over himself that he could hurt the one he loved most?

Her intense scrutiny in her room had revealed everything. She was afraid of him. He had *made* her afraid.

He pushed away from the desk, too on edge to sit still. What the devil had come over him? When he should have been comforting her in the carriage, he had lost his wits. He never should have taken her to the bloody docks. Accidents happened all the time, and yet he had allowed his pride to overrule good sense.

She needed to be sent somewhere she felt safe, at least until he could make sense of what was happening to him and gain control over himself. Ben returned to his desk to seal the letter. He wished he could claim confidence in his decision, but the thought of living apart from his wife—even temporarily—caused a sharp pang in his gut.

A knock sounded at his door. "Enter."

It was Dobbins. "Dr. Portier has arrived, sir."

Ben rose from his seat, snatching the letter from his desk. He handed it to his butler as he passed. "I will show the doctor to my wife's chambers. See this is delivered to Thorne Place immediately."

"Yes, sir."

If Ben could count on Sebastian Thorne to do anything, it was to protect Eve, especially from him.

Thirty

DR. PORTIER HELD THE WOODEN TUBE HE USED FOR listening to patients' insides against Eve's back. "Take a deep breath."

Eve did as he instructed, trying to be a good patient for her husband's sake as much as the doctor's. Dr. Portier had been her family's physician for as long as she could recall, and he was much sought after among members of Polite Society. He had studied under her grandfather, who had been a successful doctor in his own right. Eve barely remembered Papa's father since he died when she was young, but she'd been told he attended hers and Sebastian's births.

Ben stood at a distance with his arms crossed over his chest. A grimace was fixed upon his handsome face as if he were a marble statue. She couldn't help but see him every time she glanced up since he had positioned himself directly in front of her. The aloofness in his blue eyes added to her dismay, and she wondered if the doctor noticed the labored beating of her heart.

Dr. Portier was discreet enough to make no comment if he did. Sitting on the side of her bed, he moved the tube to different places on her back and had her repeatedly take deep breaths.

"Very good, madam." Dr. Portier smiled at her just as he had when she was a child, then turned to speak with Ben. "Her lungs are clear, Mr. Hillary. There is no cause for concern. It is highly unlikely she will develop a fever, but you should send for me at once if she does."

Dr. Portier's pronouncement didn't alter her husband's dire expression. "Are you certain? Perhaps you should listen again."

The doctor stood and returned his equipment to the black bag sitting on her bedside table. "I can assure you Mrs. Hillary is no worse for the experience. She will be fine."

Apparently, Dr. Portier was accustomed to handling nervous husbands, because his authoritative tone brooked no argument.

Ben conceded with a nod. "Thank you, Doctor. You have put my mind at ease."

"As it should be," Dr. Portier said with a satisfied smile. "Your wife is in good health." The doctor bid her farewell. Ben hesitated a moment, then followed him from her chambers without a word or backward glance. Her heart sank.

He truly was pulling away from her, and she didn't have the first clue how to bring him back. Worse, she couldn't even talk to anyone about him. Considering Ben's efforts to keep the wounds he carried deep inside hidden from her, she couldn't imagine he would appreciate her confiding in others. He couldn't view it as anything but a betrayal. After the horrible rumors of madness that had circulated about her father, she could understand Ben's fear of someone finding out about his spells.

When her door eased open, she swung toward it with an eager smile, but it was only Alice. "May I come in, ma'am?"

Eve's shoulders drooped and she motioned her maid inside.

Alice closed the door behind her and leaned against it. The fine lines bracketing her mouth and at the corners of her eyes appeared more pronounced. "Did everything go well with the doctor?"

"Dr. Portier proclaimed me to be in good health. I thought a positive report would reassure Mr. Hillary, but he seems as worried as he was before the doctor arrived."

"Your husband loves you a great deal. It is natural for him to be concerned for your welfare."

Eve sighed. "I know he does." Perhaps if he loved her less he wouldn't be so burdened by the day's events. He was not to blame for any of them—certainly not her fall into the river or the moment in the carriage.

Alice clasped her hands at her waist as if in prayer. "Others are concerned about your welfare too."

"Others? Surely word of my accident hasn't traveled to Mayfair already."

"I cannot say, ma'am, but Lord and Lady Thorne are below stairs requesting an audience. Mr. Dobbins settled them in the drawing room and sent me to retrieve you."

Eve pushed wearily from the bed. All this fuss over

her was becoming embarrassing. "I suppose I should go reassure them all is well."

"Are you, madam? Well?"

Alice's concern was genuine. She had been with Eve through the hardest times in her life.

For a fleeting moment, Eve considered telling her the truth, but chose not to burden her maid. "Yes, Alice. Thank you."

When Eve joined her brother and sister-in-law in the drawing room, Helena looked up from her spot on the settee. "Eve, is everything all right?"

Her brother, who had been pacing in front of the unlit fireplace, halted midstride. "What has Hillary done? Why are you returning to Thorne Place?"

Sebastian's preposterous questions left her with her jaw hanging open.

He pulled a folded sheet of foolscap from his jacket pocket and came forward, holding it out. "I received this from your husband about an hour ago. From the look on your face, I would venture you know nothing about it."

"About what, exactly?" She accepted the letter with a baffled frown.

Sebastian guided her toward the settee. "Perhaps you should sit before you read it."

Her gaze shot toward the doorway. The last time she'd had to sit down for news, she'd learned Ben was on his way to India. "Is he g—" The words stuck in her throat as her heart thrashed against her ribs.

Her brother rubbed his hands up and down her arms as if trying to warm her. "He is in his study."

"Oh, thank heavens." She lowered to the settee

before her weakened legs failed her. Helena scooted closer as Eve unfolded the sheet with shaky fingers. She read the letter aloud. "Dear Lord Thorne, I must ask for your assistance in a matter concerning your sister. Her welfare is of the utmost importance to both of us, so I know you can be entrusted with her care. I do not wish to go into details, but I believe Eve would feel more at peace under your roof until I am able to offer her safe haven."

Sebastian perched on the armrest and leaned down to tap his finger against the foolscap. "What is *that* line supposed to mean? If he has hurt you, he will answer to me."

"He has not hurt me." At least not in the sense Sebastian was implying, but sending her away was the worst thing her husband could do to her. And she wouldn't allow her brother to drag her back to Thorne Place either. She rushed through the rest of the letter, reading silently as nausea turned her stomach.

You need not worry about providing for her physical needs. My man of business will arrange to honor any debts incurred while she is in your care, but I will forever be personally indebted to you. Your servant, Benjamin Hillary.

The words blurred on the page, and Eve dropped the letter in her lap. "I cannot believe he wants to send me away. I never expected—" Her voice cracked as a sob escaped.

"Oh, Eve." Helena draped an arm around her shoulders. "There must be some misunderstanding."

"Absolutely. Hillary is mad about you, poppet." Sebastian embraced her from the other side, creating a comforting cocoon around her. "It sounds as if he doesn't *want* to send you away, but for some reason he thinks he should. Tell us what happened and perhaps we can figure this out together."

She glanced up at her big brother with a watery smile, her faith in him restored. Sebastian wasn't here to take her away from Ben. He was here to ensure she stayed with the man she loved, and she needed any help available.

Setting aside any misgivings and trusting her family to support her, she retold the story of Charlotte, Ben's nightmares, and her fall into the river—minus the part about Sir Jonathan and the man who had followed them.

Finally, she told them about her husband's heroic rescue of her, followed by his breakdown in the carriage. "Watching him suffer was excruciating. I've never felt so helpless."

Helena's blue-green eyes held nothing but compassion as she took Eve's hand. "How horrible for both of you. Is there anything we can do to help?"

If anyone else posed the question, Eve would assume they were just being polite, but Helena was the type of person to swim an ocean for those she loved.

Eve pressed her friend's hand between hers. "I cannot think of anything, but your offer warms my heart."

"How long do you think he has been having these attacks?" Sebastian asked in the most matter-of-fact manner, as if it were every day he encountered a similar dilemma.

She should have realized Sebastian would never stand in judgment of Ben. Her brother had grown up in the same household, trying to make sense of Papa's odd behaviors and changeable moods, just as she had.

He handed her a handkerchief, and she shrugged as she dabbed at her tears. "I suspect he has been trying to hide them since our wedding night, but I believe they began two years ago. The day he fled the church, he described a similar episode."

"Blast," Sebastian muttered and wearily scrubbed his hands over his face. "When I met him on the street, he appeared pale and shaken. Now it makes sense— his unexpected departure, coming back for you, his disheveled state. Devil take it! I thought—" Sebastian shook his head, his face screwed up with disgust.

Her stomach pitched. "You thought he was with another woman."

"I'm sorry, Eve. I should have allowed him to explain. I was a jackass and let my temper control me."

Helena reached across Eve to pat his knee. "The past cannot be undone, my love. No amount of guilt makes it so."

He covered his wife's hand and offered a grateful—albeit sad—smile. "But if I could, I would change everything."

"Helena is right. The present is all that matters." Heaping blame on her brother would accomplish nothing. "I love my husband. I don't want to leave him. And I am not afraid of him, but it is clear he believes otherwise."

Sebastian pressed his lips together as if debating whether he should speak up. Apparently, speaking his mind won out. "I've often wondered how our lives might have been different if our mother hadn't accepted our father's decision to retreat into himself. I know she tried to reach him, but how could she not feel defeated after a while? I cannot fault her for giving up, but I still wonder what might have happened if she hadn't."

"I cannot stomach the thought of accepting this," Eve said. "Ben doesn't want to send me away. He loves me. I know he does."

Sebastian held her hand and gave it an affectionate squeeze. "You always see the good in people, even if it is hidden, Evie. You are the most compassionate person I know, and I've always thought compassionate people must be incredibly strong to share in another's sorrow. I believe you have the strength to hold on for as long as it takes."

Tears pricked the backs of her eyes. Her brother was often generous with his praise, but he'd never before given her a compliment that made her truly proud of who she was.

He ruffled her still-damp hair, perhaps to distract her from the misting of his eyes. "I think you can set things to rights without our help, but if you would like us to stay while you speak with your husband, we will."

Ben might insist she leave with Sebastian and Helena if they stayed. In addition, she didn't want to embarrass her husband by defying him in front of witnesses, but she was not leaving her home or him. She would not give up on Ben, even if he was ready to give up on himself. "Thank you for offering, but I need to do this alone."

"I anticipated as much." Sebastian rose from his perch on the settee and offered her a hand up before gathering her in a hug. "Good luck, poppet. If you do discover you need me, do not hesitate to send word and I will be here."

Her brother's reassurance gave her strength. She exchanged a hug with Helena before her sister-in-law linked arms with Sebastian.

Eve lightly drummed her fingers against her lips and studied her brother. "Perhaps there is something you could do." With his connections in the Lords, Sebastian might have access to information about a certain evasive earl. "How well do you know the Earl of Wellham?"

Her brother grinned. "Ham and I go back a ways, although we haven't crossed paths since I stopped frequenting the Den." Before her brother met Helena, he had spent many nights at the Den of Iniquity, a gaming hell Eve wasn't supposed to know about, but did because of her propensity for snooping. "I heard he is visiting his…uh…friend in Kent." A slight flush rose in his cheeks as he shot a distressed look in Eve's direction.

She rolled her eyes. He meant Wellham had a mistress, but she would accept his explanation without pressing for details. "Would he receive you if you paid him a visit? Ben has been unable to get an audience with him, and he has a proposition for the earl."

"I see no reason Ham would turn me away. Tell me about this proposition."

❧

Ben had returned to his study after Dr. Portier departed and forced himself to stay there while Lord and Lady Thorne called on Eve. It had taken every bit of his willpower not to storm the foyer when he heard the baron and baroness taking Eve away. As the clack of the Thornes' carriage wheels on the cobblestones faded in the distance, a blanket of despair descended over Ben. The heaviness weighed him down, making holding up his head feel like a herculean feat.

He opened one of the logbooks on his desk, turning toward work for comfort. Half an hour later, however, he hadn't advanced beyond the second page. His thoughts were too sluggish to make any sense of what was written.

Dobbins entered his study and waited until Ben acknowledged him. "Mrs. Beardmore informs me dinner is ready, sir."

"Dinner?" Ben blinked up at his butler. In all the turmoil this evening, he had forgotten to send word to the kitchen. He wasn't hungry, but he couldn't refuse after Mrs. Beardmore had gone to the trouble of preparing a meal. "Very well," he said as he pushed back from his desk. "I will dine in my chambers."

Dobbins's eyebrows shot up.

"Is there something you would like to say?"

"No, sir."

Ben started for the door when Dobbins cleared his throat. "Yes, what is it?" he asked with a beleaguered sigh.

"I do not mean to pry, sir, but what should I tell Mrs. Hillary? She is waiting in the dining room."

Ben's heart kicked against his ribs. "My wife is here?"

"Yes, sir." Dobbins's cautious tone and narrowed eyes suggested he suspected Ben had bats in the belfry. "Is she planning an excursion this evening? Should I send word to the coachman?"

"No," Ben said as he swept toward the door. "I will inform you if anything changes."

He stalked to the dining room, not breaking stride as he crossed the threshold. Eve was alone. She hadn't gone with her brother as Ben had arranged. He couldn't decide if he was annoyed or heartened by her disobedience.

He locked gazes with his wife as he advanced. She stood; her lips parted on a silent gasp. He stopped inches from her, waiting for a sign that she wanted him here. She gripped the napkin in front of her, twisting the fabric square as if trying to strangle it. His shoulders sagged at the evidence of her nerves.

"I heard your brother and sister-in-law stop in for a visit," he said.

She arched an eyebrow and released one end of the napkin so it hung at her side. "That wasn't well done of you, then. Sebastian and Helena would have been pleased to see you. I thought you and my brother made peace when we married."

Ben had thought the same, but the fact Thorne hadn't granted his request suggested he had misjudged their association. "Did Thorne's visit serve a particular purpose?"

Her hands landed on her hips in agitation. "Are we going to pretend all evening, or may we get to the bottom of your attempt to send me away? And allow me to be clear: I am not leaving. Not now. Not *ever*."

Ben's lips curved into a reluctant smile. With Eve's determined stance and slightly bedraggled coiffure, she looked fierce and ready for battle. She was the most beautiful sight he'd ever seen—lively and well. Her quick recovery from the afternoon seemed a miracle too good to be true.

"Are you laughing at me?" she said, her voice rising in volume. "Because there is nothing humorous about this situation."

"No." He shook his head to clear his mind and focus on the here and now. "I'm happy you stayed. I expected you to be eager to put as much distance between us as possible."

"Why, in God's name, would I want distance? I can't imagine anything more distasteful. The past two years we've had more than enough distance between us, and I can say with confidence it only made me miserable. I believe you were no happier either." She stepped toward him, her face softening as she looked up at him. "We must stay together through good times and bad, just like we promised when we spoke our vows."

He shook his head. She had spoken her vows under false pretenses. How could he hold her to her word? "You didn't know what you were promising."

"Of course I did." Her chin hitched higher. "Do you take me for an idiot?"

"You know I think nothing of the sort. I only meant you didn't vow to love a broken man. I am *flawed*."

"You are not broken, and I have news for you. Everyone is flawed. My father was. My brother, my mother, me." She ticked off each person on her fingers. "Show me one person who claims to be perfect and I will point out *his* flaw. Either he is arrogant or delusional."

"You have no flaws, Evie." He pulled out the chair next to hers and collapsed on it. "You are perfect, and you deserve better than to be saddled with an ill husband."

A wry smile stretched across her face. "Normally, claiming I am perfect would be an effective tactic to end an argument, but I'm afraid I cannot accept it this time. Even if it were true, there are no promises I will stay this way. In truth, I won't. My hair will gray. Wrinkles will come. My hips will probably spread when I have our children. Are you implying you will toss me aside if I change? What if I become sick or face a problem I cannot overcome alone? Will you leave me in the country and forget about me?"

The notion was too preposterous for serious consideration. Ire renewed his strength, and he shoved to his feet. "Do you think I could love you any less because of gray hairs and wrinkles—or wide hips?"

She shrugged one shoulder, stirring his temper more. "Will you love me even if I grow senile and forget your name?"

"Even if I must remind you every hour that I am your husband and you are the love of my life. My word is my bond. Nothing could ever make me toss you aside." He slammed his fist down on the table. "*Nothing*."

Her eyes flared slightly in response to the startling bang. She paused with lips parted, then nodded thoughtfully. "I am not questioning your word."

She pulled something from her pocket and offered it to him.

It was the necklace he had given her two years earlier. The yellow diamonds sparkled in the candlelight as he held it up for inspection. It was a beautiful piece he had discovered years ago on a trip to India, and for some unfathomable reason, he couldn't walk away from it. When he had fallen for Eve, he knew the necklace would make the perfect wedding gift. He'd wanted nothing more than to join their lives together.

She glanced up at him with a question in her eyes. "I have heard this particular necklace symbolizes a lasting connection between husband and wife. Why did you charge Mr. Cooper with bringing it to me when you were severing the connection between us?"

Ben opened his mouth to speak, but words evaded him. He forcefully exhaled and shook his head. He didn't have a ready answer.

"You know what I believe?" she asked. "Deep down you realized we are forever joined at the heart. Even with seas between us, our connection couldn't be broken. Separation caused us to suffer. I cannot see how the result would be any different if you sent me away now." She extended her free hand toward him. "Please, allow me to be at your side while you face whatever is troubling you. *Please.* I simply want the chance to live up to my promises too. Shouldn't I be allowed to love you with the same devotion you have for me?"

Hurt shone in her brown eyes, hurt and desperation. But also, in the depths, he detected a glimmer of hope. That tiny glimmer reached out just as her hand strained toward him. It shattered the last stone in the wall he'd erected between them. Their fingertips brushed, and he tugged her into his arms. He prayed he wasn't making a mistake. "I want you to stay, Evie. I need you."

She buried her face into his neck. "Good, because I am not leaving. I need you too."

When their lips met, their kiss was filled with promise. Oddly, his burden felt lighter, as if his wife was already bearing part of the weight of his shameful secret. He broke the kiss but didn't release her.

"This could get difficult." He felt the need to warn her off, to allow her one more chance to escape, but she didn't take it.

Instead, she scoffed at the idea. "Easy is for novices. We know all about difficult." Lifting to her toes, she placed a peck on his mouth, then sat in the chair. "As long as we are discussing complications…"

She patted the upholstered seat beside her, and he lowered to the chair, waiting for her to continue.

"At the dock today, I saw the man who followed Sir Jonathan, my maid, and me to the museum."

Ben tensed. "The one you spoke with before you stumbled into the river?" In the turmoil, he had forgotten about the man.

"Yes, but he seemed as surprised to see me as I was to see him, so I believe our encounter was purely coincidental."

"Did he say anything to you?"

"I couldn't understand a word, but he seemed distressed by the whole ordeal. I am only mentioning him because I promised not to keep anything from you. Maybe we should let it be."

Like hell he would. "I will have the docks searched. I didn't have a good view. Could you give a description to the investigator I hired?"

"I am certain I could, but you said we shouldn't get involved with Sir Jonathan's affairs."

She might be right on that account, but learning the man's identity could be the key to keeping her safe. *Know your enemy.*

"Be that as it may," he said, "I would like you to speak with the investigator tomorrow."

"Very well, but there is something I would like in return. Even if you are able to purchase the property from Lord Wellham and forgive Mr. Tanney's debt, you need to call on Charlotte's brother."

Ben's chest tightened. "That seems unnecessary. I told you there is no love lost between the Tanneys and me."

"Maybe that is the source of your troubled dreams. You said they restarted when you learned about the Tanneys' situation. Making peace with Charlotte's family might help." Eve reached for his hand and laced their fingers together. "I would go with you. Please, think about it."

He didn't relish the thought of returning to Eton. His last memories of the town were ones he wanted to forget, but perhaps his wife was correct. He should at least entertain the idea before rejecting it. "I will think about it."

Thirty-one

BEN REACHED FOR EVE'S HAND AS THE ETON COLLEGE Chapel appeared in the distance. The wooden fan-vaulting on the chapel's roof jutted into the gray sky, reminding him of spearheads. He hadn't visited the school since his father mercifully allowed him to return home after Charlotte's accident and hired a tutor to complete Ben's education. The chapel was a forbidding sight.

Eve raised her gaze to his, her rich eyes assessing. "The House of Hanover: George III, George II, George I," she intoned and smiled reassuringly.

He released her hand to wrap an arm around her shoulders. She laid her head against his chest. "Thank you, but I am all right."

He'd had spells the last three days as he anticipated returning to the place of Charlotte's accident, but together he and Eve had made it through with few troubles. During the first episode of his heart beginning to run away from him, he had launched into a recital of the British monarchies in reverse order, as he'd learned to do in India. Afterward, he had been mortified, but Eve's compassion and curiosity drew him out. He had explained his method of distraction and how it worked to control his symptoms. She declared him brilliant, and the next time, she joined in the recitation. Now he was finding he had a much more effective and attractive distraction—his wife.

It had been a week since Eve's brother assisted Ben in brokering a deal with Lord Wellham to purchase the property in Eton, and as promised, he had given a lot of thought to calling on Robert Tanney and Charlotte's mother. The nervous tumble in his stomach was a manifestation of his doubts, but it was too late to change his mind. The Tanneys were expecting them.

As the travel coach lumbered away from Eton College on High Street toward the Tanneys' bakery, Eve lifted her head to peer out the window. "The village is charming. From Sebastian's letters, I always imagined something quite different."

"Did you never visit the village when you attended the Fourth of June?" The whole of London society absconded to Eton for the biggest day of celebration on the school's calendar. How was it Eve had never seen the village?

"I am afraid we never made it for Sebastian's Fourth of Junes. Papa was in a bad way before my brother left for boarding school."

Every time Ben learned something new about Eve and her brother's upbringing, the more he realized how lonely her childhood had been. This was what she meant about not marrying a man like her father. Eve wanted to escape a life of loneliness, and Ben would spend every moment of their life together making certain she never had that worry again.

He trailed the tip of his finger down the gentle slope of her pert nose. "I love you, Evie."

She beamed at him. "What brought on such a sudden declaration of the heart?"

"You. I am grateful you are with me today."

"I would not be anywhere else."

The coach slowed as they reached a section of the village most familiar to him. They had arrived at Tanney's Bake Shoppe. Tingling began in his fingers as he studied the bow window displaying tiers of sweets and breads. A yeasty scent permeated the air as he stepped onto the walkway and offered a hand to Eve.

He ran a quick eye over his investment, more comfortable focusing on the building than his coming encounter with Charlotte's family. The shop door required a coat of paint and the glass in one of the upper windowpanes needed replacement, but the roof appeared to be in good condition. Wellham hadn't allowed the building to fall into disrepair, much to Ben's pleasure.

"Shall we?" Eve asked, waiting for his approval before approaching the bakery.

He gave a brief nod. They had traveled many hours that day. It was best to get on with the task. A small bell attached to the door tinkled as Ben pushed it open. An older woman bending down behind a glass counter slowly straightened with a smile for her customers. Her hair had streaks of gray and her face bore more wrinkles, but Ben recognized her immediately.

Charlotte had always resembled her mother in appearance, and suddenly it seemed as if he was receiving a
glimpse of what his young love would have looked
like had she been allowed to grow old.

Charlotte's mother surprised him when her eyes lit
with recognition and her smile broadened. "Benjamin
Hillary, what a sight for sore eyes." She rounded the
counter and came forward to take his hands in hers.
"Robert said you would be visiting, but we didn't
know when you would arrive." Her welcoming
gaze swung toward Eve and she paused, awaiting
an introduction.

"Please allow me to present my wife. Mrs. Tanney,
this is Eve Hillary."

Charlotte's mother greeted her with a welcoming
squeeze of her hands. "What a pleasure it is to meet
you, Mrs. Hillary. How kind of you both to call."

"It is our pleasure, Mrs. Tanney," Eve said. "Ben
has spoken highly of Charlotte on many occasions,
and it is an honor to make the acquaintance of
her family."

Mrs. Tanney's blue eyes radiated with warmth.
"Thank you, madam. To know my Charlotte is
remembered fondly provides me with much comfort."

Whereas Ben might have felt ashamed for parading
his wife in front of Charlotte's mother, instead he felt a
proud straightening of his spine. Eve was gracious and
genuine in her speech, and he loved her more than
ever for caring about Mrs. Tanney's feelings.

"Let me close up shop, then we will retire above
stairs. Robert will join us as soon as he returns from
the mill." Charlotte's mother moved to the window

to place the closed sign, then locked the door. "Follow me, please."

The Tanneys' living quarters were above the bakery, and the smell of cinnamon and ginger hung on the stuffy air. The scent reminded him of Charlotte and made him smile.

"Please, have a seat at the table." Mrs. Tanney bustled to a window in the kitchen and threw up the sash, then snagged a plate of sweets on her way to the table. "Ginger biscuits can never repay your kindness, sir, but they are still warm. Would you care to have one?"

"Thank you." Ben allowed Eve to choose one first before helping himself. The biscuit melted in his mouth, the bite of ginger sharp and yet pleasant. "Mr. Tanney owes me nothing. All rents owed were cleared when I purchased the property. However, I am tempted to accept future rent payments in biscuits."

"You would hear no complaints from me," Eve said, then took another nibble from her biscuit.

As soon as the agreement with Wellham was signed and the deed was transferred to Ben, he'd sent his man of business to Eton to notify the tenants of the change in ownership. Two other businesses occupied the building besides the bakery, and Mr. Yearwood, the hatter next door, had fallen behind on his rent by a quarter as well. The Earl of Wellham had raised rents at the beginning of the year in an attempt to clear his own debts and, in doing so, created a hardship on the tradesmen. While in Eton, Mr. Davis had been under orders to research the average cost of rent on High Street. All slates were wiped clean and now the tenants' payments were on a par with their neighbors'.

The door to the living quarters flew open and banged against the wall, causing the women to startle. Robert Tanney stood in the threshold with two uneven red splotches covering his face. "Pardon me. The breeze caught the door."

Mrs. Tanney smiled at her son and waved him to the table. "Come. Allow me to make introductions." Charlotte's mother played the perfect hostess while Robert Tanney stood with his hat in his hands and rocked from foot to foot. "Sit down, Robert," his mother scolded.

He hung his hat on a peg by the door and hurried to do his mother's bidding, choosing the seat across from Ben. He sat with his eyes downcast, which was far from the scornful man Ben had expected to meet today. Robert Tanney was nothing like his father. "Mother and I are honored to receive you and Mrs. Hillary, and we are deeply humbled by your generosity."

When Tanney glanced up, Ben saw determination burning in his eyes.

"I swear I will repay everything owed, sir. The bakery's business has improved since the start of the half at the college, and if I add a little more to my payment each month, I should be able to clear our debt in a year."

Ben leaned back in the chair with a slight frown. "You owe no debts, Mr. Tanney. As long as you make your rent next quarter, you are in the clear. In truth, I am not here to discuss the bakery." A lump rose in his throat, but he forced his words around it. "I wish to speak about Charlotte. I never had a chance to apologize for what happened that day or make amends to your family."

Tanney and his mother wore matching looks of bewilderment. "Make amends? Whatever for?" Tanney asked. "My sister's death was an accident."

Eve eased closer to Ben's side, lending him strength.

Ben cleared his throat and started to explain. "I was with her before the accident. She was troubled, and we had words. If I hadn't upset her, she would not have run away or been too distraught to notice the coach coming around the bend."

Charlotte's mother pursed her lips. "Mr. Hillary, I do hope you haven't been carrying this burden all this time. We do not hold you responsible."

"Mother is right. The coach was traveling too fast around the bend, and for such a narrow lane. It is no wonder poor Charlotte was struck. May she rest in peace."

Ben didn't know what to say. The coachman hadn't driven the team of four with recklessness, as Charlotte's brother suggested. Perhaps her mother and brother were altering their memories of the past simply to placate him. He now held their lease, and therefore held some sway over them.

Eve spoke up on his behalf. "Please forgive my interruption, but I understood that Mr. Tanney senior blamed my husband for Charlotte's death."

"It is easier to point the finger elsewhere than face the truth," Robert Tanney said, then addressed Ben. "The moment Father noticed a spark of interest between you and Charlotte, he began asking around about you. He reasoned because your grandfather was a tradesman, you would be more amenable to marrying a baker's daughter. You seemed to be the answer to his financial troubles, so he encouraged a flirtation. He was rather insistent about it."

Mrs. Tanney shot her son a chiding stare and swept an imploring hand toward Ben. "Please do not think Charlotte played you false, Mr. Hillary. She cared a great deal for you, but she was also vulnerable to suggestion. She was still a girl and infatuated with a handsome young man. I was not surprised she preferred to listen to her father's false hopes than reason, but anyone with any sense knew your gentleman father would not allow a match with a tradesman's daughter with no dowry."

Ben reached out to pat her hand in reassurance. "I never doubted Charlotte's sincerity, and while I appreciate your generosity, I do not deserve to be regarded as blameless. Charlotte was upset with me. I should have taken better care with her feelings."

Mrs. Tanney planted her palms against the table and slowly pushed to her feet with a soft grunt. "The kettle is likely ready." She moved to the hearth, turning her back to them.

"You were not responsible for her state of distress," Robert Tanney said. "She was already high on the ropes when she sought you out."

"May I ask what was troubling her?" Eve spoke softly, as if concerned she might be overstepping her bounds, but Ben appreciated her involvement and slipped his arm to the back of her chair in a show of inclusion.

Charlotte's mother returned with a tray bearing a simple white teapot and chipped teacups. "My husband had a difficult time accepting that a match between you and Charlotte was not made in the stars. When he heard news of your return to school, he sent Charlotte straightaway to find you."

"But not before he fed her worries and filled her head with nonsense," Robert Tanney spat, ignoring his mother's chiding glance. "She left on a mission to bring you up to scratch. Father warned that he would not accept no for an answer and neither should she. It was her duty to catch a wealthy husband. I hold *him* responsible for her death, Mr. Hillary. My father killed her."

Tanney's dark glower and venom left Ben taken aback. Eve sat stiffly at his side, and he gently touched her shoulder for reassurance. Tanney's fury was not directed at either of them, but it was palpable and uncomfortable all the same.

Mrs. Tanney poured a cup of tea and slid the saucer and cup to Eve. "Would you like another biscuit, madam?"

"No, thank you," she murmured and sipped her tea, studying Tanney over the rim.

Charlotte's mother tried to pass Ben a cup as well, but he declined. Changing the topic to Eton's cricket matches—something slightly less volatile, although Tanney had strong opinions on this as well—allowed Eve to finish her tea in relative comfort.

"We should find the inn," Ben said after the requisite time had passed to leave without appearing rude. "Our trunks have already been delivered, and I imagine my wife is ready to rest after our journey."

Eve took his cue and thanked their host and hostess for their hospitality. Charlotte's mother and brother responded graciously and insisted on seeing them safely back to the walkway outside the bakery.

At the front door, Mrs. Tanney stopped Ben with a light touch to his elbow. "Mr. Hillary, if I may be so bold... You have never required our forgiveness, but I suspect you need to forgive yourself. Our Charlotte was just a girl and you were only a boy. Perhaps you could show that young boy a bit of compassion. It does not seem right to make him pay such a steep price for wanting to honor his father's wishes."

Ben's eyes widened. He had never considered that he had been punishing a mere boy all this time. Inclining his head in thanks, he ushered Eve from the bakery and headed in the direction of their lodgings.

That evening he shared a quiet meal with his wife before they retired to bed early. As they cuddled under the covers, he reflected on the afternoon and Mrs. Tanney's suggestion that he forgive his younger self.

"I think I should return to the place where Charlotte died. It may sound morbid, but..." He didn't know how to finish his thought.

Eve placed a tender kiss on his cheek. "I think it sounds like the right thing to do, my love."

❦

The next morning Eve held her husband's hand as they strolled along a narrow country lane. Green meadows, sprinkled with yellow and white wildflowers, rose gently over hills and sloped down the other sides. Azure skies with nary a cloud were perfect for a day of frolicking and laughter, but she and Ben moved in somber silence.

His fingers tightened around hers as they neared a bend in the dusty lane. They must be approaching the site of the accident. Eve closed her eyes and said a silent prayer for Ben. She supported his need to revisit the location, but couldn't help fretting over how it might affect him.

He slowed his step until eventually he stopped before rounding the curve. She stood still, holding her breath. Releasing her hand, he hugged her to his side, and when she looked up to determine if he wanted to turn back, he smiled ruefully. "Many wives wouldn't humor their husbands like this."

"If that is true, they are a sorry lot. Furthermore, I am not humoring you. I am standing by your side, and there is no place else I would rather be."

Tiny crinkles appeared at the corners of his eyes when he smiled. "That was my poor attempt at saying thank you for being at my side." Leaning down, he placed a soft kiss on her lips, lingering and sharing one slow and steady breath. When he straightened, his blue eyes reflected strength and determination. "I am ready."

Eve's stomach churned as she accepted his arm. When Ben suffered, so did she. Yet she wouldn't shy away from being his lifeline if he needed one. As they walked around the curve, her breath left her in a relieved whoosh. She didn't know what she had expected to see, but there was nothing but more meadow and a row of wizened oaks standing haphazardly along one side of the lane.

Ben silently surveyed the area, while she couldn't shift her gaze from him. She watched for any hints of distress with such vigilance, her own hands began to tremble. Her husband looked toward the field, then back at the road several times before nodding. "It looks nothing like my nightmares anymore."

"Oh?" Her whisper was nearly lost on the breeze.

"It is beautiful and peaceful. The trees are large enough to cast shade, and I can hear the birds."

She wondered what he heard in his nightmares, but she refrained from asking. All that mattered was he didn't hear it now.

"Charlotte loved wildflowers," he said.

"Should we gather some to place on her grave?"

"No, I do not believe she is there." Ben guided them toward a massive tree before looking up at the green canopy. "All around, I see Charlotte's spirit. In the sway of the branches. The butterflies flitting about the field. Even the scent of sunbaked earth reminds me of her." His mouth curved up gently as he turned to Eve. "This is a better way to remember her, to honor her life."

"Oh, Ben." Tears clouded Eve's vision. Perhaps her husband could find peace at last. She retrieved a handkerchief from her reticule and dabbed at her eyes.

"I am grateful you encouraged me to return," he said. "You were right about my need to say good-bye, but now it is time to look toward our future." He gathered her to his chest and rubbed his hands slowly up and down her back as she rested her head on his shoulder. "I love you, Evie, and I am enthusiastic about loving you for the rest of our lives."

"Likewise, Mr. Hillary." Eve slid her arms around his neck and flashed a playful smile. "Likewise." And then she pulled him toward her for a kiss that demonstrated just how enthusiastically she intended to love him forever.

Epilogue

EVE GRIPPED THE SHIP'S RAILING, HER GLOVES PROTECT-
ing her hands from the rough wood. "Is that land?
Dear Lord, are we nearing Lisbon at last?" Relief
diminished the wave of nausea that had almost overpowered her moments earlier, driving her husband to
usher her onto the quarterdeck for fresh air before she
tossed up her accounts yet again.

"We have reached Portugal," Ben confirmed and
slipped his arms around her from behind, supporting
her against his chest and keeping her from dissolving
into a quivering puddle on the deck. "Soon we will
sleep in a real bed and enjoy a decent meal."

She groaned at the mention of food.

"My apologies, love." He chuckled under his
breath. "I only now realize my words could have been
better timed."

"I will likely feel different later this evening, but at
the moment..." Closing her eyes, she melted against
him as the men went about their duties on the main
deck. She had been beyond pleased to learn Ben had
kept his promise to provide work for the young men

who had grown too old to remain at the foundling hospital. Two of the young men were members of the *Eve Lorraine*'s crew.

"I am looking forward to our stay in the villa," she said. She hated to admit it, but she was not the hardy traveler she had hoped she would be. Seasickness had been troubling her every morning since they had sailed from London, and a month on land sounded heavenly. With the way she felt at the moment, Ben might have a hard time convincing her to step foot on the ship again to continue their journey.

Of course, that would mean Mama, Sebastian, Helena, and Gracie must come to her if she never left Lisbon, because she couldn't imagine a life without seeing them as often as she liked. Already they had been apart longer than at any other time in her life.

She'd said a tearful good-bye to her family nine days ago when she and Ben had seen them off to Scotland. By now, her loved ones would have reached Aldmist Fell and were likely settling in at the castle Helena had inherited from her late husband. Eve would miss Sebastian and Helena's first Christmas together, but she was where she belonged—standing with the man she loved.

She cracked open one eye for another glimpse of Portugal. The clear blue waters and soaring cliffs along the shoreline were breathtaking. Her stomach pitched as the deck beneath her did the same. She held back another groan, not wanting to worry her husband. Having abandoned her bonnet in their cabin, Eve welcomed the salty wind blowing through her unbound hair. Ben kissed her temple, his presence and loving care fortifying.

Fortunately, he hadn't needed her help weathering one of his episodes since they had returned from visiting Charlotte's mother and brother, for she had been in no condition to support him. She was quite useless lately. He still had bad dreams on occasion, but he no longer cried out or woke gasping for air.

"Are you recovering, dearling?" he asked.

"By degrees. I am comforted knowing I will wake on land tomorrow, and this incorrigible seasickness will end."

Ben eased her from his hold and turned her to face him. Strong brows lowered over his smoky-blue eyes. "You do not know?"

Her heart dropped. "Please tell me we will reach Lisbon tonight."

A sly smile played across his face. Taking her elbow, he guided her toward the stern of the ship away from the activity onboard. "You haven't recognized the signs, have you, Kitten? No wonder you've said nothing to me. I suppose there has been too much excitement these past few weeks."

Eve frowned, not understanding what signs she was supposed to recognize and what too much excitement had to do with their stay in Lisbon.

Her husband's smile widened. "The nausea in the morning? The soreness in your breasts?" He lowered his voice to a whisper. "When was the last time you bled, Evie?"

She gasped. "Good heavens! I never thought to calculate…" Could it be true? If so, her husband was correct. She had been too preoccupied with preparing for their voyage and fretting over leaving her family.

The shock of possibly missing evidence of one of the most joyful moments of her life caused gooseflesh to rise along her skin. "Do you think I am with child?" she whispered too.

"It has been at least five weeks since your last cycle. It seems very likely."

Her cheeks flamed. "You pay a little too much attention to what I've always considered a private matter."

He laughed and tugged her into his arms. "I beg your pardon then. If it is any comfort, I cannot help noticing all manner of things about you, like the way you glow after the sickness has passed, or how your hips are beginning to round the slightest bit. I can barely keep my hands off you." Sliding his hands to her derriere, he fondled her apparently expanding backside and nuzzled her neck, his whiskers tickling.

"*Barely?*" She laughingly tried to extract herself from his hold. "You show no restraint at all, sir."

He stopped nuzzling her neck, but he didn't release her. "It is not my fault you are irresistible."

"I beg to differ. I might not have recognized the signs, but I do know you are responsible for my condition."

His smile faded and he brushed the hair back from her face with both hands, burying his fingers in her wild locks. "Are you pleased to be with child?"

Her throat burned with unshed tears. How could she be anything except ecstatic to carry his child? He was the love of her life. Her heart's true desire for as long as she could recall was to be a mother, but the reality was even more joyful than she could have imagined. "Pleased does not adequately capture how I feel. I am elated, Ben. We are having a *baby*."

The thrill of that word raced through her and she tossed her arms around his neck.

He laughed again, lifting her off her feet and planting a smacking kiss on her lips.

"Will we return home before it is time to give birth?" she asked.

He set her back on her feet. "I cannot imagine you would wish to be anywhere else, and you will want your mother and possibly Helena too."

"And you."

He blanched. "Me?"

"Perhaps. Amelia said your brother was in attendance when she birthed their son."

"That blasted whelp is forever trying to outclass his older brothers," Ben said with a wink. He bent down to surprise her with a sweet, loving kiss. When their lips parted, he leaned his forehead against hers. "There is only one place I plan to be when you bring our child into the world, by your side. Nothing will ever keep me from you, Kitten."

"Oh, Ben," she managed to choke out as tears filled her eyes. "You are turning me into a watering pot."

"Watering pot or not, I will always love you, Evie. I wonder if we will have a boy or girl."

"Does it matter?"

He grinned and slipped his arm around her waist. "Not one bit. I can sing and dance with either one."

She laughed. "Just don't make the mistake of holding our baby overhead unless you want a surprise."

"Yes, Toby Boy taught me that lesson."

They remained at the railing side by side, their arms wrapped around each other, happily chatting about their bright future as Lisbon loomed on the horizon.

She laid her head against his shoulder and sighed. "I love you, Ben."

"I love you too." He placed a kiss on her hair. "I never thought I could be this happy, Evie. You are my everything, and always will be."

Author's Note

For the sake of the story, I chose to create a fictional orphanage in London where the heroine is involved in charity work. In reality, there was only one foundling hospital in London in 1819. My research indicates infants were sent to live with foster families in the country, where it was believed to be a healthier environment for the babies. I am sure they were correct, given the unsanitary conditions in the city. In this story, however, I've chosen to create a nursery in the foundling hospital where the babies are cared for by nurses and wet nurses.

Acknowledgments

Every time I finish writing a book, I pause to reflect on how many people are involved in the entire process from the moment the seeds of an idea begin to develop until the reader is holding the book in her hands. The number of people involved can be mind-boggling, especially when writing a book feels like such a solitary task. I'd like to take a moment to thank a few of these wonderfully supportive people I'm lucky enough to have surrounding me.

Thank you to my husband, kids, and extended family members who have been very understanding when I've needed to miss time together to finish the book by my deadline. It's never a pleasant task to plant myself in front of the laptop rather than spend time with family, but your enthusiasm and understanding makes everything a little easier. I appreciate you more than words can express.

Thank you to fellow Regency author and critique partner Heather Boyd. Her feedback has been invaluable. From the first page to the last, she has been with me during this entire process.

A special thank you to my street team, the Social Graces. Not only do the ladies help spread word about my stories, they are excited about my current projects. Sometimes an author needs an extra boost of encouragement to keep going, and these ladies are a godsend.

Next, I would like to thank the group at Sourcebooks who create beautiful covers, edit my work, and help make my books visible to historical romance readers: Cat Clyne, editor; Skye Agnew, production editor; and Becca Smith, publicist. These women are just the tip of the iceberg. There are many others involved behind the scenes, but Cat, Skye, and Becca are there for me whenever I need help, and they make this experience a very pleasant one.

Finally, I would like to thank my agent, Nephele Tempest, for lending her expertise. She is a delightful person to know, and her support is equally important and appreciated.

One Rogue Too Many

by Samantha Grace

From the betting book at Brooks's gentlemen's club: £2,000 that Lord Ellis will throw the first punch when he discovers Lord Thorne is wooing a certain duke's sister.

All bets are off when the game is love

Lady Gabrielle is thrilled when Anthony Keaton, Earl of Ellis, asks for her hand. She's not so pleased when he then leaves the country without a word. Clearly, he has changed his mind and is too cowardly to tell her. There's nothing to do but go back on the marriage mart…

When Anthony returns to find his ultimate rival wooing Gabby, his continual battle of one-upmanship with Sebastian Thorne ceases to be a game. Anthony is determined to win back the woman who holds his heart.

Praise for Samantha Grace:

"Grace's flair for crafting engaging characters and light touch when it comes to humor and charm result in another sexy Regency." —*Booklist*

"A merry romp… Grace captures the essence and atmosphere of the era." —*RT Book Reviews*

For more Samantha Grace, visit:
www.sourcebooks.com

In Bed with a Rogue

by Samantha Grace

He's the talk of the town

The whole town is tittering about Baron Sebastian Thorne having been jilted at the altar. Every move he makes ends up in the gossip columns. Tired of being the butt of everyone's jokes, Sebastian vows to restore his family's reputation no matter what it takes.

She's the toast of the *ton*

Feted by the crème of Society, the beautiful widow Lady Prestwick is a vision of all that is proper. But Helena is no angel, and when Sebastian uncovers her dark secret, he's quick to press his advantage. In order to keep her hard-won good name, Helena will have to make a deal with the devil. But she has some tricks up her sleeves to keep this notorious rogue on his toes…

Praise for *One Rogue Too Many*:

"Filled with humor and witty repartee… Grace woos readers in true Regency style." —*Publishers Weekly*

"Charming…Grace captures the essence and atmosphere of the era." —*RT Book Reviews*

For more Samantha Grace, visit:
www.sourcebooks.com

Lady Vivian Defies a Duke
by Samantha Grace

The Naked Truth

Lady Vivian Worth knows perfectly well how to behave like a lady. But observing proper manners when there's no one around to impress is just silly. Why shouldn't she strip down to her chemise for a swim? When her betrothed arrives to finally meet her, Vivi will act every inch the lady—demure, polite, compliant. Everything her brother has promised the man. But until then, she's going to enjoy her freedom…

A Revealing Discovery

Luke Forest, the newly named Duke of Foxhaven, wants nothing to do with his inheritance—or the bride who comes with it. He wants adventure and excitement, like the enchanting water nymph he's just stumbled across. When he discovers the skinny-dipping minx is his intended, he reconsiders his plan to find Lady Vivian another husband. Because the idea of this vivacious woman in the arms of another man might be enough to drive him insane—or to the altar.

"An ideal choice for readers who relish smartly written, splendidly sensual Regency historicals." —*Booklist*

For more Samantha Grace, visit:
www.sourcebooks.com

Never Resist a Rake

A Somerfield Park Romance

by Mia Marlowe

— ❦ —

Can he fool his new family?

John Fitzhugh Barrett, surprised to learn he is heir to an estate, is determined his new status won't mean giving up his freedom. But as families from all over England descend upon Somerfield Park for the shooting season, their unmarried daughters are lining up to bag the newest trophy buck—him.

Or is he only fooling himself?

John's instinct for self-preservation inspires him to divide his attentions between a scandalous young widow, and beautiful Rebecca Kearsey, daughter of a destitute baron. The charade gives John the illusion of controlling the game, but when he loses his heart to Rebecca, all bets are off.

— ❦ —

"Marlowe's delightful tale is replete with unexpected characters, a wonderful romance, and a page-turning plot. Marlowe cleverly turns a rascal into a hero readers will adore, while adding a depth of emotion that will touch their hearts." —*RT Book Reviews*, 4.5 Stars

For more Mia Marlowe, visit:
www.sourcebooks.com

The Beautiful One

Book 1 in the Scandalous Sisters Series

by Emily Greenwood

---~✤~---

A picture says a thousand words...

The *ton* is buzzing about *The Beautiful One*, a scandalous book of nude sketches making the rounds of the town. Only two men know the true identity of the striking woman depicted, and they are scouring the countryside, determined to find her.

But not the most important ones

The unlikely center of the scandal, Anna Black, flees her home. Her tomboy heart and impertinent tongue serve her well when she meets most brooding Will Halifax, Viscount Grandville. When the viscount's outrageous teenaged ward arrives, he presses Anna to take on her care. But Anna knows that the more she loves, the more she has to lose.

---~✤~---

"Greenwood weaves some unique threads into her Regency romance, heightening the sexual stakes and rendering a wholly satisfying happy ending for this touching love story." —*Kirkus Reviews*

For more Emily Greenwood, visit:
www.sourcebooks.com

About the Author

Historical romance author Samantha Grace discovered the appeal of a great love story when she was just a young girl, thanks to Disney's *Robin Hood*. She didn't care that Robin Hood and Maid Marian were cartoon animals. It was her first happily-ever-after experience and she didn't want the warm fuzzies to end. Now that Samantha is grown, she enjoys creating her own happy endings for characters that spring from her imagination. *Publishers Weekly* describes her stories as "fresh and romantic" with subtle humor and charm. Samantha describes romance writing as the best job ever.

Part-time medical social worker, moonlighting author, and Pilates nut, she enjoys a happy and hectic life with her real-life hero and two kids in the Midwest. To learn more about Samantha's books, visit her at www.samanthagraceauthor.com.